Praise for earlier Cram myste

Brighton-based murder mystery is a delight." *Peter Lovesey,* **Crime Writers' Association Diamond Dagger winner**

"It read like a breath of fresh air and I can't wait for the next one." *Little Bookness Lane*

"By the end of page one, I knew I liked Colin Crampton and author Peter Bartram's breezy writing style." *Over My Dead Body*

"A little reminiscent of [Raymond] Chandler." *Bookwitch*

"A rather fun and well-written cozy mystery set in 1960s Brighton." *Northern Crime*

"The story is a real whodunit in the classic mould." **crime author** *M J Trow*

"A fast-paced mystery, superbly plotted, and kept me guessing right until the end." *Don't Tell Me the Moon Is Shining*

"Very highly recommended." *Midwest Book Review*

"One night I stayed up until nearly 2am thinking 'I'll just read one more chapter'. This is a huge recommendation from me." *Life of a Nerdish Mum*

"I highly recommend this book and the author. I will definitely be reading more of this series and his other books." *The Divine Write*

"Bartram skilfully delivers one of the most complex cozy mystery plots I've read in years." *Booklover Book Reviews*

The Family Tree Mystery

A Crampton of the Chronicle adventure

For Mhianda Santey

The Family Tree
Mystery

with best wishes

A Crampton of the Chronicle adventure

Peter Bartram

Peter Bartram

Deadline Murder Series Book 7

THE BARTRAM PARTNERSHIP

First published by The Bartram Partnership, 2022

ISBN: 9798360197591

For contact details see website:
www.colincrampton.com

Text copyright: Peter Bartram 2022
Cover copyright: Red Nomad Studios 2022

Text and Cover Design: Red Nomad Studios.
www.rednomadstudios.com

Chapter 1

Dateline: Brighton, England, 3rd July 1967

My girlfriend Shirley Goldsmith threw her arms around me. She hugged me tight and pressed her lips to mine.

Her kiss lingered, sweet and clinging, soft and luscious, like a dewy peach. The kind of kiss to make you think you're the only man in the world - while it lasts.

And that you're not, when it ends.

Because Shirley broke our embrace and threw back her head, her lips still slightly parted. Her cornflower blue eyes sparkled with fun.

"Guess what, big boy?" she said. "It turns out I've got a half-uncle."

"Couldn't you afford a whole one?" I asked.

"Ha, bloody, ha."

"Perhaps I should have asked which half?"

"You better take this seriously, bozo. I've got family I never knew about."

"The best kind," I said.

Before I became crime reporter on the Brighton *Evening Chronicle*, my own life was shadowed by flatulent uncles, rebarbative aunts, and twin cousins as useless as a pair of busted bookends.

We were in Shirley's flat. It was early evening. I'd called in after a tough day at the paper to find Shirl celebrating. She'd popped the cork on a bottle of *Asti Spumante*. It had been in the back of the fridge since Christmas. She poured herself a glass.

She was wearing pillar-box red slacks and a top circled with red, yellow and black stripes. It looked like she'd been laced in multi-coloured ribbons. She'd pinned her blonde hair back with an Alice band made out of scarlet beads. Every inch the savvy

1

photographers' model.

If her long-lost half-uncle could see his half-niece now, he'd know for sure he'd got the best of the bargain.

I asked: "Serious question: what exactly is a half-uncle?"

"He's the half-brother of one of your parents."

"Half-uncles... half-brothers... there are too many incomplete people floating around here."

"Look, this isn't difficult," Shirl said. "It turns out my Ma, Barbara, had a half-brother who was the son from her mother's first marriage."

"I get it. With a different father."

"And Barbara's half-brother is my half-uncle."

"So, not exactly a sturdy branch of the family tree. More of a leafless twig."

I reached for the Italian fizz and poured myself a glass.

"How long have you known about this half-uncle?" I asked.

"Since this morning. A package arrived in the post."

"Unknown relatives who turn up from the past – especially in packages - usually want only one thing," I said.

"My moolah," Shirl said. "Not this guy. He just wants to meet me."

"So, who is he?"

Shirley moved over to the table. Grabbed a large buff envelope and we sat side-by-side on the sofa. She reached into the envelope and pulled out a paper.

"Evidence," she said. "Isn't that what you're looking for when you write your newspaper stories?"

Shirl handed me a long thin document. An Australian birth certificate issued in the state of Victoria. It recorded that Hobart Jocelyn Birtwhistle had been born on the eighth of December 1917 at Ballarat. His father was one Jonathan Birtwhistle (deceased) and his mother Bella Caroline Birtwhistle.

I said: "Just because you've got a guy's birth certificate doesn't mean it's been sent by the same guy. I could get a certificate for Paul McCartney but it wouldn't make me a member of The Beatles."

"I know that. There's more. The guy's sent a letter, too."

Shirl reached into the envelope again and pulled out a sheaf of Basildon Bond blue notepaper. It was covered in scrawled black writing.

"He says he'd been researching his family's background and didn't realise until a few months ago that he had a half-sister. My Ma."

I put my hand gently on Shirl's shoulder. Barbara Goldsmith, a bold brassy bundle of life, had died just a few months ago. With her father already gone, Shirley had been deeply upset.

I still had the damp hanky from a tear-stained evening when we'd huddled together on the sofa and Shirl had told me Barbara's life history.

Her Ma was the daughter of Bella's second marriage to one Eddie Green, a railway engineer. It was, apparently, a tempestuous match. Bella was plagued by bouts of deep depression and Green by outbursts of drink-fuelled violence. As soon as she could, Barbara took the bus from Erskineville, a suburb of Sydney, and headed for Adelaide. She never looked back.

At the bus station, she met Jack Goldsmith, a sheep farm equipment salesman. By the time they'd reached Adelaide, Barbara had fallen for the handsome seller of halters, lambing ropes, warming boxes and prolapse harnesses. It was like a plot out of Mills and Boon. But, hell, it's nice sometimes when real life imitates art.

I said: "Does Birtwhistle say why he's getting in touch?"

Shirl turned over a page of the letter. "He says he has 'information which may be to my advantage'."

I smacked the palm of my hand to my forehead. "Not that hoary old chestnut. The old con-man's party trick."

"He seems genuine."

"They always do."

"He says it's all quite urgent."

"Never give the sucker a chance to think it might be a con."

"Wants to see me tomorrow morning."

"Force the sap's hand and they'll end up helpless."

"So, you're going to leave me to my fate?"

I drained the last of my wine. "Would I ever?"

Shirl leaned towards me. Her arms sinuously slipped around my neck. Her lips met mine in another lingering kiss.

She pulled away and grinned. "I don't know how I can ever thank you."

My gaze strayed to the bedroom door. "I might be able to suggest a way," I said.

We made an early start the following morning.

As the sun was shining from a summer sky, I folded back the roof on my white MGB and we headed into the Sussex countryside. By nine o'clock, we'd put the ruins of Lewes castle behind us and hit the open road towards Ringmer.

Hobart Birtwhistle lived in a remote hamlet called Muddles Green. Given its name, perhaps it had got there by mistake. I'd never heard of the place. It was not much more than a dot on my Ordnance Survey map.

I depressed the accelerator and the MGB responded with a pleasing growl. We cleared the last houses in Ringmer and flashed between high hedges on either side of the twisty road.

I glanced sideways at Shirley. She pressed her lips together in a gesture I knew meant she was thinking hard.

She said: "I wonder why Hobart simply didn't say in his letter why he wanted to see me."

"Personal matter, perhaps?"

"I don't see that can be right. I didn't even know the guy existed until yesterday. How could there be anything personal between us?"

"Who knows what might be lurking in that half-uncle connection?"

Shirl tapped my leg in an irritated way. "You've worried me now."

I took one hand off the steering wheel, reached across, and gave her arm a reassuring squeeze.

"I'm sure there's nothing to worry about. After all, Hobart told us a lot about himself in that letter."

I'd read the lengthy letter last night. Hobart's story would have made a lively episode of the TV show *This Is Your Life* – always assuming Eamonn Andrews had been able to surprise the fellow with his big red book.

Hobart's father, Jonathan Birtwhistle, had been a dashing lieutenant with the Fourth Australian Brigade. He had met Bella while he was training in Britain during the First World War. The pair had married on New Year's Day 1917, just one week before Jonathan was posted to the front-line in France, near Arras. Meanwhile, Bella set sail on the long journey to the new home she would make in Australia with Jonathan after the war. It turned out Jonathan had not wasted the days before he left his new bride. By March, Bella was writing to him that she was expecting their first child. But Jonathan was never to see his son. He was caught in the crossfire during the disastrous Battle of Bullecourt in the early days of April.

No doubt Bella grieved, like so many war widows. But, it seems, it was not long before she became a merry widow. By the end of her first year in Australia, she'd met and married Eddie Green.

Green was apparently pleased to take on the widow, but not her wailing baby. The infant Hobart was sent to live with the late Jonathan's own parents. So, Hobart grew up in Melbourne. It seemed he'd made something of his life. He'd worked for the National Australian Bank. Was posted to Britain to run the bank's London office. Decided to stay on in Britain when he retired from banking. Reading between the lines, he'd done well for himself. He'd moved to Muddles Green a few years earlier.

I slowed the MGB behind a tractor pulling a trailer loaded with bales of hay.

I said: "That letter Hobart wrote about his early life might explain a lot about why you never knew you had a half-uncle."

Shirley shot me a puzzled look. "Why do you say that?"

"I was just thinking about what he said. It was a lot of personal information to share with someone he's never met before."

"Perhaps that's why he shared it," Shirley said. "Maybe the fact his mother rejected him has been a cross he's carried all his life. Probably waited for years to share it with someone."

I nodded, but unconvincingly. "That's another point I don't understand."

Shirley pointed at a fingerpost by a crossroads. "Turn left for Muddles Green," she said.

The tyres squealed on the Tarmac as the MGB roared into a narrow lane.

A couple of minutes later I pulled the car into the side of the road by a neat village green.

We climbed out and stretched our legs.

Shirley turned a circle to view the place. "Guess old Hobart wanted a quiet life when he chose this spot," she said.

A couple of dozen houses were grouped around the green. His own place, he'd told us in the letter, was at the north end of the village.

We found it, a two-storey cottage with a sagging slate roof and wisteria growing around the windows.

There was an unruly privet hedge around a small garden. A brick path led up to the front door. I gave the bell chain beside the door a sharp tug.

Somewhere inside the cottage a bell jangled.

We waited for the door to open. Looked at one another uncertainly.

No answer.

"Have we got the right day?" I asked.

"No, bozo, I just took a chance."

I tugged the bell chain more irritably.

No answer.

I said: "Perhaps Hobart is in the garden at the back."

We brushed past some soaring hollyhocks and walked down a narrow passage at the side of the cottage.

At the back of the house, there was a small conservatory, packed with ferns, cacti and succulents. The door was ajar.

I knocked and called out: "Mr Birtwhistle."

No answer.

Shirley and I exchanged an anxious glance.

She pushed the door further open, stepped inside, and said: "Follow me."

The conservatory opened into a large kitchen. A pine table in the middle of the room was loaded with the pots and pans of what looked like last night's dinner. Lamb chops and carrots.

Shirley called out: "Uncle Hobart, it's Shirley."

No answer.

We crossed the kitchen and stepped into a small hallway.

The door off to the left led into a parlour. There were two easy chairs and a sofa – a G-Plan three-piece suite. A bookcase lined the far wall. To the side, a window gave a good view of the garden.

A couple of worn Axminster carpets covered the ancient floorboards. The boards creaked as we advanced into the room.

A man was sitting in one of the chairs. He had his back to us.

Shirley said: "Uncle Hobart. It's Shirley. Sorry to wake you if you're asleep."

She crossed the room and put her hand gently on his shoulder.

Hobart moved sideways. He slipped in the chair. His head slumped forward and he slid onto the floor.

Shirley shrieked.

I crossed the room in a couple of steps. Knelt down beside Hobart's crumpled body.

He was dead.

His eyes bulged from their sockets. His lips were swollen. His tongue lolled from the side of this mouth.

I turned away and felt that familiar churn in my guts whenever I see a dead body.

I stood up and put my arms around Shirley. Her face was taut with strain. Her body shook as I held her tight.

She clung to me like I was a lifebelt.

"Looks like I'll never know now what Hobart wanted to tell me," she said.

Chapter 2

I took Shirley's hand gently and led her out of the room back into the conservatory.

She was breathing deeply. Her face had turned pale.

I sat her down in a basket chair.

She said: "I thought Hobart was asleep. I never thought... Do you think he died of a heart attack?"

I knelt beside the chair and stroked her hand. I thought it would calm her. Or perhaps me. I could have done with it. My mind was buzzing like a chainsaw.

It wasn't going to take a cardiologist to tell that poor old Hobart hadn't died from a heart attack. Not unless a heart attack involved being clubbed with a blunt instrument, then strangled by a monster with giant hands.

As soon as I'd knelt beside Hobart's body, I'd seen the dented abrasion on his forehead. Then I'd noticed the deep bruises around his neck and throat. The kind of marks made by a man whose hands could have choked a gorilla. Cross the giant from Jack and the Beanstalk with the Boston Strangler and you'll get an idea of what I was thinking.

Shirley let out a long sigh. "I'm feeling a little better now. What a pity we didn't visit yesterday. If we'd found Hobart poorly, we could have called an ambulance."

"He could've done that himself. Besides, I don't think he would've had the opportunity. He was murdered."

Shirl's body tensed and she sat up straight. "That's not a good joke."

"It's no joke." I told Shirley what I'd seen.

"We must call the cops," Shirley said.

"Yes, but not yet."

"The sooner the cops come, the sooner they can track down the killer."

"The killer is long gone by now. My guess is that Hobart died yesterday evening. An extra half hour isn't going to make a difference at this stage of an investigation."

Shirl gave me a hard look. "And don't tell me. You'll use the time to get a story for your paper. You're a cynical bastard."

"Stories like this don't often fall into a reporter's lap," I said.

"Says the reporter who has stories fall into his lap."

"I wasn't thinking so much of a story as whether we could find the information Hobart was going to give you."

Shirl nodded thoughtfully at that. Decided I'd passed the test. Just. And stood up. I was pleased to see she'd regained her colour and looked better.

"So, if we're going to search the place, where do we start? The body?" she asked.

"No, we won't find anything we need to know there. And looking at Hobart as he is now, you may give yourself nightmares. No, the place a good reporter starts in a case like this is the same place our subject – Hobart – regards as his most private domain."

"Which is?"

"I'm guessing it's his study."

"If he has one," Shirley said.

"I'm betting he does as he lives alone."

"You don't know that."

"I think we can tell. First, he didn't mention anyone else living here in his letter to you. If there were anybody else here, they'd have surely raised the alarm by now – or died themselves at the hands of the killer. And, finally, the furniture in his sitting room was arranged to suit one person. His chair, the one we found him in, was the only one positioned so he could look out over the garden. There was a coffee table nearby, but not next to the other chair and sofa. And the clock on the mantelpiece was angled so that he could see the time while sitting in his favourite chair."

Shirley shrugged. "I guess I'll buy that. But just remember one thing. He's my half-uncle. I've got proprietorial rights around here."

I nodded. "Let's find the study."

We walked back into the passageway which led along the length of the house and found the study at the far end. It occupied a single-storey extension. It looked as though it had been added quite recently.

The study was furnished in a modest style. Think small-town solicitor. There was an old desk mottled with ink stains. There was one of those chairs on wheels behind it. The padding on the chair had split and stuffing hung out. The desk held a telephone and a tray containing pens and pencils. There was a wire basket holding a dozen or so sheets of paper – mostly bills that were due for payment. Nothing overdue. No threatening red letters. As a former banker, Hobart evidently kept his financial affairs in good order.

Don't we all?

I reached into my pocket and pulled out a pair of surgical gloves (one shilling and nine-pence at Boots, the Chemists). I make it a habit to carry a pair just in case I come across a crime scene. I don't want to contaminate it with my own prints.

"Don't touch anything in here," I said to Shirley as I rolled them on.

"Jeez, you sure come ready for action," she said.

I flipped through the bills in the basket. "I don't see that these tell us much," I said.

I tugged open the desk drawer. Inside there were half a dozen pencils and one of those little sharpeners with a blade mounted in a plastic holder. There was a bottle of black Waterman's ink. And two books. I picked them up. The first was a 1967 diary. The other a leather-bound address book.

"Perhaps these will help," I said.

Shirley moved closer as I flipped the diary's pages to the day's date. And there it was in the same black spidery writing we'd seen in his letter: "Morning: Shirley Goldsmith." Underneath the spider had added: "I hope she will come. I can't take this on by myself."

Shirley read the words, then gawped at me. "Take what on?"

I shrugged and turned to earlier pages in the diary.

It was clear that Hobart was not a busy man. Most pages had no entries. Others merely little domestic notes: "Pay milkman."

However, two weeks earlier an entry read: "Visit BNL, Colindale."

Shirley said: "Who is BNL?"

"It's what rather than who. I think BNL stands for British Newspaper Library which is at Colindale in north London. The place archives copies of newspapers published in Britain."

"Why would he want to go there?" Shirley asked.

I pulled a sheet of paper that had been slipped inside the back cover of the diary.

"This may tell us."

I unfolded the sheet. It was a copy of a cutting dated February 1967 from the foreign news pages of *The Times*. A headline in modest type read: "Australia's double murder mystery".

Shirley snuggled closer to me and we read the cutting together.

The story told how police in Melbourne were baffled by the double murder of a father and son. First, father Fletcher Woodburn had been knocked out and strangled at his apartment near the Yarra river in the Spotswood district of the city. Then, hours later, son Jake was killed in the same way at his lodgings at Upfield. Cops were apparently working on the theory that the killer was someone with a grudge against the family. But people who'd known the father and son said they were both well liked, with a wide circle of friends.

"They were killed the same way as Hobart," Shirley said.

"Without knowing the forensic details, we can't be sure," I said. "Let's look through the rest of the diary."

Hobart had not been busy since his trip to the British Newspaper Library.

But two days earlier he'd had a visit from a Victoria Nettlebed. She was due at two-thirty but there was no other information about her.

And the day before that, Hobart was due to meet a Lionel Bruce. Underneath the entry Hobart had scrawled: "May be late. Arriving on one-forty train."

I flipped back over earlier pages. "According to the diary, these were the only two people Hobart arranged to meet in the seven days before his death," I said.

"Only two people and we don't know who they are," Shirley said.

"This may help." I opened the address book and flipped to the page for N.

"Well, we know where we can find Victoria Nettlebed," I said. "She's listed here as professor of Australian history with an address at Sussex University."

I took out my notebook and made a quick note of her contact details.

I flipped to the page for Bs. Nothing. Just a jagged tear where the page had been roughly torn out.

"No information about Lionel Bruce," I said.

Shirl's face registered shock. "And you think Bruce tore the page out? That would make him..."

"...the murderer," I said. "But I don't think so."

"If he was acute enough to remove evidence from the address book, surely he would have done so from the diary as well?"

"You'd have thought so," I said. "But if he is the killer, perhaps he was too flustered to think of the diary."

Shirl cocked her head to one side while she considered the point. She looked cute.

But we had work to do. And there'd be time for cute later.

There was a metal filing cabinet up against the wall. I stepped around the corner of the desk and tugged on the cabinet's drawers. All locked.

On top of the cabinet, there was an office spike. It was just like the ones we impaled copies of our stories on in the *Chronicle* newsroom. I took a look at the spike, but it was so crammed with documents, there were too many to read. And if I tried to take them off, I'd have to thread them back through the original holes. Impossible. Even Brighton's finest would spot they'd been tampered with. Which would mean trouble.

I turned to Shirley. She was staring at something on the floor on the other side of the desk.

"Look at this," she said.

It was a wastepaper basket. In it were two pieces of paper.

They'd originally been one sheet which had been torn in half. I reached into the basket for them and laid them on the desk together. The jagged tear ran down the middle.

I recognised the spider writing. Looked like Hobart fancied his chances as a poet – or perhaps a songwriter. Shirley and I leant over the desk and read his take on *Waltzing Matilda*:

Once a half-way uncle lived in a cottage neat,
Lived like a poor man who just wanted peace.
He learned as he watched and waited while some others died,
You'll come a Waltzing Matilda, half-niece.
Waltzing Matilda, Waltzing Matilda,
You'll come a-Waltzing Matilda, half-niece.
He learned as he watched and waited while some others died,
You'll come a-Waltzing Matilda, half-niece.

As I read the last lines, I felt Shirley's hand reach for mine and grip it hard.

We finished reading at the same time. Turned to one another.

"What does it mean?" she said in a voice that quavered with uncertainty.

"It means it's time to call the cops," I said.

***

"I can't understand why Hobart wanted to go waltzing with you," I said. "If it was me, I'd want to tango. Or perhaps salsa. Besides, I'd never have you down as a Matilda. Much too frumpish."

It was five minutes later. Shirl and I were sitting in the conservatory waiting for Brighton's finest to show up. I'd used Hobart's phone to call the cop shop. I'd removed the surgical gloves and shoved them in my inside jacket pocket before picking up the telephone receiver. The cops are suspicious when they find fingerprints that shouldn't be there. But they ask awkward questions if your prints aren't where they should be.

"You need a crash course in Aussie slang," Shirley said. "The 'Matilda' in the song is a backpack – a bedroll and a few odds and ends. And the 'waltzing' means walking about with it – hiking around the Outback. In the song, it's a 'jolly swagman' - I guess the Yanks would call him a hobo - who camps by a 'billabong', a stagnant pool. He stuffs a 'jumbuck', a young sheep, in his 'tucker bag', his food store. And he jumps into the billabong to avoid arrest by the 'troopers', the cops."

Shirley shrugged. "What I can't figure is why Hobart wrote an extra verse aimed at me."

"Perhaps he intended to show it to you when you met."

"Then why did he tear it up?"

"Second thoughts, perhaps. Not really in good taste to give a young woman a risqué poem at a first meeting. You wouldn't catch me doing that."

Shirl arched an eyebrow. "And we all know you're the perfect gentleman."

She paused and gave me a quizzical look.

"But you can't help wondering whether there is some deeper meaning in it," I said.

Shirl nodded. "It's that line about watching and waiting while others died that gets to me."

"I've been thinking about that too."

"The brainbox come up with any theories?"

"I was wondering whether the other dead might be Fletcher and Jake Woodburn mentioned in the press cutting."

"You think he knew them?"

"I don't know. But he obviously went to a lot of trouble to get a press cutting about their killing from the back issue of a newspaper."

I wasn't going to worry Shirley about that, but I'd already decided I needed to know more about the Woodburn murders. And I'd thought of a way of getting the information.

I said: "The main thing is we need to find out what Hobart planned to tell you. I've got a hunch Victoria Nettlebed and Lionel Bruce may have something to do with that. I'm going to track them down."

Shirley nudged me sharply in the ribs. "Don't forget who's the main shareholder in this enterprise. Little me."

Behind me, a gruff voice said: "I might have guessed you'd be mixed up in this."

I swung round. Detective chief superintendent Alec Tomkins had just stepped through the conservatory door. He was wearing a blue serge suit, a red and white polka-dot tie, and a satisfied smirk which made his face look like a deflating balloon.

Behind him, a couple of his forensic team clumped in without wiping their feet.

I said: "You'll find the body in the sitting room. If you wish, I'll introduce you as you've not met before. And then Shirley and I will be on our way."

"Having done our duty as upright citizens," Shirley chipped in.

Tomkins loomed closer. "Just a minute. I need to take a statement from you two."

I pointed at the two forensic guys heading into the passage that led to the rest of the house.

"You might want to stop them contaminating the crime scene.

They've obviously stepped in something rural outside in the lane. They're leaving a trail of brown footprints which would've had Sherlock Holmes whipping out his magnifying glass."

Tomkins' head swivelled so fast I expected to see a couple of screws fly out of his neck.

"Come back, you idiots," he screamed.

But the forensic guys were already half-way down the passage.

Tomkins forgot about us and bundled after them.

I winked at Shirley. "Let's quit while we're ahead. We can make our statements to Tomkins later."

Chapter 3

I arrived back at my desk in the *Chronicle* newsroom two minutes before midday.

I hadn't spared the gas as I'd powered the MGB through the Sussex lanes. I'd dropped Shirley off at her flat and offered to stay with her. Behind her Aussie confidence, I could tell she'd been shaken by the morning's events. But she insisted all she wanted was a strong coffee and the latest issue of *Vogue* magazine.

I'd left her with a kiss and a promise that I'd pick her up in the evening.

In the newsroom, I pulled my Remington towards me and started to pound the keys. I had a hell of tale to tell. Man found murdered in remote cottage. Killing had same *modus operandi* as two in Australia just months before. Mystery in a tiny hamlet with a funny name.

The only thing that worried me was how much of the tale to reveal. There are only two kinds of murder stories. Those where you know within days or even hours who did it. And those where you haven't a clue about the means, motive and opportunity – or the killer. My story fell firmly into the second category.

It was going to take time to get the answers I needed, so I decided to stick mostly to the facts which the cops would put in the public domain. Knowing Tomkins, there wouldn't be many of them. So, I could spice up my story with a few details the other hacks wouldn't have. They hadn't seen Hobart with his head caved in and a giant's hand-prints around his neck.

Most of all, I wanted to keep Shirley out of the story. It's not that Shirl is the shy retiring type. A girl who's in heavy demand for fashion and promotional photoshoots won't be Miss Modesty. Shirl was proud of her assets and not shy to flaunt them. Photographers knew that, when they clicked their shutters, she would provide them with a lens-full of loveliness. And it would come with a wink and a blown kiss for anyone who saw the pictures.

No, what worried me was that I simply didn't know how Shirl fitted into this story. I didn't know why Hobart had wanted to see her. I had no idea how he had tracked her down. Even though he had said in his letter to Shirl that he'd been researching his family tree. I drew a blank on what it was that would be to Shirl's "advantage". I hadn't a clue what the connection, if any, was between Hobart and the murdered Woodburns. And I found the *Waltzing Matilda* verse that Hobart had written weird and spooky.

So I was thinking hard as I pounded those keys.

I tugged the last folio from the typewriter's carriage, and signalled for Cedric, the copy boy, to take the story up to the subs.

My telephone rang.

I lifted the receiver and a voice that sounded like a rusty rake dragged over a fallen tombstone said: "My office."

Frank Figgis, my news editor, was apparently in desperate need of my company.

I said: "Your office. What about it?"

"You're not in it."

"Is there any reason I should be?"

"If you're not here in twenty seconds, I won't sign off your expenses."

Eighteen seconds later, I barged through Figgis' office door without knocking. There are some things too serious for badinage. And my weekly expense sheet is one of them.

Figgis was sitting behind his desk folding an empty Woodbine packet into the shape of a yacht.

I said: "I didn't know you were into origami."

He said: "I don't like Japanese food."

As there was no answer to that, I sat down in the visitor's

chair.

Figgis put his Woodbine yacht aside. He was a small man with a pallid skin tone and a smoker's cough. The lines on his face looked like the isobars on a weather chart when a gale was blowing in. He had dark black hair which he parted right down the middle with mathematical precision. If Isaac Newton had been a hairdresser, he wouldn't have been able to make it more precise – even with the aid of a fine-toothed comb and calculus. Figgis' false teeth squeaked a bit when he was excited and made a grinding sound like a rusty gear when he got annoyed. At the moment, the sound was somewhere between the two. He seemed ill at ease. Usually, I'd be the cause of that. But, today, I didn't think so.

I said: "I've just sent a murder story up to the subs. I think it should lead the afternoon extra edition."

Figgis picked up a copy of the midday edition from his desk.

He said: "If you'd phoned in your copy from the scene of the crime, we could already have the story on the streets."

I said: "The cops arrived and I couldn't use the phone."

"What's wrong with a public call box?"

"I was in a place called Muddles Green, deepest rural Sussex. It's a miracle they've even got electricity."

Figgis grunted and tossed the paper into a wire tray. He reached for his Woodbines and shook one out. Tapped the end on his desk to settle the tobacco. Parked the fag behind his ear. I'd never seen him do that before.

He said: "There's something you're not telling me."

He was right about that. I hadn't mentioned Shirley's role in the drama.

I wouldn't be able to keep it from him for ever, so I sat there and spilled it all out.

The teeth grinding gave way to more squeaking.

I ended: "So that's why I want to keep Shirley out of the story for the time being."

"Rival papers may find out – and you know where you'll be then."

I did indeed. A rival rag would splash Shirley's role in the story in the most damaging way they could. Even though they knew Shirl and I were going out – the most enjoyable bits of which were staying in. In the newspaper trade, dog does eat dog. And the gobbled-up mutt is expected to wag her tail while it happens.

I said: "The cops won't want to spread it around that Shirl and I found the body. Makes them look like they're not doing their job. Besides, I think we've got enough of an inside-track on this story to keep us ahead of the pack."

Figgis picked up a paperclip and started to bend it out of shape. He gazed out of the window. This definitely wasn't like him.

I said: "Are you feeling all right? Why don't you light your Woodbine? But better take it from behind your ear first."

Figgis looked back at me as though I'd just asked him to jump out of the window. "Woodbine? Oh, yes."

He took the fag from behind his ear and rummaged in his jacket pocket for his matches. He struck a match, lit the ciggie, and took a long drag. He relaxed a little.

"I was telling you about how we could develop the murder story," I said.

"Oh, that. Actually, there's something I need to talk to you about."

"About the Muddles Green murder?"

"No, this is more important."

"What's more important in our trade than an exclusive front page splash?"

Figgis took another drag on his fag and blew out a perfect smoke ring. "What I'm about to tell you stays within these four walls."

"That leaves the windows and the door to let it out."

Figgis banged his hand on his desk. "This is no matter for one of your so-called witticisms."

"Then get to the point," I said, more testily than I should've.

"There's something I need to tell you."

"Tell away."

"It's strictly confidential."

"My lips are sealed with cement."

"It's vital that no one else knows."

"We two shall be the world's most secret society."

Figgis took a nervous drag on his fag. "I've written a book."

My heart should have raced. My eyes should have bulged. And I should have barked with derisive laughter. But I didn't do any of those things. Because I'd had a suspicion for some weeks that Figgis was up to something.

For a start, he'd moved the typewriter he usually parked on top of his filing cabinet to the extension at the side of his desk. A pile of blank copy paper had appeared by the side of the typewriter. And on a couple of occasions, I'd caught him late in the office, well after the time he'd normally leave for the Coach & Horses.

I said: "Congratulations! Don't tell me, you want to keep schtum because it's a story of sex and violence. Like Harold Robbins' steamy tale *The Carpetbaggers*."

Figgis stubbed out his Woodbine and shook his head. "It's not a novel and if Mrs Figgis even thought I'd written anything like Robbins she'd banish me to the spare bedroom."

"So, what kind of book is it?"

"My memoirs."

I couldn't help it. This time, I just rocked back in my chair and roared with laughter.

The lines on Figgis' forehead deepened. "I don't know what you find so funny."

With a bit of effort, I controlled my merriment. "Sorry. It's just that it wasn't what I'd expected. I take it your colleagues in the newsroom remain mere ghosts. Many of us wouldn't like our scams and tricks to form part of your narrative."

"After thirty years as a newspaperman, I know what I can say. And what I can't," Figgis snapped.

"When do you expect the book to come out?"

"We come to the point. It's not going to – because the manuscript has been stolen."

This time, I leaned forward with a serious look on my face. "When did this happen?"

"I'm not sure. The past few days. I'd stored the manuscript in the top drawer of the filing cabinet over there by the wall. I kept the drawer locked."

I swivelled my head to view the cabinet and show I was keeping up.

"When I came to look for the manuscript yesterday, it was gone."

"And the filing cabinet locked?" I asked.

Figgis shook his head. "I'd unlocked it earlier to get some files out of one of the other drawers. Must have forgotten to relock it. I was out of the office for half an hour having another time-wasting meeting with His Holiness."

Gerald Pope was the public-school twit who'd become editor of the *Chronicle* because his father had known the proprietor's father. He was obsessed with minor typos in the gardening notes and whether the odds on the two-thirty at Goodwood were correct. Pope and Figgis detested one another. But they pulled together like a pair of horses in harness because they knew each needed the other. Pope needed Figgis to get out the paper with exclusives that beat the rivals. And Figgis needed Pope to provide cover from the proprietor when there was trouble over a story.

I said: "I can't understand who'd have a motive for stealing your manuscript."

Figgis' voice dropped to a whisper. "I can. Anyone who

wanted to make trouble for me."

"That could be a long list," I said.

Figgis nodded.

"Reporters you've fired. Crooks you've exposed in the paper. Publicans you've rubbed up the wrong way. Need I go on?"

I didn't need to mention crime reporters who'd had their stories spiked.

Figgis shook his head. "I'd rather you didn't."

"Perhaps the manuscript will turn up. As a well-thumbed copy with some edits."

Figgis shivered. "I hope not. You see, I may have allowed my prose to run away with me."

"I get it. Payback time for anybody that ever tried to cross you. And for some who only thought about it."

Figgis' lips twitched into a sinister little grin. "Every time I'd screwed one of those bastards in a few well-chosen words, I felt better. It's an unbelievable feeling. But the book can't be published yet. When I'm dead and buried, perhaps. That's why I want you to get it back."

I didn't like the sound of that at all.

I said: "For recovery of stolen goods, you need a private detective. Besides, I'm too busy to do personal sleuthing for you. I've got a hot murder story to cover."

Figgis reached for his Woodbine origami and crumpled it in one hand. "The consequence of that manuscript surfacing in the wrong place could be bad for all of us."

"You mean… I'm mentioned in it," I snapped.

Figgis held up his hands to placate me. "Only in the most flattering way. But I have revealed some of the scams you've pulled along the way. There are people around who'd turn dangerous if they read it."

"Like detective chief superintendent Tomkins?"

"Yes."

"And the *Chronicle's* proprietor?"

"Yes."

"And certain figures in Brighton's underworld who don't court publicity?"

Figgis shrugged. "I don't like it any more than you."

I was annoyed. No, I was full-on angry. That doesn't quite cover it. I was spitting fire.

But Figgis had me cornered. If he'd written what he'd said about me, that could cause – would cause - a lot of trouble in the wrong hands.

I said: "Do you have any idea who might have taken the manuscript? Where should I start looking?"

"Most thefts are committed by people close to home."

"By which you mean the newsroom?"

"They're most likely to have the means, motive and opportunity," Figgis said. "Isn't that what you're always writing?"

I didn't answer that. When it came to Figgis' memoirs, the less I said, the better.

I trudged back to the newsroom feeling like old Hercules who had to carry out twelve labours.

At least, I only had three impossible tasks. I had to cover a murder story in which Shirley was the central character (apologies to the corpse) without mentioning her. I had to find out what secrets poor old Hobart Birtwhistle planned to whisper in Shirl's shell-like. And I had to recover Figgis' manuscript without letting on to anyone what I was about.

Still, if Hercules could clean the Augean stables and still manage another eleven labours, perhaps I could perform three.

And I would start by spending the least possible time on Figgis' manuscript. Because I knew exactly what the outcome would be. But he'd need to think I was busy at the task. I'd start by making an attempt at narrowing down the list of suspects.

I swivelled around in my captain's chair and viewed the rest of the newsroom. Twenty-three reporters. Figgis' suspicious mind would suspect all of them. Even me. Which of them might bear Figgis some kind of grudge? I made a quick assessment. The answer: twenty-three.

So much for trying to narrow the field. But Sally Martin, who edited the women's page, had wanted to step up to deputy editor last year. Figgis had opposed the move on the grounds Sally couldn't be spared from the women's beat.

Then there was Phil Bailey. One of the paper's old timers, and still stuck as a general reporter. Some said that's what he liked. But I knew Phil had pressed Figgis many times to get the town hall beat. No joy.

And my final principal suspect was business reporter Susan Wheatcroft. Susan had been head-hunted by one of the nationals last year. She reckoned she'd have landed the job had Figgis not penned a lukewarm reference because he didn't want to lose her.

But what was I thinking? Figgis had me suspicious of my newsroom colleagues when I was sure that none of them would have snatched his wretched book. Even so, I had to put on a show. Every newsroom has its sneaks. They'd report back on whether it looked like I was taking the case seriously.

And that irked me. Because I should have been spending my time following up the Birtwhistle murder story.

And as for the threat Figgis' manuscript posed to me? Well, it would have to be a case of "tell the truth and shame the devil". Perhaps I could even shame the devil without telling the truth. The search for the manuscript would prove that.

Meanwhile, I had two names from Hobart's diary – Victoria Nettlebed and Lionel Bruce. Hobart had also recorded Nettlebed's address and telephone number in his contacts' book. Bruce's details may have been on the ripped-out page.

I reached for my telephone and dialled Nettlebed's number. The phone was answered after six rings.

A voice that was half BBC news-reader and half railway ticket office clerk, said: "Nettlebed. If you're asking for an extension to hand in your history essay, the answer's no."

I said: "Colin Crampton here."

"You're not one of my students."

"No, I'm one of the *Evening Chronicle's* reporters."

"A journalist? As G K Chesterton said, 'Journalism largely consists of saying Lord Jones is Dead to people who never knew Lord Jones was alive.'"

"As an historian, you should know that journalism is the first draft of history."

"With a mass of crossings out and corrections before the final story is told. Anyway, what do you want?"

"An interview."

"About what?"

What indeed? I should have thought about how to play this request before making the call. I couldn't come straight out and say I wanted the interview because her name was in the diary and address book of a murdered man.

"Er... I want to get your perspective on Australia's plan to change its constitution."

The country had just voted in a referendum to give indigenous people – the aborigines, as they called them – the right to be counted in the country's censuses. Big of them. Pity they hadn't yet given them the vote or a fair share of the country's wealth.

"I'm surprised a Brighton newspaper is interested the referendum result," Nettlebed said.

"We have a lot of Australians living in Brighton," I lied. I had a brainwave. "I could bring one with me."

"Very well, then. Tomorrow morning, at the university. Ten-thirty. My office. Ask at reception."

The line went dead.

I replaced the receiver and wondered how I'd tell Shirley I'd lined her up for a meeting with a bolshy history professor.

Chapter 4

I met Shirley three hours later in Prinny's Pleasure.

The pub occupied a corner site in the North Laine part of town. The outside had crumbling brickwork, a front door with flaking brown paint, and a loose drainpipe that banged in a high wind.

Inside, the green flock wallpaper had little patches of moss growing on it. The carpet squelched as you trod on it. The place smelt of stale beer and desperation.

Jeff Purkiss, the landlord, was propped on a stool as Shirley and I walked up to the bar. Purkiss was a beanpole of a man with cadaverous eyes and a nose that had once been broken in a fight. He was wearing a sweaty singlet and a pair of grey trousers held up by braces.

He looked up as we approached the bar and sniffed dismissively, like we weren't good enough for the place.

I said: "Were you expecting royalty?"

Jeff sniffed again. "There was a time when the highest in the land would take ale here."

Jeff was convinced that back in the eighteenth century the place had once been a secret rendezvous for the Prince Regent, the future king George the Fourth, and his favourite squeeze, Mrs Fitzherbert. Jeff had put up a blue plaque outside announcing the fact in the hope it would attract sucker tourists. A council inspector had ordered him to take the plaque down on account of it was totally inaccurate. Jeff had argued that the ghosts of the Prince and Mrs Fitzherbert still haunted the place on stormy nights. He told the inspector he could hear their bed's headboard banging against the wall upstairs as the pair consummated their love. But the inspector pointed out it was the loose drainpipe.

I said: "Forget the highest in the land, Jeff. You're stuck with us. Make with the gin and tonic. One ice cube and two slices of lemon."

"And Campari soda for me," Shirl added.

We took our drinks to the corner table at the back of the bar.

Shirl sipped her Campari and said: "I really don't know what you see in this place."

"Nobody. No nosey regulars. No fussy tourists. And that's the point. When you're a crime reporter you meet plenty of shady characters. And that's just the cops. You don't need an audience."

I took a pull at my G and T. "I've a confession to make," I said.

"If it's the kind where you end up buying me another Campari, go ahead, big boy."

I told Shirl that I'd fixed us up for a joint appointment with Victoria Nettlebed in the morning. I expected her to tell me she'd already arranged something else.

In fact, I needn't have worried. Shirley jumped at the idea of meeting a professor of Australian history.

"I may be able to put her straight on one or two points," Shirl said. "Do you think she'll shoot the breeze on why she had a meeting with Hobart?"

"I don't know. It'll be tricky to raise that with her without admitting how we knew. She sounded like a no-nonsense type on the phone. And one with no particular love of journalists."

"A smooth-talking bastard like you will have her waving her knickers in the air just for the pleasure of seeing you smile," Shirl said. "Anyway, right now I'm famished. Where shall we chow?"

"Somewhere fast. I have to get back to the office this evening."

Shirl pulled a disappointed face.

"Urgent job," I said. "I'll tell you about it afterwards. Say, why don't we meet tomorrow morning? Breakfast at Marcello's? The full English. I'm paying."

Shirley grinned. "Gee, I'm going out with the last of the big spenders."

My reason for heading back to the office had nothing to do with Figgis' manuscript thief and everything to do with Hobart Birtwhistle's killing.

I'd been puzzling over the newspaper cutting about Fletcher and Jake Woodburn's double murder. From the entry in his diary, it looked as though Birtwhistle had gone to a lot of trouble to get a copy from the British Newspaper Library. I needed to know more. *The Times* cutting had been brief. But the local newspaper – in this case the Melbourne *Herald Sun* - would know more.

When I finally got a connection to Melbourne, I spoke to Charlie Field, the night editor. He told me the story had originally been covered by Henry Truelove, the paper's crime reporter. Unfortunately, Truelove wasn't in the office. It was five in the morning Melbourne time, and his star reporter would be tucked up with his teddy bear.

But I sweet-talked Charlie into giving me Truelove's home number on the strength of sharing a new angle on the Woodburn double murder. Like one journalist helping another. Hands across the sea and all that.

So, there I was, sat at my desk, the receiver clamped to my ear, and with the sound of a phone ringing in a Melbourne suburb, ten thousand miles away.

A sleepy voice answered: "Henry Truelove. Unless you're trapped in a fire or cornered by a mad gunman, rock off. I'm fast asleep and intend to stay that way for three more hours."

I said: "I have a new angle on the Woodburn double murder."

"Forget the foregoing. Who the blazes are you? Is this for real?"

"I'm Colin Crampton, crime reporter on the Brighton *Evening Chronicle*."

"Jeez. Dear old Blighty! G'day, Colin."

"And a very good morning to you. And, yes, it is for real. I have the facts on another murder with the same M O as the Woodburns'. All yours for a front-page headline. In return, I need a briefing on everything you couldn't use in your original *Herald Sun* piece."

(Crampton, master negotiator. Give a little to get a lot.)

"Sounds okay to me, sport. Shoot."

So, I told Truelove about Birtwhistle's murder. I mentioned the similarities – the victims knocked out, then strangled. And I told Truelove that Hobart had a press cutting about the Woodburn killings.

I said: "Did you know there were people outside Australia taking an interest in the case?"

"We'd had a couple of enquiries from the American press but nothing from Britain."

"Did the name of Hobart Birtwhistle crop up in the case?"

"Not on anything I saw."

"I can't figure out what the motive for the Woodburns' killing was."

"Neither can the local cops. At first, they played the gangland killing card. Father and son killed on the same day – the sort of revenge slaying one of the downtown gangs might pull. But the cops haven't been able to link Fletcher or Jake Woodburn to any gang. The pair seem to have led a blameless life – not so much as a parking ticket between them."

"In my experience, blameless people don't normally end up murdered," I said. "Certainly not as part of a double killing on the same day. Did you run your own background check on the pair?"

"Sure. Fletcher had married a Maria Borlotti just before the war. Baby Jake popped out in 1938. All was well for a few years, but Maria joined the heavenly choir back in the fifties. No violence, the big C. Fletcher was devastated but carried on bringing up Jake himself. The lad turned out well. Was working as a motor mechanic at a garage on the outskirts of the city. Fletcher was a retired electrical engineer."

"There has to be more to this than a couple of motiveless random killings," I said. "The fact they were murdered on the same day must mean the killer planned his attacks in detail."

"That's what the cops here think. Trouble is they've tried to find witnesses who spotted some sinister guy hanging round Fletcher's or Jake's pads. No dice."

"Of course, the best way to hide is in plain sight. Like you're someone who you'd expect to see. No street sweepers, window cleaners, or delivery guys who raised suspicion?"

"Not that I know about."

"What about people Fletcher and Jake knew? Most murdered people are killed by someone they know."

"True. The cops looked at friends and acquaintances. But none raised suspicion. Didn't have a motive to kill one, let alone both of them. And certainly not the opportunity for a double killing."

"So, two violent deaths in the Woodburn family - both unexplained."

"You speak of a couple but, in fact, the Woodburn family have had three deaths this year - Francesca Woodburn, Fletcher's mother. She was a 72-year-old widow."

"Another murder?"

"Not unless you count being eaten by a shark while swimming off Bondi beach."

I thought about that for a moment.

"Is there any way her death could have been the trigger for the killings?"

"In what way?"

I shrugged. Felt foolish because Truelove wouldn't have seen the gesture.

"I don't know. Just a thought," I said.

"Sure. We could do with some more on this case. Now, if you don't mind, I'd like to get another couple of hours kip before I head for the office. But keep in touch, Colin. G'day."

The line went dead.

It was almost midnight by the time I arrived back at my lodgings.

I had a suite of rooms on the top floor of a house in Regency Square. "Suite" sounds a bit posh. There was a small sitting room with squeaky floorboards. There was a bathroom where the cold tap dripped. And there was a bedroom tucked under the eaves, where I lie awake at night listening to the seagulls scrabbling around on the roof.

The place was presided over by Mrs Beatrice Gribble, known to her tenants (behind her back) as the Widow. Her husband Hector had expired, probably from boredom, a few years earlier. There was a photo of him on the mantelpiece in the Widow's parlour. He looked like he wanted nothing so much as the earth to swallow him up.

After Hector's death, the Widow was faced with keeping a five-storey house going without any income. So reluctantly, she turned to the landlady game. She got her own back by making her tenants' lives a constant battle for sanity – not least in my case.

I inserted my key in the lock and turned it silently. As I opened the front door, I applied a well-practised upward force to the handle to stop the hinges creaking. I closed the door behind me and crept towards the stairs.

I had my foot on the first tread when the Widow shot out of her parlour. She was wearing a royal-blue quilted dressing gown that came down to her ankles and pink pom-pom slippers. She'd put her hair in curlers under some sort of net arrangement. She'd smothered white cream on her face so she looked like the lead in *The Ghost and Mrs Muir*. On second thoughts, perhaps not. In the film, the ghost was played by Rex Harrison wearing a full beard. The Widow only had a thin moustache along her upper lip.

She said in the ingratiating tone she usually saved for titled ladies and bank managers: "Mr Crampton, you're a man of the world."

I said: "Actually, I'm an alien from Mars and I'm just going back to my mother ship to sleep."

The Widow's face cracked into what may have been a smile. "You know I don't have aliens here. Or travelling salesmen."

"I thought we were missing something good."

"Can you spare a minute?"

"As days on Mars are thirty-nine minutes longer than Earth, I suppose I might manage one."

It was usually quicker to let the Widow have her say.

The Widow said: "My cousin Christine in Solihull has passed on."

"You'd told me before she was moving to Cleethorpes."

"She's been called to a higher place."

"Skegness?"

"Mr Crampton, Christine is dead."

"She'll have to cancel the Cleethorpes move, then."

"And now there are arguments about who should inherit her portrait of Lady Amelia Fogge. It's by that artist who sounds as though he was in the army. Corporal, was it?"

"Do you mean Sargent?"

"Yes, I think he was the brush twiddler."

John Singer Sargent was more than a brush twiddler. He'd been a top player in the paint-your-portrait game. Everybody who was anybody in Edwardian society at the turn of the century had their ugly mug slapped on a canvas by Sargent in his finest oils. Now he was long dead, a decent portrait by him could easily sell for twenty or thirty thousand pounds. No wonder the Widow wanted to get her grubby fingers on it.

I said: "Surely, Christine's will sets out who gets the picture."

"She didn't have a will."

"She died intestate?"

"No, in a nursing home."

"If there's no will, her goods and chattels go to her next of kin. Is that you?"

"It could be."

"What relation were you to Christine?"

"Sort of a cousin."

"What sort?"

"The sort that couldn't stand her. She always had her nose stuck in the air. The type that thinks she's better than anyone else."

"You didn't like her but you want her picture," I said. "Isn't that just a teensy-weensy bit hypocritical?"

"I didn't say I didn't like the picture."

I shrugged. "Well, I can't see why you need my help."

"Because Christine kept the picture in a vault. A bank vault. I rang up the bank manager today, but he wouldn't let me have it. I want you to write him a letter. On my behalf."

"Much better you do it yourself."

"I wouldn't know what to say – how to put it right. You have a way with words."

The Widow gave me a big blousy wink. "There'd be something in it for you," she said. "That new rug for your bedroom you've been going on about."

I staged a long yawn to show how unimpressed I was. "I'll think about it," I said.

I powered up the stairs. Behind me, I heard the Widow slam the door to her parlour.

The following morning, I arrived at Marcello's before Shirley.

I was well into the full English – bacon, sausage, tomatoes, mushrooms and fried bread – before Shirl steamed through the doors. She practically danced across to my table. Waved to

Marcello and ordered coffee and toast.

"No fry-up?" I asked. I leaned across the table and kissed her gently on the lips.

Shirl pointed at my plate. "I'm so excited I couldn't possibly eat all that." She grabbed my sausage and took a bite. "You won't believe my news."

"Go on."

"I had a phone call this morning from a guy called Harry Peccinotti."

"Harry who?"

"Peccinotti. He's a photographer who's been hired for the Pirelli calendar."

"I never tire of looking at it."

"Ha, bloody, ha. They dropped the tyre photos after the first couple of calendars. Incidentally, they call it the Cal. Now it's just the girls who feature in the shots. And Harry wants me as one of the models for next year's calendar – the one coming out in 1968. They didn't have one this year for some reason."

"That's great news. The Cal is building a big reputation. And not just because it features the world's most beautiful women wearing barely enough to keep the goosebumps at bay."

The tyre company had hit on a cunning marketing plan. They printed a limited number of the Cal and gave them away as promotional gifts. Because the Cal was in short supply, having one became a status symbol. There were guys who would willingly sacrifice a testicle to get one. Pirelli had only conceived of the calendar wheeze in 1963 – and already it was a winner.

And Shirley was going to be in it.

"They're shooting the next Cal in Tunisia," Shirl said. "They want to fly me there in about a month's time. But before then, I've got lots of tests and studio work."

Marcello stepped up to the table with Shirl's coffee and toast.

"I'm gonna be on a calendar," she said.

"Which month?" Marcello asked.

"Don't know. But I'll ask for April. It's my favourite time of year."

"*Un bel mese per una bella ragazza.*" Marcello swooned like he was Romeo climbing the balcony for a kiss and cuddle with Juliet.

"Isn't that your coffee machine I hear hissing, lover boy?" I brought him down to earth. He sloped off to his counter.

Shirl grabbed a slice of toast and took a bite.

I said: "Better mangle that toast, calendar girl. We have an appointment in the groves of academe."

Shirl pulled her snooty face when I talked posh.

"And there was me thinking we were going to the university," she said.

Chapter 5

Shirley leaned back in the passenger seat of my MGB.

The wind streamed through her hair. We were on the road to the University of Sussex.

She was still fizzing with excitement about the Cal. She was wearing a pair of jeans which looked like they'd been sprayed on and a T-shirt with the slogan: "Make Love Not War (It Costs Less)".

She said: "Guess I should have dressed in a black gown and one of those square hats for the university. But when I got that call from Harry, I just felt I had to slip into something that shows those tyre guys what they're getting."

I changed up a gear as we headed on the road out of Brighton. "You'll look great. And Sussex University isn't one of those stuffy places out of the dark ages, like Oxford. It's only been around for six years and got a modern image."

"Sure, like everyone thinks Latin is cool."

"Seriously, Sussex has built a trendy vibe – largely thanks to the Jay twins, Helen and Catherine. They're daughters of Douglas Jay, who's president of the Board of Trade in the Labour government. They were into groovy music and fashion. Even got their picture on the front cover of *Tatler* magazine. Only left the university last year."

"Let's hope Victoria is with it, too."

I nodded. "I think Professor Nettlebed may live up to her name. She sounded like a tough customer when we spoke on the phone."

"The harder they come, the harder they fall."

"We'll see." I pointed ahead. "And soon. There's the turn-off for the university."

We parked our car and walked towards the main building.

Inside, the reception desk directed us to an office on the first floor, third door from the lift. Under Professor Nettlebed's nameplate on the door, a hand-written note held in place by a drawing pin, read: "Come to ask for extra time to finish your essay? Leave fast if you value your life."

Shirl read it, looked at me, and said: "Nice. I don't think."

I knocked on the door and a voice said: "Enter."

Victoria Nettlebed was sitting behind a long desk which held a row of books between two bookends. The spines were turned towards her.

She was a well-built woman – not exactly fat but more like one who can't resist that extra biscuit. I put her at around fifty - or perhaps an old forty. She had dark brown hair with some early streaks of grey. She'd tied her hair back in a bun. She had grey eyes with heavy lids which made her look like she couldn't be bothered with life. She was wearing a cream- coloured blouse and a small red scarf looped around her neck. She had pearl earrings but no rings on her fingers. She had a pince-nez perched on her nose. She was studying the pages of a fat tome on her desk.

She looked up as we walked in and removed the fancy eyepiece. It hung comfortably on a cord between her breasts.

She viewed me with a not over-friendly eye and said: "You must be the reporter." Her gaze moved to Shirley. "And you must be the Australian."

Shirl grinned: "Does it show that much, prof?"

"Given what you're wearing, it's about the only thing that doesn't. And don't call me prof."

"If you've got it, flaunt it, sister."

Nettlebed frowned. "Or sister."

"I'm Colin Crampton and this is Shirley Goldsmith," I said to cool the temperature.

"You'd better sit down," Nettlebed said.

As we made our way to the chairs on the guest side of

Nettlebed's desk, I glanced around the office.

There was a bookcase along one wall. It was untidily filled with books on their sides and piles of learned journals. Beside the bookcase was one of those wall clocks with a large second-hand. It makes you feel your life is slipping away as it ticks remorselessly round each minute.

Below the clock, a vicious looking club – a stout stick, smoothed and polished, with heavy carved head – was mounted on a couple of fancy wall brackets. It looked like the kind of ethnic artefact a tourist would pick up from a gift shop - and then wonder what the hell to do with when they'd got it home.

On one wall, a collection of cheap frames held a selection of photographs.

I nodded towards the snaps and said by way of an opener: "Your own work?"

(Crampton, master of small talk.)

Nettlebed's eyebrows lifted a little. I guessed that might be a substitute for a smile. "I took the photographs during my travels around the country, earlier this year."

That woke me up. "You've been to Australia this year?" I asked.

"That is what I have just said, Mr Crampton. Do I need to repeat myself? But to add detail to my statement, I returned to this country at the end of May."

I pointed at the club on the wall. "And you brought that back as a souvenir, too?"

"It is called a *waddy*. In some indigenous tribes, a *nulla-nulla* or *boondi*. They could be used as a throwing stick for hunting animals. They were also used in hand-to-hand combat and could be lethal."

And very handy for knocking out half-uncles before strangling them, I didn't say.

Instead, I said: "Were you in Australia for long?"

"Four months. It was an academic trip. I was researching

source materials on the early Australian gold rushes. It was the subject of my doctorate – but there is still much we don't know about the topic."

"Did you find anything new?"

Nettlebed shifted uncomfortably in her chair. "Yes, I did. I found a trove of documents I'd not previously seen – maps, press cuttings, letters - in the library at the University of Adelaide."

"My town," Shirley chipped in.

"You studied at the university?" Nettlebed asked. With the hint of a sneer.

"Nah. I had a scholarship to Harvard," Shirl lied.

Nettlebed looked like she'd just swallowed a duck-billed platypus.

I tried to hide my grin. But I also had plenty to think about.

Nettlebed would have been in Australia at the time the Woodburns were killed. Could she have felled them with the club on the wall? It would land a hell of a blow, and Nettlebed packed a bit of muscle in the shoulders. But I was getting carried away. Nettlebed couldn't have strangled the Woodburns with giant hands. Hers were small and bony. But perhaps she worked with a partner. And he provided the giant's hands.

Nettlebed leaned forward and said: "I understood, Mr Crampton, that you wished to question me about this year's referendum in Australia."

This wasn't going to make any copy in the *Chronicle*. But it had got me through the door to meet Nettlebed. Now I had to justify the ruse.

"Yes, the referendum." I took out my notebook. I licked the tip of my pencil to look serious. "Were you surprised by the ninety per cent yes vote in May?"

"Not really. It is an outrage that indigenous people have not been included in population counts before now."

"Too right, Sheila," Shirley chipped in.

"And don't call me Sheila," Nettlebed snapped.

"You're the boss, cobber."

Nettlebed shook her head in mock despair.

I said: "We're interested in getting some background on the history of Australia. For instance, how important were the gold rushes for the country's growth?"

Nettlebed relaxed a little. We were on her own territory. She stood up from behind her desk and, for the first time, we saw that she was wearing baggy tan slacks.

She strolled over to the window and looked out across the countryside. Turned to face us. Took a deep breath. She was preparing to give us a lecture.

"In 1851, the population of Australia was 430,000. Then a prospector called Edward Hargreaves found gold at a place called Orange in New South Wales. People had found gold as early as the eighteen-twenties but not on this scale. It started the first Australian gold rush. Of course, they'd already had them in California."

"A miner forty-niner… Oh, my darling Clementine." Shirley broke into song.

Nettlebed turned a basilisk stare on her. "To continue, between 1851 and the end of the century, there were thirty-five clearly defined gold rushes in Australia. No wonder the population had grown nine times to nearly four million by the turn of the twentieth century. But the numbers don't tell the whole story. In the mid-nineteenth century, Australia was still a penal colony, a place where Britain dumped its ne'er-do-wells. Not until 1868 did the last ship of convicts arrive on the fatal shore. Most of the newcomers were adventurers, men and women determined to make their way in a new life – and to win in the gold fields as part of that. The character of Australia as a country was shaped during those fifty years of gold rushes."

Nettlebed strode back to her desk and sat down. Lecture over.

While she'd been spouting her history, I'd been wracking my brains. I needed a way to bring the dead Hobart Birtwhistle into the conversation.

I said: "I once met an Australian called Hobart Birtwhistle."

Well, I didn't say he was alive when I met him.

"I'm sure he'd take exactly your view of the country's history," I added.

I'd watched Nettlebed very carefully as I'd mentioned Birtwhistle. She hadn't put her hands to her face in shock. She hadn't blushed. She hadn't done any of those sideways glances that show up the liars.

So I added: "Have you ever met Hobart Birtwhistle?"

"Er... I meet so many people."

"If you haven't, you missed out. He died two days ago."

Nettlebed banged her hands down on her desk. "That was hardly the way to introduce Mr Bartwhustle into the conversation."

She'd deliberately mis-pronounced his name. A guilty give-away in my book.

"Why would Birtwhistle have your name and contact details in his address book?" I asked.

Nettlebed sprung to her feet. "This is an outrage. You've tricked me."

"Why did you have an appointment to see him four days ago?"

"That's my business."

"It's also the cops' business," Shirl chipped in.

Nettlebed strode over to the door. Flung it open.

"You will leave now, or I will call security to have you thrown out."

She eyed the club on the wall. It was a formidable weapon.

We stood up and hustled towards the door. I stepped out into the corridor.

Shirley lingered. Faced up to Nettlebed.

"We'll be back when you're ready to tell the truth. Prof."

**

Frank Figgis leaned across his desk and whispered: "Have you found it yet?"

I gave him my wide-eyed look. "Found what?"

"The manuscript."

"As the cops would say, enquiries are continuing."

It was a couple of hours after Shirley and I had quit Victoria Nettlebed's office in a hurry. I'd dropped Shirley off at a beauty parlour before heading back to the *Chronicle*. With Figgis on my back, I wished I'd stayed away.

"That document is dangerous," Figgis said. "I want it returned."

"Easier said than done."

"Have you interrogated the newsroom?"

"I can't use the bright lights and thumbscrews on them. They're our colleagues. But I'm having a crafty word here and there."

"If I find one of them has snitched that manuscript..." Figgis left the rest of the threat unsaid.

I said: "Apart from chasing down your naughty book, I've got a murder to cover."

"The cops seem baffled," Figgis said.

"When don't they?"

"But we don't seem to be doing better. I'd hoped to lead the front page with a new twist in the tale today."

I told Figgis about my meeting with Nettlebed. About her interest in Australian artefacts. Especially ones you could bash people with.

He lit a Woodbine and sucked thoughtfully on it.

"A learned professor at Sussex University has refused to say why she had a meeting with Hobart Birtwhistle two days before he was murdered," Figgis said. "How about that for an intro to your story?"

"As an intro it leads the reader to believe Nettlebed was somehow implicated in Hobart's killing. But we haven't a scrap of evidence to back it up."

"What about the club on her wall?"

"She'd say it was a souvenir. Everyone brings back rubbish when they go abroad. If you go to Paris, you come back with a model Eiffel Tower. Doesn't mean you're going to brain someone with it."

"So where do we go from here?"

"There was another name mentioned in Birtwhistle's diary – Lionel Bruce. But the page with Bs in the address book had been torn out. I'm wondering whether Bruce did that so that he couldn't be traced."

"Why not tear out the page with the appointment in Birtwhistle's diary?"

"Perhaps an oversight. A killer in a panic to flee the scene of the crime, maybe. But I'm going to try and track Bruce down."

"I hope you're more successful at that than finding missing manuscripts."

"If I didn't know you better, Frank, I'd say there was a hint of resentment in that remark."

"You're catching on fast," Figgis said.

If Lionel Bruce was Birtwhistle's killer, he'd left behind an important clue.

Under the Bruce appointment in the diary, Hobart had written: "May be late. Arriving on one-forty train."

There was no railway station at Muddles Green, where Hobart lived. But there were three not far away – Lewes, Uckfield and Polegate. Bruce could have used any of them.

I was willing to bet that when Bruce arrived at one of those stations, he then took a taxi to Muddles Green. If I could trace the taxi driver, he might be able to provide enough information for me to track down Bruce. After all, taxi drivers are talkative types with an unhealthy interest in their passengers' business. At least, the ones I get always are.

But which station had a train arriving at one-forty? Possibly they all did, which wouldn't be much help. Lewes had the most frequent services. Uckfield was a terminus, so trains could only arrive from one direction. But Polegate was the nearest to Muddles Green.

I needed a comprehensive set of railway timetables. And the place to find them was the *Chronicle's* morgue.

I'd never found a dead body in the morgue, but there were thousands of press cuttings carefully filed under people, places and organisations. And shelves full of reference books. Despite its nickname, the morgue was a living library which we reporters used every day as we researched our stories.

As I pushed through the door, Henrietta Houndstooth, who ran the place, was carrying a pile of box files across the room. Henrietta was something of an institution at the *Chronicle*. She knew everybody's secrets but had the tact to keep mum.

She dressed for summer in the same way she did for winter – in a tweed skirt and jacket. It was a combo that seemed to keep her cool in hot weather and warm in the cold. It certainly kept the crofters on the Isle of Skye happy.

She put the box files on top of a filing cabinet and turned to meet me.

I said: "I presume you keep railway timetables in here."

"British or continental?"

"Home-grown British Rail. Snail rail. The delays because of leaves on the line rail."

Henrietta raised her eyebrows. "Why is nothing ever simple for you?"

"Because if it were, life would be too boring."

Henrietta pointed to a bookcase on the other side of the room. "Third shelf down," she said.

I walked over and pulled the Southern Region timetable from the shelf. I flipped the pages.

Lewes and Polegate stations were on the same line, which ran from London to Hastings. Trains coming from London would stop at Lewes first, then move on to Polegate. I turned to the timetable. A train from London stopped at Lewes at one-twenty-seven. No joy. But a few minutes later the same train reached Polegate at one-forty. I checked the timetable for Uckfield. No train reached the town within fifteen minutes of one-forty.

So, did Lionel Bruce alight at Polegate five days ago for a meeting with Hobart Birtwhistle? A meeting he wanted to keep secret.

And did Bruce return three days later to kill Birtwhistle?

If I could trace Bruce, I might get an answer.

Back at my desk in the newsroom, I lifted the receiver and called Tom Huxtable, the *Chronicle's* Eastbourne reporter. Polegate was also on Tom's beat. He told me the main taxi service in the town was run by one Steve Turner under the trade name Speedy Cabs.

I called Speedy Cabs. A woman with a nasal twang in her voice answered.

I asked: "Is Steve Turner around?"

"No."

"Who am I speaking to?"

"Marlene."

"You've got a lovely voice, Marlene."

"Yeah, I've often been told I sound like that actress – you know, the one who's in all those films."

"Irene Handl?"

"Audrey Hepburn."

"Of course. Perhaps you can help me? Do you know whether Steve picked up anyone off the one-forty train last Saturday?"

"Couldn't say."

"He went to a place in Muddles Green for a meeting. Perhaps he also asked Steve to pick him up afterwards."

"As it happens, I do remember that now. The bloke just marched in here and demanded a cab on the spot. Steve had just got a hot sausage sandwich from the café round the corner. Said he'd run the bloke up to Muddles Green after he'd eaten it. But the bloke was insistent he went straight away. Quite shirty about it, too. Anyway, when Steve got back, his sausage were cold."

"You don't happen to know who the bloke was?"

"Someone who was no respecter of Steve's lunch break."

"Nothing else?"

"Well, he had this flash umbrella with a big curved handle. And an expensive briefcase. Leather job. Set him back a bit. Had a name embossed in some kind of writing on the front of it."

"Lionel Bruce?"

"No. It were some company name. Global something or other."

"Anything to do with gold?" I asked.

"I don't think so. But now you mention it, the other word was something to do with metals. Yes, Global Metals."

"That's terrifically helpful, Marlene. Next time I'm in Polegate I'll buy Steve a sausage sandwich. Get you one, too."

"I like plenty of sauce in mine," Marlene said.

"I thought you might."

I replaced the receiver.

But Marlene had been wrong.

Not about the sauce on her sandwich. The name of the company on the briefcase.

When I searched in the London telephone directory, there was no company called Global Metals. But I didn't leave it there. A lot of companies like to call themselves Global something – especially when they're one man and a mongrel. I looked through all the globals and found a firm called Global MegaMetals. A call to Companies House, revealed that Lionel Bruce was the sole director.

I picked up the receiver and dialled his number.

Chapter 6

As the phone rang, I built up a mental picture of what a company called Global MegaMetals would look like.

It would have a prestige office in the City of London, perhaps somewhere like Cornhill or Threadneedle Street. There would be a smart reception with an old oak desk and leather-covered chairs. It would be presided over by a svelte secretary. She'd have long auburn hair that shone because she'd been taught to brush it one hundred times before she went to bed at night. She'd answer my call in a voice that would be a mix of Cheltenham Ladies College and a manor house in Norfolk. There would be…

"Hello. Speak your name and state your business." The phone was answered by a man with a strong cockney accent.

I said: "Colin Crampton. Brighton *Evening Chronicle*. I was expecting the phone to be answered by a secretary."

"Monica's off sick with her Chalfont St Giles."

"Her what?"

"Chalfont St Giles. Piles. Haemorrhoids. Up her bum, poor girl. It's like the third world war going on up there – or so she tells me. Anyway, if you're ringing about advertising, you can sling your hook."

"Later perhaps. This is more of an editorial enquiry. Can you put me through to Lionel Bruce?"

"You're speaking to the gaffer."

"You're Lionel Bruce?"

"The one and only. Numero uno."

Clearly, I'd got the wrong idea about Global MegaMetals. I took a breath and decided to dive in from the top board.

"Why did you have a meeting with Hobart Birtwhistle at Muddles Green five days ago?"

"Who says I did?"

"Birtwhistle for a start. The meeting was listed in his diary."

"Tom tit!"

I had no trouble translating that cockney rhyming slang.

"You travelled to Polegate railway station and then took a taxi to Muddles Green."

"So what if I did? You sound like the kind of bloke who might stick his nose in once too often. If you get my drift"

"I do – and it's a drift I've been threatened with many times before. And yet here I am."

"Well, you can take a hike."

"Were you aware that Hobart Birtwhistle was murdered three days after your visit?"

"Now, look, that's going too far. What do you think I am? Some kind of crazed killer?"

"That's what I'm trying to discover."

I heard Bruce take a deep breath. His tonsils rattled as he sucked in the air. Or perhaps it was a fault on the line.

He said: "Okay, I'll come straight. I might have visited Birtwhistle."

"Might?" I said sharply.

"Did. I'll admit we had a meet. Hobart was as lively as a dog with two dicks when I left him. There's no way you can pin his killing on me."

"That's the police's job. Mine is to write stories for the *Evening Chronicle*. We need to meet."

"No way."

"I want you to tell me every detail of your meeting with Birtwhistle."

"You can stuff that, you know where. And climb up after it."

"You want to tell the tale to the cops instead?"

"Rozzers bring me out in a rash."

"I'll do a deal with you. The old Bill doesn't know about your close association with Hobart Birtwhistle yet. If they did... well, you could hardly blame them if they drew the wrong conclusions. After all, you didn't come forward when you heard he'd been murdered."

"Look, can we keep the filth out of this?"

"Had trouble with the police before?"

"That's for me to know and you to wonder."

"Best, then, we keep this between ourselves for the time being. Shall we say eleven o'clock tomorrow morning? Your offices."

There was a brief silence at the other end of the line. "If you say so. But no men in blue breaking the door down."

"You have my word as a journalist and a gentleman. Until tomorrow, then. Best wishes to Monica. Hope her Chalfont St Giles get better."

I replaced the receiver.

A voice behind me said: "I never knew that."

I whirled round in my captain's chair. The damned thing very nearly did a full circle.

Susan Wheatcroft had evidently snuck up behind me while I was talking to Bruce.

I said: "What didn't you know?"

"That you had a girl called Monica on the side. And that she lives in Chalfont St Giles. I bet Shirley doesn't know you're cheating on her."

I grinned. "I'm not. You've got the wrong idea. Monica is secretary to a sharp type called Lionel Bruce. And I'd never cheat on Shirley."

Susan's lips pouted in a moue of disappointment. "Worst luck."

"But, say, suppose I take you for a drink after work?"

Susan was one of the reporters I thought Figgis might believe had stolen his manuscript. It was nonsense, of course. She was a big bouncy bundle of fun and collected men the way some people collect stamps. Rumour had it, she kept photos of her conquests in an album. All nicely mounted. In the album, I mean.

Susan had a twinkle in her eye. "You're not one of those guys

51

that ply a girl with strong drink and then..."

"No, I'm not one of those guys," I interrupted.

Susan treated me to one of her big fat winks. "Pity. But I'll come anyway. So, what'll it be? Champagne in the Starlight Room at the Metropole hotel?"

"The tipple of your choice in Prinny's Pleasure."

Susan shrugged. "Can't wait."

We met at Prinny's Pleasure shortly after the place had opened for the evening session.

I'd already ordered my gin and tonic before Susan waltzed in a couple of minutes later. She wore a light grey raincoat over a figure-hugging black dress with a fancy lace collar. She'd changed out of her office flatties into four-inch heels. She'd freshened up her lipstick and smelt of Yves Saint Laurent *Rive Gauche*.

She looked ready for the kind of action I hoped we could avoid.

I ordered Susan a large malt whisky and water. We took our drinks to the corner table at the back of the bar.

Susan raised her glass and inflicted some serious punishment on the scotch.

She leaned back on her seat and grinned. "Not often a girl like me gets a date with a desirable guy like you."

I shifted on my seat and took a sip of my drink. "I've got something to ask you."

"Does it involve a ring?"

"Afraid not."

"I'm desolate." Susan clapped the back of her hand to her forehead. The despair pose actresses used in the days of silent movies. "My life stretches before me like an endless desert."

"There's always an oasis just over the horizon."

"I wish."

"What I wanted to talk to you about concerns the *Chronicle*."

"Just work?"

"Not exactly. It involves Frank Figgis' private life."

"Now I feel sick."

I'd decided the only way I could do this was to take Susan into my confidence. She was the one person in the newsroom who knew how to keep a secret.

I took a bracing pull at my gin and tonic. "The fact is that Figgis has had a document taken from his office. And he wants me to get it back."

"What document?"

"The manuscript of his memoirs."

Susan's eyes popped. Her cheeks bulged. And then she laughed. Not just a chuckle, either. A full-throated roar.

"You've got to be kidding." And then the implications hit her. And her eyes became searching and serious. "You're not kidding."

"The memoirs deal with his years at the *Chronicle*. What he thinks about the reporters, past..."

"...and present."

"The methods we've used to get our scoops by fair means..."

"...and foul."

Together we reached for our drinks and drained our glasses.

"So, you see if these memoirs ever got published, we'd have our own secrets held up for all the world to see," I said.

Susan shook her head. "That's terrible. But if Figgis gets the manuscript back, surely he'll publish it?"

"He's told me it won't see the light of day until he retires."

"And Figgis will never retire."

I nodded.

"So, we're in the clear."

"You can count on it. I knew you wouldn't be someone who'd take something that didn't belong to you from a colleague."

Susan smiled. "Wait while I polish my halo."

I felt mean that I'd loaded the burden of a new secret on Susan.

She didn't deserve that. Silently, I cursed Figgis. He had put me in a difficult position which even he couldn't have understood. But I was just going to have to live with it.

Susan whipped a compact out of her handbag, looked at herself in the mirror, and gave a contented sign of satisfaction.

She grinned. "So, now we can get down to business – about our future."

"My heart belongs to Shirley."

"Fair enough. If it means I can have the rest of your body."

"Would you take another large malt as a substitute?"

Susan mocked a shrug. "Looks like I've no choice."

An hour later I met Shirley at English's Oyster Bar.

She'd been to the beauty parlour. She looked like a girl who'd just stepped off the cover of a glossy magazine. She'd had her hair trimmed and fashioned so it curled round the sides of her face.

She was wearing a pale blue Zapaka dress with what she later told me was a Peter Pan collar. It had a fancy bow on the left shoulder. She had black elbow-length evening gloves.

She was sitting at a table in English's downstairs room sipping a Campari soda.

I sat down opposite her and said: "You look sensational."

Shirl pouted. "Don't feel it," she said. "A man followed me from the beauty parlour."

"Just the one? Looking like that, I'm surprised you weren't leading a procession."

"You better take this seriously, big boy."

"Do you know who it was?"

Shirl shook her head. "I stepped out of the parlour – it's Margarita's in Queens Road - and headed towards the North Laines. I glanced back and there was this guy wearing one of those raincoats with a belt and a slouch hat pulled down over his forehead."

"Could you tell his age?"

"Not really. He was too far back. But after I turned into Sydney Street, I looked back again and he was still there. I thought I'd walk on a bit and then stop and look in a shop window. So, I did. But when I glanced up the street he'd gone."

"Must have stepped into one of the shops."

"That's what I thought. So I walked back the way I came. Couldn't see him anywhere."

I thought about that. The follower could have been a random guy who just happened to be going the same way as Shirl for a few streets. But she'd had a feeling about it – and her instincts were often right.

I asked: "He made no attempt to speak to you?"

"Too far away."

"And he didn't follow you to your destination."

"I think the bozo knew I was on to him."

"Could be – if you'd looked back a few times."

"He had these weirdly rounded shoulders."

"Enough to recognise him again?"

"I reckon so. Since I saw Hobart all dead, I've been all shook up."

"And not like Elvis Presley."

Shirl forced a smile.

I signalled to a waiter. "Let's eat. How about a grilled lobster and some champagne to celebrate your Pirelli job?"

"Sounds good."

I gave our order to the waiter.

I said: "It's not a surprise you're all shook up. You've seen a dead body. It must be worse when it's someone related to you. And doubly worse as you were to meet Hobart for the first time."

Shirl nodded. "I guess I was expecting too much from the meeting. I hoped I might learn some more about my own family background. My Ma, bless her Aussie tush, never wanted to talk about where we came from. I guess she knew most of our family were trouble and wanted to keep me away from them."

Not a moment too soon, the waiter glided alongside the table and poured the champagne.

We clinked glasses and drank – but without the zest the *Veuve Clicquot* deserved.

I put my glass down and asked: "Was your father distant, like your mother?"

"Not as much as Ma. He was fun to be with. As a kid, he made me laugh at jokes. Well, one joke at least. What do you get if you cross a sheep with a kangaroo?"

"A woolly jumper," I said.

"Yeah, every time he asked me, I pretended I didn't know the answer. He'd tell me and I'd laugh so much I'd roll around on the floor."

"Couldn't you ask your Pa about the things your Ma wouldn't tell you?"

"I did. He told me all about his own family and how he came to meet Ma. But I'm not sure how much he knew about her family. Whatever it was, he didn't want to share it with me. He'd just tell me the joke."

The waiter appeared again, this time with the grilled lobsters.

We picked up our knives and forks and attacked the food.

"Perhaps tomorrow I'll get some answers from Lionel Bruce," I said.

Chapter 7

Shirley and I took the eight-thirty Brighton Belle train to London the following morning.

We eschewed the kippers in favour of tea and toast. Too much lobster and champagne the previous evening were taking their toll.

We parted at Victoria station. Shirley headed for her meeting with the Pirelli calendar guys. I dived down onto the Circle Line to take the tube into the heart of the City of London.

After my telephone call with Lionel Bruce, I'd trimmed my expectations about Global MegaMetals. But it turned out, not enough. The company was based in a run-down Victorian building not far from Spitalfields Market. I pushed through a heavy black-painted door into a small hallway. The hall was lit by a dusty chandelier. Only two of the bulbs were working. The place smelt of damp and disappointment.

A faded notice pinned to the wall listed the occupants floor-by-floor. Global MegaMetals shared the third with a company called Coffin Handles Ltd. The lift was out of order. I trudged up the stairs wondering whether Monica was back on duty or still off sick with her Chalfont St Giles.

Global MegaMetals' office had a brass plate mottled with age. I resisted the temptation to give it a quick polish, opened the door, and stepped inside. The office was empty. No sign of Monica or Lionel Bruce. The walls had been painted a pale green. Someone had hung up a promotional calendar from a car hire firm. On the right side of the room, there was a desk with a telephone, a typewriter, and a tower of wire baskets that overflowed with papers. On the floor beside the desk, a pile of old copies of the *Financial Times* quietly gathered dust.

On the left side, a door with a frosted glass window led to a kind of inner office. I opened it and entered without knocking.

Lionel Bruce was on his hands and knees with his head under a desk. He glanced sideways, saw my shoes, and crawled out.

He looked up at me and said: "Dropped a tanner. Needed it to pay for my coffee at Stinky Pinky's."

He grabbed the side of the desk as he staggered to his feet. He was a thin man with narrow shoulders and a neck which jutted forward so that he looked a bit like a tortoise. He had a wide mouth but eyes that were too close together. His thinning brown hair was combed back from his forehead. He was wearing a crumpled blue pin-stripe suit fraying at the cuffs. He had a red and blue striped tie. Might have been some regiment. More likely, something he'd picked up cheap in Spitalfields Market.

He shot me a friendly look and said: "Who the hell are you, my old cock?"

I fished a card from my jacket pocket and handed it to him.

He looked at it like it was covered in the Black Death and handed it back.

He said: "You're that nosey parker from the linen draper."

I nodded. "I am indeed the reporter from the newspaper."

"You want to stick your garden hose in on my business with that bloke in Muddles Green. The one who ended up brown bread."

"We don't call it sticking our nose in. We call it investigative reporting. And Hobart Birtwhistle is, indeed, dead."

Bruce shrugged and sat down on the seat behind his desk. "Yeah! Well, if you must, you must. Park your bum on that chair." He gestured at an upright job in hard wood. It looked like the penitent seat you'd find in a strict Baptist chapel.

I eased myself onto it as requested and took out my notebook. I asked: "What exactly does Global MegaMetals do?"

"We trade in metals," Bruce said uninformatively.

"Which metals?"

"Gold mostly. Some silver. Rarely platinum. I dabble in copper sometimes if I'm feeling adventurous."

"You've always been a specialist in metals?"

"Nah! I used to dabble in a bit of this and bit of that. As you do. Then one night, I met this bloke in the Horse's Head. He was in the metals game."

"A bit of this?" I asked.

"Nah! A bit of that. Called himself a metals futures trader. Turns out he used to do deals to buy metals in, say, a year's time at a tasty price. Then he'd find a geezer to sell the same metals to in a year at a big profit. If it all worked out, he'd make a mint. Futures trading, he said. Was going to be big. Sounded like something I could make a few quid on myself. He'd had a few and was scotch mist – well gone - so I pumped him on the basics. Over the next couple of weeks, I set myself up as Global MegaMetals trading futures in metals."

I looked around the room. Beside the desk and chair there was a filing cabinet, a bookcase with a broken shelf, and a couple of clocks on the wall. One told London time, the other New York. The New York one had stopped. There was a hat stand with a raincoat, a trilby hat, and an umbrella with a heavy curved handle. The kind of handle that would leave a nasty dent if it whacked a forehead.

I said: "Futures trading didn't quite work out for you."

Bruce waggled his head from side to side as though he wasn't sure. "Turns out if you wanted to trade in futures, you didn't need a past."

"And what kind of past would that be?"

Bruce shrugged. "A couple of little misunderstandings down the Snaresbrook magistrates court."

"What kind of misunderstandings?"

"The kind that gets you three months in Wandsworth, then six months in Pentonville."

"I meant what offences?"

Bruce clenched his fists on the desk and leant forward.

"First time for handling stolen goods – to wit, an Ekco

television set. Second time for obtaining a pecuniary advantage. Specifically, helping an old dear collect her pension from the post office, but forgetting to hand over the money. You really need to know all this? I've had enough of my little misunderstandings spread all over the newspapers in the past."

"This is for background."

"If you say so."

"But you're still trading?"

"I wasn't going to be beat. So now I trade in metals on the knocker."

"I don't understand."

"I call door-to-door asking if the householder has any old metal they want to turn into bees and honey."

"Money."

"Yeah! I always pay a fair price, of course. And then I sell it on when I can. I suppose you could still call it a form of futures trading."

"How did you come to meet Hobart Birtwhistle?" I asked.

"He rang up."

"Just like that?"

"Yeah! Out of a clear blue sky. I'll admit I don't get many calls from potential clients on account of the newspapers reporting about my porridge."

"And Birtwhistle asked to see you?"

"Yeah! I was reluctant to go at first, Birtwhistle's place being in darkest Sussex. But he offered to pay my train fare – third class, worse luck – and said his interest was in gold. So, what did I have to lose?"

"When you visited, what did Birtwhistle want to talk about?"

"Strange guy. Bit of a ducker and diver on the quiet, in my humble opinion. It takes one to know one – don't write that bit."

"But why had he asked you there?"

"He wanted to know how to sell gold discreetly. Well, I didn't like the sound of that. If the gold was hot, I could be done again for handling."

"That would be entrapment."

"Too right, squire. And me the mug in the trap. So, I told the geezer I wasn't interested. Gave him a lughole full about wasting my valuable time. To do him credit, he apologised. Said he would be frank with me."

"And was he?" I asked.

"He said he expected to be the beneficiary of an inheritance."

"Of gold?"

Bruce nodded. "I asked him, how much gold? He said he wasn't sure. I asked him what form it was in – jewellery, plate, coins, ingots. Well, you could have bowled me over with a downy duck's feather. You'll never believe what he said."

"Try me."

"Nugget."

"What?"

"He said the gold would be in the form of a nugget."

"Do they really exist?" I asked.

"As sure as my name's Lionel Bruce. Some of them can be monsters, too. Take the Welcome nugget, found in Australia's Victoria gold fields. It weighed in at more than 150 pounds, or nearly 70 kilograms, if you'll pardon those fancy foreign measures. Worth a tidy bit, too."

"How much?"

"Well, I did a bit of research. It all depends on how many Troy ounces of gold are in the nugget. But you could be looking at around £115 per Troy ounce. So, a nugget weighing, say, 900 Troy ounces would be worth…"

"More than £100,000," I interrupted.

"Enough to buy a nice little Ford Cortina. Always fancied one to run down to Southend of a weekend."

"Enough to buy a hundred of them," I said. "Or thirty average priced houses," I added.

The previous day Susan Wheatcroft's business page had

reported the average price of a house in Britain was £3,500.

I stood up. Strode over to the window. Looked out into the street below. An empty Smith's crisp packet was blowing down the gutter.

I was trying to make sense of all this. Birtwhistle had asked a metals dealer to advise him on the discreet sale of a gold nugget. And two days later Birtwhistle was dead.

I turned back to Bruce.

I said: "Did Birtwhistle say when he hoped to inherit the nugget?"

"No."

"Or from whom?"

"Family."

"Did he say whether he'd mentioned it to anyone else?"

"He said not."

"Have you mentioned it?"

"Buttoned Lips is my name."

"Did you agree to help him sell the nugget when he obtained it?"

"The conversation didn't get that far. He said he'd be in touch again when he was ready to move."

"And you left it at that?"

Bruce shrugged. "I had no other choice."

I sat down again and squared up to Bruce.

"Did you kill Birtwhistle?"

"Now that question is out of order. Why should I? I stood to make a good commission if the nugget sale came off."

Bruce was right. He had no motive. And, seemingly, no opportunity either. Only the umbrella with the heavy handle hanging from the hat-stand could have provided a means.

I said: "What will you do now there's no nugget to sell?"

Bruce blew out his cheeks. Glanced at his watch. "I think I'll leave it an hour, then go and knock on some doors in Hoxton. Might find someone who's discovered a couple of gold sovereigns up the back of an old drawer."

He brightened up a bit. "There's opportunity everywhere you look. If you know how."

Shirley and I met up at Victoria station just in time to catch the lunchtime train to Brighton.

Shirl bubbled with excitement about her meeting with the Pirelli photographer. She was awed by the prospect of the location shoots (exotic and expensive). Stunned by the clothes she would wear (not very many). Thrilled by the poses she'd strike (would make a vicar blush).

But she fell to earth when it was my turn to tell her about the meeting with Lionel Bruce.

Her eyes widened and she leaned forward in her seat. "You mean Hobart Birtwhistle – my newly discovered half-uncle - has a gold nugget to sell?"

"Had," I said. "Past tense. Remember, he's dead. And we don't know whether he had a gold nugget when he was alive. The way Bruce told it, made it sound like Hobart expected to get the nugget in the future. Certainly, the cops haven't said anything about a nugget. And even if Tomkins tried to keep it secret, one of the plods would've leaked the news. There are guys there who'd snitch on their wives for a couple of pints down the pub."

Shirley shook her head. "I don't know what to make of it."

"Neither do I. But there are three points which seem most important. First, besides Bruce, Hobart had a meeting with Victoria Nettlebed. We know she's an expert on Australia's history – special subject, Aussie gold rushes. So, did Hobart tell her about the gold nugget? If he mentioned it to Bruce, I think it's logical that he'd have said the same to Nettlebed. But she never mentioned it to us."

"Sneaky cow. I never liked the look of her."

"I think we need to pay her another visit. This time,

unannounced."

"Sure. Let's do it as soon as we reach Brighton."

I nodded. "But let's not forget my second point. Hobart is now dead – murdered. Was he killed by Nettlebed or Bruce because of the nugget? Or had Hobart mentioned it to anyone else? Is there a third person, perhaps even a fourth, who'd be willing to kill for a fortune in gold?"

"That spooks me," Shirl said.

"Me, too. Because here's the third point. Bruce said Hobart had told him the ownership of the nugget was an inheritance issue. That suggests it comes down through a family. And you are a member of that family, too."

Shirl stared out of the window in a reverie. Like she was watching scenes from the past. Or perhaps from the future. She shivered. Wrapped her arms around herself in a bearhug.

The train's whistle blew as the Belle raced into the Clayton tunnel.

Shirl looked back at me. "Do you think I'm in danger?"

"I don't know," I said. "Perhaps our meeting with Professor Nettlebed will tell us more."

We stomped into Nettlebed's office half an hour after stepping off the train at Brighton station.

She looked up and removed the pince-nez from her nose. Like she wished it was a pistol and she could finish us with a couple of shots.

She said: "I'd hoped to have seen the last of you two."

"Nice to see you, too," I said.

She let the pince-nez dangle on its cord and reached for her phone.

"And before you call security, consider what tale you'll tell the police when they ask you why you discussed the fate of a valuable gold nugget with Hobart Birtwhistle," I said.

She pulled her hand back from the phone. Sat back in her

chair and glared at us.

"You can forget the affronted innocent look, too," I said. "We've been doing some research into Australian gold as well. Might not gain an A grade as a student essay, but it certainly poses some tough questions for you."

"And we want some answers," Shirley added.

A pink flush had bloomed around Nettlebed's neck and cheeks. Her eyes were fixed like little chips of granite. Her hands gripped the arms of her chair like she wanted to strangle it.

I said: "I'll make it easy for you. I'll tell you what we know and why it's important. Then I'll want some information from you."

So, I gave Nettlebed an edited version of my meeting with Lionel Bruce. I told her how Hobart Birtwhistle had questioned Bruce about the value of gold nuggets. I outlined how he'd hinted he could become the owner of a nugget – and how that may have led to his death.

And I explained how Shirley was related to Hobart – and now feared for her life. All as a result of a vague conspiracy which we knew little about.

I said: "When we were here yesterday, you refused to talk about your meeting with Birtwhistle. Now you know why it's important. You can either tell us or have it out with detective chief superintendent Alec Tomkins. I'd guess that Sir Hartley Shawcross QC, the university's chancellor, won't take kindly to the plods with their size tens clumping all over the campus. Besides, as Sir Hartley was the British prosecutor at the Nuremburg War Crimes tribunal, he's more than used to extracting information from the tight-lipped."

The flush around Nettlebed's cheeks had faded during my little speech.

I said: "You seem a little pale. Would you like a glass of water?"

"No, thank you."

"Why did Hobart Birtwhistle contact you?" I asked.

"He'd heard about my research into Australian gold rushes. He said he wanted to know more."

"Did he tell you he expected to inherit a gold nugget?"

"Not specifically. But I assumed his interest in Australian gold was not merely academic."

"What did you tell him?"

Nettlebed stood up. Walked over to the window. It looked out towards the whale-backed hump of the Downs hills. She rubbed a hand thoughtfully around her chin. Turned back to us and took a deep breath.

"We're going to get another lecture," I whispered to Shirley.

"Better take notes," she hissed back.

But I'd already whipped out my notebook.

Nettlebed said: "I told Mr Birtwhistle that about twenty years ago, I received an old trunk which had been rescued from a boarded-up country house. The house had an old barn that was being demolished. It was purely chance that I happened to be holidaying in the village at the time. The trunk was packed with old documents, newspapers, letters, maps, photographs and notebooks. All the material was about Australia and dated to the period between the 1880s and the start of the First World War."

"Who gave you the trunk?" I asked.

"The workmen who demolished the barn. They drank at the inn where I was staying as a paying guest. They were friendly with the landlord. He knew I was a young historian. As no one knew who owned the trunk, he suggested I might take it off their hands. I paid them ten pounds for it."

"Who'd lived at the house?"

"The workmen didn't know. It had been boarded up since well before the Second World War. In any event, the contents of the trunk sparked my interest in Australian history. In such ways do random events shape our lives."

"What we want to know is how this all relates to my half-uncle Hobart," Shirley said.

"There was a huge amount of material in the trunk, most of it unreferenced. Over the years, I worked on it alongside my regular academic duties. Much of the material was about the gold mining industry. There was a rich seam of material about Australia's gold rushes – and the discovery of gold nuggets. One particular gold nugget turned up in several of the newspaper cuttings and some of the notebooks and letters."

"Which nugget?" Shirl asked before I could get a word in.

"The Teetulpa nugget, discovered in the South Australian gold field, just north of Adelaide."

"Jeez. Must've been worth a fortune," Shirl said.

Nettlebed fixed her pince-nez on her nose and glared at her.

"The Teetulpa nugget did not bring great fortune to all of those who discovered it," she said. "It was found in 1897 by two prospectors called Ned Hambrook and Roderick Tuff. The nugget contained nearly 900 Troy ounces of gold, enough to keep both of them in luxury for the rest of their lives. Unfortunately for Tuff, his life was short. He was dead within weeks of the discovery being registered."

"Dead? How?" I asked.

"That is the great mystery," Nettlebed said. "Tuff was found dead at the bottom of a mineshaft. The trunk had dozens of press cuttings about the case. Everyone had their own theory. Some said Tuff had fallen while prospecting in the mine in an unsafe shaft. Others suggested he had been attacked – murdered even. That must have been a hard blow for Tuff's family. He left a wife and child."

Shirl and I gawped at one another. We turned to Nettlebed. She walked back to her desk and sat down.

I asked: "Did the cuttings suggest who had killed Tuff?"

"Some writers thought another prospector, jealous at Hambrook and Tuff's finds," Nettlebed said. "Others suggested

Hambrook himself was responsible. Tuff's wife never doubted her husband had been killed by Hambrook. After Tuff's death, Hambrook disappeared."

"Disappeared where?" I asked.

"If anyone had known where, Hambrook wouldn't have disappeared," Nettlebed replied tartly.

"What I meant was – were there any theories?"

"Many. Some fantastic. Others speculative. Perhaps he lived the life of a jolly swagman for a few years and then returned to a city in another part of Australia. The consensus of opinion was that Hambrook had left the country. But how could he do that – especially in secrecy? He would've needed funds to buy his passage out. He had a priceless nugget but no cash."

"And you can't walk into a shop, buy a packet of fags, slap the nugget on the counter and say, 'have you got change for that?'," I said.

"If he left the country, he'd want to go somewhere he'd fit in," Nettlebed said.

"South Africa," I said. "It also had a prosperous gold mining trade at the end of the nineteenth century. It was one place in the world where he could turn up with a gold nugget and expect to sell it."

"Your theory is one I've considered myself. But in my research, I found no trace of Hambrook, or anyone like him, in South Africa. It's disappointing. For years, I've been hoping to write a book. I plan to call it *The Teetulpa Gold Nugget Mystery*. However, I have the mystery but no answer to it."

"Anyway, even if Ned Hambrook lived to be a hundred, he'd be dead by now," Shirl said.

"But gold nuggets never die," Nettlebed said.

"So where is it?" I added.

For a moment, we sat and gazed at one another. As though one of us would suddenly produce an answer.

"I guess it will remain one of the unsolved mysteries of our time," Nettlebed added.

Not if I have anything to do with it. The thought was speeding around my mind like a racing greyhound after a hare.

Trouble is, the greyhound never catches the hare.

Chapter 8

Frank Figgis smoked two Woodbines while I sat in his office and told him about the unsolved mystery of the Teetulpa gold nugget.

It was an hour after Shirley and I had left Victoria Nettlebed. I'd dropped Shirl in Bond Street where she'd seen a pair of summer sandals she'd wanted to buy, then headed for the *Chronicle*.

Figgis stubbed the last of the Woodies out on the edge of his desk and tossed the dogend into his waste basket.

He said: "Human nature, eh? Never ceases to amaze me how people can be greedy, dishonest and violent. What would we write about in our newspapers without those foibles in our fellow citizens?"

"So, I have your go-ahead to spend some time looking into the story?"

Figgis reached for his fag packet, opened it, realised he'd smoked all the ciggies. Tossed the packet into his bin.

"Not so fast. The story of the Teetulpa nugget died when that Ned Hambrook drew his last breath. Who knows when that was? Or where?"

"If we could answer both those questions, we'd have a scoop."

"You could spend weeks looking into that and come up with nix. Meanwhile, I've got empty columns to fill. Speaking of which I need another two from you on the Birtwhistle murder."

"There's nothing new to say. I'd just be repeating myself."

"Since when has that stopped you?"

"Now, Frank, that's unfair."

Figgis held up his hands in an apologetic gesture. "I spoke hastily. But there must be something new, surely?"

I shook my head. "I've interviewed both Lionel Bruce, the so-called metals dealer, and Victoria Nettlebed, the expert on

Australian history. They've both admitted they met Birtwhistle. But both say it was at his invitation and that they'd never heard of him before. Difficult to see why either would have a motive for killing him. Unless they've hidden something we don't know about."

"What progress have the cops made?" Figgis asked.

"With Tomkins running the case? Is that a joke question?"

Figgis reached for a pile of galley proofs. "So, we have a story going nowhere. Time to look for another murder, methinks."

I stood up and made for the door. "I don't commit them."

I opened the door and stepped outside. "But I could be tempted," I mumbled under my breath.

In journalism, it can seem like you've reached a dead end.

That you've run out of juice. That you're going nowhere.

Then something unexpected opens up the road ahead.

I had just reached my desk when the phone rang.

I scooped up the receiver and a voice said: "Listen up. You know whose flat feet lurk around my office."

The voice urging me to lend him my ears belonged to detective inspector Ted Wilson, one of my contacts in the Brighton cops. My only reliable contact, to be honest about it. And speaking of honesty, Ted was one of the few among Brighton's finest who didn't demand the folding stuff for tip-offs. Even so, he wasn't averse to a large scotch. But, hey, that's perks not corruption.

Ted was a mournful man who looked like he'd dressed from a jumble sale. He had sad eyes and a bushy black beard that usually harboured a bit of bacon from his breakfast.

The flat feet to which he referred belonged to detective chief superintendent Alec Tomkins, his boss. And the bungler of the Birtwhistle investigation.

"I've only got time to say this once," Ted whispered.

"Better get on with it, then."

"It's the Birtwhistle murder. You'll recall that spike in his office stuffed with papers."

"Reminded me of the ones we've got here."

"Well, we finally got round to going through all the papers on the spike. Terrible job. Scratched myself on the bloody thing three times. I don't know how you do it."

"Get on with it. Remember the flat feet."

"Near the top of the spike..."

"So only recently put on," I helpfully added.

"We found a slip of paper with the date of the second of July and the words 'S Ballantyne, six-thirty'."

I cursed myself. I'd considered taking the papers off the spike but decided it would be obvious someone had tampered with them.

But I didn't let my annoyance show as I said: "The date being the day before we suspect Birtwhistle was murdered."

"You've got it."

"So S Ballantyne could be the last person to have seen Birtwhistle alive."

"Without doubt - if Ballantyne killed Birtwhistle," Ted added.

But I'd already worked that one out.

"Any leads on who this S Ballantyne is?"

"Not yet."

"Male or female?"

"Definitely one of them."

"You can cut the stand-up comedy."

"I've called because I thought you may have seen the same slip of paper."

"How would I do that if it was impaled on a spike?"

"Don't play me for a patsy. You'd have searched the place before you called us. I know you carry those surgeon's gloves around with you."

"Would I have withheld vital evidence?"

"I won't answer that question to avoid the risk of causing offence."

"Let me know if you hear anything."

"I can hear Tomkins bellowing at a plod in the corridor, so I'll ring off."

The line went dead.

I leaned back in my captain's chair and thought about that.

Birtwhistle hadn't entered the appointment in his diary, so had it been a last-minute thing? Had he arranged the appointment or had Ballantyne instigated it? Impossible to be certain. But my gut feeling was that as Birtwhistle had scribbled the date and time on a scrap of paper, he hadn't had his diary to hand when the call came in. If he'd been fixing the call, he'd have the diary open in front of him so he didn't double book himself.

Then there was the fact that the page with the B entries had been torn out of Birtwhistle's address book. Ballantyne was a B name. If Ballantyne had killed Hobart, he or she would only have needed to tear out the B page in the contacts' book. Perhaps it had been entered before Ballantyne called to make the six-thirty appointment. Which would imply that Hobart had known Ballantyne for some time.

It was all speculation.

I needed to turn it into fact.

I headed for the morgue.

Half an hour later, I emerged feeling frustrated. I'd found only two S Ballantynes in the press cuttings file. One was a warehouse man who'd died in a car crash eight years ago. The other was a retired chaplain from the village of Cackle Street, north of Hastings. Seemed an unlikely killer, but I'd made a couple of calls from the phone in the morgue. The reverend gentleman was now in a nursing home in Winchelsea. He was expected to book his appointment with St Peter in the near future. Dead end. For him and for me.

Then I'd tried the phone books. Only three Ballantynes in the Brighton area directory, but none with the initial S. Of course, Ballantyne could be listed in any of the dozens of phone directories that covered the British Isles. But I didn't have time to go down that route now.

Who's Who, one thousand pages of the kingdom's notables, provided no viable Ballantynes. Nor did half a dozen other directories covering accountants, solicitors, chartered surveyors, estate agents, auctioneers and bank managers. They listed Talbots, Hartingtons and MacPhersons. Even a few Smiths. But no Ballantynes. At least, none that could be lined up as a heartless killer.

I leaned back in my captain's chair and looked around the newsroom.

Over by the door Phil Bailey was batting out a lengthy piece on his typewriter. He was one I'd fingered as a straw man manuscript thief. Same with women's editor Sally Martin who was on the phone to a contact. Sally was a wizard when asked to knock out five hundred words on ten ways to use left-over chicken. But steal a manuscript? Forget it. Still, I'd have to pretend to interrogate them – thumbscrews and all – to keep Figgis happy.

In the meantime, I puzzled over the identity of S Ballantyne.

More out of frustration than anything, I stood up and called out round the newsroom. "Listen up, you loafers. Anyone know of an S Ballantyne?"

From different parts of the newsroom a dozen heads turned in my direction.

"Who's S Ballantyne?" Phil Bailey wanted to know.

"What's the S stand for?" Sally Martin asked.

"Could be sexy," Susan Wheatcroft yelled.

A head appeared over the partition which screened off the sports reporters' desks. Fred Youngman needed to change his name as he was now pushing sixty. He had one of those smiling faces with intelligent grey eyes magnified behind strong wire-rimmed glasses. His brown hair was thick but turning white around the ears. The overall impression was of an ageing swot.

Fred said: "Actually, if it's who I think, the S stands for Scarlett."

All eyes turned on Fred.

"As in Scarlet Pimpernel?" Sally asked.

"More like scarlet woman if Colin knows her," Susan jeered.

"To be precise, neither as she spells her name with two Ts," Fred said. "At the end. As in Scarlett O'Hara. The main character in *Gone with the Wind*. As played by Vivien Leigh in the film."

I crossed the newsroom to the sports desk.

"Who are you talking about?" I asked Fred.

The grey eyes blinked twice behind the glasses. "Scarlett Ballantyne," he said.

"And who is Scarlett Ballantyne?"

"She's the captain of the Australian women's cricket team," Fred said. "They're currently touring England."

"Would you like me to start with Ballantyne's batting average?" Fred Youngman asked.

"Perhaps later," I said. "We'd like to know something about her life in Australia and why she's in England."

It was early evening and I'd asked Fred to join Shirley and me in Prinny's Pleasure. Fred may have been a bit of a swot, but he was a great sports reporter with a memory for facts and figures. He'd spent an hour in the morgue pulling together the gen about Scarlett Ballantyne.

"Spill the beans on the secret Scarlett," Shirley said.

Fred lifted his glass of beer and took a good pull at it. He wiped the froth from his upper lip with the back of his hand.

"Not that many beans to spill," Fred said. "But I found an article in a back issue of *The Cricketer*. It seems by the time she was eighteen, she was already making a mark as a batter in the junior women's game. That would be in Queensland. Picture in the mag showed quite a looker, too. There were hints that she was on friendly terms with some of the men's Ashes team

– the guys who whopped England in the first test at Brisbane in December '46 by an innings and 332 runs. Talk about bowl a maiden over. She was the original maiden."

"I suppose you wish you could have been the third man," Shirl said.

"By all accounts, Scarlett was already on to her fourth, fifth and sixth men by then. And despite the fact she'd married the year before."

"She was hitched and playing the field?" I asked.

Fred said: "She'd taken her marriage vows with a Jeremy Ballantyne. He was a true Brit who'd served in the Royal Air Force, out east between 1941 and 1945. Married an Aussie girl, Scarlett Maguire, at the end of the war. It was her second marriage – first husband was killed in the hostilities. Anyway, after the war, Jeremy took a job flying transport planes across Australia and the Pacific. Kept him away from home a lot. Convenient for Scarlett's affairs. Jeremy died last year. By then, it was a loveless marriage. It seems Scarlett barely noticed Jeremy was dead. Her life revolved around her cricket and man chasing."

"This Ballantyne – does he have any history?" I asked.

"Not much that I could find," Fred said. "His parents Reginald and Dorothy Ballantyne were back home here. There was a hint of some society connection, but nothing I've had time to follow up."

"A belted earl in the background?" I asked.

"Don't knock it," Fred said. "There have been strange stories of people inheriting titles they've never heard of."

I took a swig of my gin and tonic and said: "Back to the cricket. What's Scarlett's story there?"

"The usual path you see in the game. She started off playing for a women's club team in Brisbane. Became a nifty middle-order batter and useful wicket-keeper. Combine those two skills and you become a mainstay of the team. Scarlett certainly did. She made it into the Queensland state team. And it was a short hop, skip and a jump from there into the women's Australian side. For the past four years, she's been the team's skipper. She'll soon be the wrong side of forty. Bit old for a test-match level player. But wicket-keepers seem to last longer in the game than bowlers. Godfrey Evans played tests until he was thirty-nine."

Fred drained his glass. "You'll want to buy me another when you hear this bit," he said.

"Go on."

"Scarlett and the team are playing a warm-up game for the tests tomorrow at the Saffrons."

"The cricket ground in Eastbourne," I said.

I turned to Shirley. "I think this news calls for more drinks. How do you feel about a day at the cricket tomorrow?"

I signalled to Jeff behind the bar. "Large ones all round."

It was sunny but with a threat of rain – typical cricket weather – when Shirley and I set off for Eastbourne the following morning.

The road was clear and I pushed the MGB up to sixty as we cleared Peacehaven, on the cliff-tops east of Brighton.

"This Scarlett isn't the only gal that knows one end of a cricket bat from the other," Shirl said.

I gave her a quick glance. She'd dressed for the day in a yellow dress with black polka dots and a matching scarf.

"You've played a bit?" I asked.

"Just a bit. I batted number five for Adelaide Typhoons. It was a team for teen girls. We even took on the boys from time to time – and I don't just mean for a kiss and cuddle behind the pavilion."

"What was your top score?"

"One hundred and four not out. Used to get my name on the scorecard with a few run-outs, too. Could hit the wicket with one throw from twenty yards."

"Impressive," I said.

"Just fun as far as I was concerned."

"It won't be much fun finding a way to ask Scarlett why she visited Hobart Birtwhistle."

"And did you croak the old boy while you were there? See what you mean."

"We can't even be sure she visited Hobart at his house."

"You have a note with date and time."

"But not place. Hobart could have met her at a different rendezvous and then returned to his house."

"Where he was killed by someone else."

"Exactly," I said. "I think that's unlikely because the meetings with Lionel Bruce and Victoria Nettlebed were both in Muddles Green. So it's possible Scarlett's was, too. But possible isn't enough to persuade a jury."

"I can't figure out why she'd want to kill Hobart," Shirley said. "Had she even met him before?"

"We don't know. Just as we don't know of any motive she'd have for wanting to see Hobart dead. All we have is a series of killings by a blow to the head and strangulation. And the common factor is they all have links to Australia."

We passed a fingerpost: Eastbourne five miles.

"I've never visited the town," Shirley said. "Does it swing?"

"Not so you'd notice. On a Thursday, pension day, the queues at the post office are said to be the longest for miles around. Not like Folkestone up the coast where ferries leave for Europe every day."

"So not exactly groovy."

"As they say: Folkestone for the continent; Eastbourne for the incontinent."

Chapter 9

When we arrived at the Saffrons, I parked next to a large poster announcing the match.

It read: *Australian Women's XI versus Eleven Ladies of Eastbourne. One day limited overs match: 40 overs each side.*

As we climbed out of the car, an old boy with a walrus moustache hobbled up. He was dressed in a one-piece brown overall and a flat cap. He carried a bucket of paste and a large brush.

He unrolled a long strip of paper printed red with the word: CANCELLED.

Shirl and I exchanged worried glances.

I walked up to the guy and said: "The sun's still shining Why is the match off?"

He looked at me with watery eyes. "One of the sides can't muster a full team."

"Which team?" I asked.

"Eleven Ladies of Eastbourne. Only ten of them have turned up."

"Couldn't both teams field one short and get the game going?"

The watery eyes hardened. "That would be like ripping up a copy of *Wisden*."

Shirley stepped forward. "Do all the Ladies of Eastbourne come from the town?"

"They're supposed to. But I happens to know that Muriel Belcher comes from Hailsham and Freda Lovejoy has a flat in Polegate." The old guy patted the side of his nose. "They keeps quiet about it."

Shirley switched on a 100-watt smile. "So if another lady came from close to Eastbourne, she could play? Especially if she kept quiet about it."

The old guy rubbed his chin. "Not my place to say, but you

could ask Isobel Maynard, the skipper."

"And where will we find Isobel?" Shirl asked.

"The pavilion."

Shirl and I exchanged a glance. She gave me a tiny nod and a broad grin.

"Roll up your notice," I said to the old guy. "'Cancelled' has been cancelled."

But it didn't prove quite as easy as that.

I sat on a bench outside the pavilion and watched the ground staff push the heavy roller up and down the wicket. Meanwhile, Shirl went into the Eastbourne Ladies' dressing room.

She came out twenty minutes later. The yellow polka dot dress had gone and she was wearing whites. White skirt, white jumper, white socks.

She sat down beside me.

I nodded at the white kit. "Where did that gear come from?"

"Muriel Belcher loaned me her spare kit."

"Anyway, you're in," I said.

"By the skin of my brilliantly flossed teeth," Shirl said. "It was like negotiating the test ban treaty in there."

"Rather than a friendly cricket match?"

Shirl grinned. "I don't think it's going to be that friendly. No love lost between Isobel Maynard and Scarlett. Turns out they've faced up to each other in a match before. The goss in the pavilion is that Scarlett is a cheat. In cricket as in love. Isobel caught Scarlett in the slips in a previous match. But Scarlett didn't walk even though she'd edged the ball and everyone heard it. The dozy umpire was looking the other way. Because he didn't see it, he didn't raise his finger. Scarlett went on to make a brisk 50 and win the match. Talk in the dressing room was Scarlett had fixed the umpire."

"With money?"

"With sex," Shirl said.

"So the umpire actually got to bowl a maiden over."

"Yeah! Not often that happens by a guy wearing only his socks."

"But both team captains have agreed to let you play. So all is sweetness and light."

"Not exactly. According to Muriel, there was a bit of a barney earlier when Scarlett and the Aussie women turned up with their cricket bags. The Eastbourne ladies tried to make them welcome by showing them to their dressing room and helping them with their bags. Scarlett had left her bag on a bench so Muriel hefted it into the dressing room to try and be helpful. Scarlett went mad. Accused Muriel of trying to sabotage her kit. Said she was quite capable of carrying a cricket bag herself. Told Muriel in some ripe language that if she wanted help, she'd ask for it. And, until then, Muriel could clear off to her own dressing room. Didn't say 'clear off' either."

"Sounds like Scarlett had lost it."

"Yeah! And here's the thing. Muriel said she thought some of the Aussie girls looked a bit embarrassed by their skipper's behaviour. Not only that. Muriel said Scarlett's bag was the heaviest she'd ever carried. You usually allow for your whites, a bat, a ball, some cricket pads and boots and a couple of personal items like deodorants. But Scarlett's bag bulged with other stuff."

"What happened to the bag?"

"Muriel isn't sure. But her bet is that Scarlett will have stuffed the whole bag into her locker. Apparently, the captain's locker is larger than the rest. It's the one furthest from the door, nearest to the showers."

"And the locker will be locked," I said.

If eyes could flash like warning lamps, Shirl's would have been full-on red.

"I hope you're not thinking what I'm thinking," she said.

"I have to take a look in that cricket bag."

"Impossible. Scarlett, or one of the team, could come into the dressing room at any time."

"Not when the Eleven Ladies of Eastbourne are batting. The Aussies will all be on the ground fielding."

"Not the twelfth woman."

"She'll watch the game from the pavilion. Her job is to come on as a reserve if a team member is injured."

"And collect anything the team need. Like a sun hat from the dressing room." Shirl paused. "At any time," she added with a warning frown.

I thought about that. "When I'm ready to move, I'll give you the signal. You can make sure none of the Aussies go back to the dressing room for five minutes."

Shirley raised her eyes to heaven. But she wasn't going to find any help up there.

"What's the point? To get into the locker, you need a key. You can be sure it's firmly tucked into Scarlett's pocket."

"I've already thought of that. There'll be a spare set of keys for all the lockers. Embarrassing if a player lost their key and couldn't retrieve their kit. I expect the spare key will be in the secretary's office."

"And he's just going to hand it to you?"

"Not exactly," I said.

At that moment, the ground Tannoy crackled into life and a plummy voice said: "The captains are about to attend the toss in front of the pavilion."

Over by the pavilion, we watched a small crowd crane their necks as a silver coin flicked high into the air.

One of the Aussie women stepped forward and punched the air with both fists.

"That's Scarlett Ballantyne," Shirley said.

"Looks like the Aussies have won the toss," I said.

The Tannoy confirmed the news and added that they had elected to field.

"Looks like the Eastbourne Ladies will be batting first," I said. "That's good. The Aussies will all be fielding. I'll wait until you're in. Then I'll rely on you to keep the focus right on the field and away from the dressing rooms."

Shirl jogged on the spot. Limbered up her shoulders.

"You look like a real sportswoman going for gold," I said.

"Don't let the confidence fool you, big boy. I'm no Richie Benaud."

As Shirley jogged over to meet her team-mates, I made my way to the pavilion.

There was a small crowd of spectators in the deckchairs in front of it. Some of them had already fallen asleep.

I took a seat a couple away from a retired colonel type who was snoring. I fished out my notebook ready to make notes.

During the next half-hour I made like a real cricket reporter. I recorded what happened with each ball and the score. It looked like the Eastbourne Ladies were being outclassed by the Aussies. Three quick wickets went down for only 24 runs. Muriel Belcher came to the crease. She whacked the first delivery for a six. And for a time, it looked as though the Eastbourne Ladies might make a competitive score. But then Belcher was clean bowled.

The Tannoy announced: "Eastbourne Ladies have scored just 69 runs for the loss of seven wickets. A new player Shirley Goldsmith is coming to the crease."

And about time. I'd noticed in previous overs two of the Aussie players had left the field at different times and gone into the pavilion. I couldn't be sure what they were doing. Chances were they'd come in to give attention to a small cut or a bruise. Cricket balls are hard.

Now I had to rely on Shirley to keep everyone focused on the field of play.

I stepped inside the pavilion and followed a small corridor to the back of the building. I found the secretary's office at the other end from the dressing rooms.

A notice on the door read: Major Robert Urquhart, secretary.

I knocked on the door, waited until a gruff voice said "enter", and stepped inside.

Urquhart was sitting behind a desk. He was scratching his head over the *Daily Telegraph* crossword.

I came to attention like a squaddie on parade and said: "A moment of your time, Major."

Urquhart looked up from his crossword and said: "Well, isn't that the limit!"

I frowned. "I've only just walked into the room."

"You misunderstand. 'Well, isn't that the limit!' is a clue. Eight letters."

"Boundary," I said.

"Good man," he said.

"In that case, perhaps I could beg a favour."

"Beg away."

"I won't get down on my knees. But could I use your telephone?"

"Public call box outside the ground."

"That's the point. It's public. My call is confidential."

"Hush-hush, eh? Used to get that in the army. Mind you, nobody took any notice."

I handed Urquhart my business card. "Newspaper scoops. We like to keep them under our hat until they're on the front page."

"Understood. I'll give you five minutes. There's the phone."

I moved towards it. Coughed politely. "The call is, er, confidential."

Urquhart looked up from his crossword. "Quite so. I'll take a look at the cricket."

He stood up. Moved towards the door. Put his hand on the doorknob and turned towards me. "Five minutes – not a second more."

He went out.

Five minutes. To find a key in an unfamiliar office. A key which might not be there anyway.

I stood in the middle of the room and turned a full circle. Felt a bit giddy and decided not to try that again.

I needed to think this problem out. Like the crossword clue.

There would be at least a dozen lockers in both the home and away dressing rooms. Perhaps more. So that could mean as many as 24 keys. Again, perhaps more. Each would need to be clearly labelled and readily accessible in an emergency. Such as when a player had lost their key and just stepped naked out of the team bath.

All that suggested the keys would be hanging from hooks in a special cabinet. I looked around the room again. There was nothing that looked like a key cabinet. Nothing that didn't look like a key cabinet but could have been one. There was a large bookcase with glass doors.

There were a couple of wooden filing cabinets. And a large item, with two doors, which looked like a wardrobe.

I opened the doors.

It was a wardrobe. Inside it, on hangers, were a tweed overcoat, a pair of grey flannel trousers, a pair of white cricket flannels, and a double-breasted blue blazer with silver buttons.

And a lady's bra.

Size 40C. Not the major's size I would have said. But then I wasn't going to whip out a tape measure and ask him to step forward with his arms stretched out sideways.

I wasted unnecessary seconds wondering whether the major had a lady friend who obliged in the office. But that thought led nowhere.

I reached out an arm to close the wardrobe doors and brushed against the blazer. Set it swinging on its hanger. And noticed something behind. I pushed the clothes to one end of the hanging rail.

A flat cupboard was screwed onto the back of the wardrobe. It was about two feet square. It had double doors each with a little plastic knob. There was no keyhole so it wasn't locked. I moved closer and opened the doors.

The keys were hanging from hooks in neat rows. One side was marked "Home". The other, "Away". I reached in and took the first key on the away side. It had a fob with a label: "Captain's locker".

I shoved the key in my pocket. I took the captain's key from the home side and hung it on the away hook. That way, when Urquhart found a key missing, he'd worry that there'd been a mix-up. He'd know someone had been in the secret key cupboard, but he'd also know they'd seen the bra. He wouldn't want to make too much of the incident. He'd quietly get a replacement key cut and hope the intruder would keep quiet about his private fetish.

These thoughts flashed through my mind at the speed of light as I closed the key cupboard doors. Then shut the wardrobe.

I hurried back to the major's desk and lifted his telephone. The five minutes had only seconds to run.

The door opened and the major stepped into the room.

The dialling tone buzzed in my ear as I said: "So we'll splash on the front-page next week and keep quiet about this scoop until then."

I replaced the receiver and rounded my shoulders like a bloke who has done good work and is satisfied with life.

I said: "Thank you, Major. All done."

He said: "Back to the crossword, then. Life is full of puzzles."

"Don't I know it." I went out of the door and closed it behind me.

I was back in the corridor which linked the different parts of the pavilion.

From outside, I heard the sound of applause.

I felt like taking a bow, but hurried down the corridor towards the dressing rooms.

There was nobody about. Another round of applause with a few cheers suggested the match might be hotting up. Well done, Shirl.

The door to the away team dressing room was at the far end of the corridor.

I sauntered up to it like a guy who looked lost. If anyone appeared, I'd tell them I was looking for the toilets.

I tried the handle and the door didn't budge. I felt a hot flush around my neck. I hadn't bargained for the dressing room door to be locked.

It wasn't - just stiff. It opened on whining hinges. I took a last furtive glance down the corridor and slipped inside.

The place was a long thin room painted white, with windows set high into the wall on one side. Down the left side, there were rows of hooks, most of them hung with the team's day clothes.

There was a row of lockers on the right side. It didn't take me long to locate the captain's. I took out the key and opened the door.

A green jacket with gold piping – the team's colours - hung from a hanger. A large cricket bag had been bundled on its side on the locker's floor. I heaved the bag out and unzipped it.

Inside were two cricket bats. One was a Kookaburra, well-oiled and ready for use. The other was wrapped in a large brown towel. I flipped open the towel. The bat was a Kingsport Deadly. It hadn't been oiled and polished like the Kookaburra and someone had removed the rubber hand-grip from around the handle. It wouldn't be unusual for a cricket pro to have two bats in case one broke during a match. But surely, both bats should be ready for use?

Alongside the bats were a pair of batting gloves and two pairs of wicket-keeper gloves. The last were larger than those used for batting and had webbing that connected the thumb to the index finger. I rummaged in the bag. Under a couple of towels, I found another pair of wicket-keeper gloves. These were tightly packed in a transparent plastic bag, like they'd just come from the makers. I picked up the bag and turned it over. The gloves were stained and didn't look new.

I heard women's voices in the corridor.

I tensed up, felt my heart go bumpety-bump. Took a deep breath to steady myself.

I repacked the bag with trembling hands. I fumbled for the words I'd say when the women burst into the room.

One voice said: "I'll just go and collect something."

I shoved the bag back into the locker. Slammed the door shut and locked it.

I stood up and hurried towards the door. Pressed myself against the wall so that when the door opened, I would be behind it.

The voice said: "I'll join you in front of the pavilion."

A door opened. But not the door to the away dressing room. The home dressing room. The door closed and a single set of footsteps faded as the other person disappeared towards the front of the pavilion.

I opened the door and peered down the corridor. Empty. I slipped out and closed the door silently behind me.

I hurried down the corridor and stepped out of the pavilion just as Shirley launched a cover drive. It sent the ball speeding past mid-on for four.

The figures moved on the scoreboard. Shirley had already scored 49. One more for a half century. I settled in one of the deckchairs in front of the pavilion to enjoy the fun.

Shirl saw me take my seat and gave a friendly wave with her bat. She settled down in the crease and prepared to take the next delivery from the bowler. I took a quick glance at the scoreboard. The bowler was Sonia Bradman. I briefly wondered whether she was any relation to the late, great Sir Donald Bradman. He'd retired from his career with the highest test match batting average ever.

Family trees! I was becoming obsessed by them.

Sonia started her run-up. Accelerated as she approached the wicket. Threw every ounce of energy into delivering the ball.

The ball pitched just over a length and turned into an outswinger. Shirley moved swiftly on to her back foot and drew her bat away. I heard a faint flick as the ball brushed Shirl's left pad outside the off-stump.

"Owzat!" a lone voice shrieked.

Behind the wicket, Scarlett Ballantyne held the ball in her gloved hand. She tossed the ball high into the air and recaught it.

"How is that for a catch?" she demanded of the umpire, Winifred Purcell, a small woman with grey hair tied back in a ponytail.

Every other player on the field looked puzzled. None of them had appealed. No chorus of "owzats!". Even Sonia stayed silent. It was clear the ball hadn't connected with Shirl's bat. So she couldn't be caught out.

Scarlett marched down the wicket towards Purcell. "Are you deaf as well as blind? Didn't you hear the ball flick the bat?"

"I, er, wasn't sure…" Winifred stammered.

Scarlett strode up to the umpire and looked straight into her face. "Be sure now," she said in a low menacing voice.

"Of course. I, er, may have missed…"

Poor Winifred looked around Scarlett and raised her finger towards Shirley. The umpire's sign for out.

A disgruntled buzz of conversation started around the ground. The Aussie players gathered in groups on the field and shook their heads. Outside the pavilion, I could hear spectators expressing shock at the decision.

At the wicket, Shirl gave Winifred a long hard stare, tucked her bat under her arm, and walked from the field.

I stood up and moved to meet her as she approached the

pavilion.

Shirl was calm. But I could tell from the pink flushes on her cheeks that she was angry.

"Scarlett Ballantyne is a cheat and a bully," she said.

"You deserved that half century," I said.

"Yeah! But I'll get my revenge when Scarlett bats. I'm going into the pavilion to shower and take my pads off."

"Not in that order," I said.

I could tell how angry Shirl was. She didn't even pretend to laugh.

It was nearly an hour before Shirley came out of the pavilion.

While she was taking her shower, the remaining Eastbourne Ladies' wickets had fallen. The team had been dismissed for the modest score of 137.

The players had trooped into the pavilion for lunch. I'd assumed Shirl had joined them. I'd found a tea tent on the other side of the ground and munched a stale cheese sandwich.

Shirl seemed in good spirits when she re-joined me.

"Just had a great chicken salad for lunch," she said.

"Lucky you," I said.

"The girls in there are really worked up about my dismissal. They're fired up to take the battle to the Aussies when they have their innings this afternoon."

"Did you pick up any information about Scarlett?" I asked.

"Not much. The Aussies sat at their own table for lunch. It didn't look like they were about to toast Scarlett with champagne. More like they wanted to slip her a poisoned cup."

"The last thing we want in this match is a dead body. Always confuses the scorers."

"Ha, bloody, ha. But seriously, I had a quick word with Sonia Bradman. She was cut up about the decision. Said she liked to take her wickets fair and square. I mentioned you're a reporter and you'd like to know more about Scarlett. Sonia said she'd slip out for a quiet word before the innings starts."

As if on cue, Sonia appeared on the pavilion steps. She took a furtive look around and hurried over to us.

She had a bouncy walk like she had springs on the soles of her shoes. She had an athletic build, but with the strong shoulders of a formidable fast bowler. She had short brown hair, cut in a bob. Her wide mouth was set in a warm smile but her eyes glanced warily about.

"Let's go and talk behind the scorers' hut," she said. "I don't want you-know-who to see me talking to you."

"It's a free country," I said.

"Yeah! That's the theory," Shirley said.

We walked swiftly over to the scorers' hut and formed a tight group behind it.

Sonia said: "I've already told Shirley I don't regard her dismissal as a fair wicket."

Shirl put her arm around Sonia and gave her a hug. "Hey, it's only a game."

I said: "That's not what Harold Pinter says. He thinks cricket is a microcosm of life."

Sonia said: "Yeah! The sun is shining and you're on top of the world. And then it all comes to an end because of a lie from a cheat."

This philosophical chat was making the conversation a bit heavy. So I said: "I get the impression your team-mates don't think much of Scarlett Ballantyne."

"Yeah! That's putting it mildly. Fact is, nobody thought she was coming on this tour – let alone as the skipper."

"How did that happen?"

Sonia grinned. "For a start, we've got a women's team, but the selectors are mostly men. Can you credit that?"

"And Scarlett didn't earn her place by showing her skills in the cricket nets?" Shirley asked.

"Yeah!" Sonia said. "When you're batting at the crease you

have to keep your legs together."

"So, Scarlett earned her tour place in the bedroom," Shirley said.

"And Scarlett is to bedrooms what crocs are to swamps," Sonia said.

"So why don't the other players do something about it?" I asked.

"Because she's a bully. As captain she has the last word on who gets into the team. And anyone who gets up her fanny might as well leave their kit at home. That's not the only cross we bear. There's her son, Rod. Makes his mother look as bright and friendly as the Queen of the May."

"He's on the tour?" I asked.

"As baggage master, can you believe? Like his Ma, he's a bounce."

"A bully," Shirl translated.

"With a mind like a dunny."

"Toilet," Shirl said.

"His trick is to come into the girls' dressing room just as we're getting our kit off. Accidentally on purpose, of course. Thankfully, he's not here today."

I said: "You know I'm a reporter. Do you think Scarlett will agree to an interview?"

Sonia looked upwards like she was searching for the right answer."

"You can always ask," she said. "It'll be like asking a great white shark not to eat you. And now I need to get back before I'm missed."

And with a nod of her head, she slipped away.

"Looks like I'll have to take on Scarlett after the match," I said.

"If there's anything left after I've finished with her," Shirley said.

Chapter 10

I sat in a deckchair in front of the pavilion and watched Shirl and her team-mates take the field for the afternoon session.

If Shirl was right, the match, which was billed as a "friendly", wasn't going to be so chummy after all. Exactly what Shirl had planned for Scarlett's nemesis, she wouldn't say.

But I'd learnt in the years I'd known her, that Shirl was not a girl you wanted to cross.

After having scored only 137 runs in the morning session, the Eleven Ladies of Eastbourne faced a tough task if they were to win the match.

On the face of it, a crack international side like the Aussies could knock off those runs in a couple of hours while whistling *Waltzing Matilda*. It could be a short afternoon for the Eastbourne Ladies.

But that was their problem. Mine was getting close enough to Scarlett to ask her some pointed questions. At the moment, she was sitting on a bench outside the pavilion, padded up and ready to go in to bat.

I was worried about two things. One was how I could get Scarlett on her own so I could ask her why she visited Hobart Birtwhistle. But the second was whether, in fact, she had visited Hobart. After all, the only evidence for this was a slip of paper found on Hobart's spike. If Hobart spiked the paper after his meeting with Scarlett, he was evidently still alive. Which would mean she hadn't killed him.

But the other possibility was that he'd spiked the paper before the meeting. The question that nagged at my mind was: why should he do that? Could it be that he wanted to keep some evidence that Scarlett had visited him? And, if so, why did he need that evidence?

I hoped that Scarlett might be able to provide some answers

to those questions.

But not now. On the pitch, the first Aussie wicket had fallen – a run-out. It was Scarlett's turn to bat.

She strode out to the wicket with a swagger. Took time taking her guard. Looked around the field like she owned the place.

The last wicket had fallen at the end of an over. So Scarlett would have to face the first ball of the new over.

Shirley had been fielding at cover point. She sprinted across the pitch to Isobel Maynard. Put her arm around Isobel's shoulder. Whispered something into her ear.

Isobel shook her head. Shirley said something more urgently. Emphasised her point by clapping her hands together.

Isobel shrugged. Tossed the ball to Shirley.

It looked as though Shirl would bowl the over to Scarlett.

This would be worth watching. Shirl had not mentioned earlier that she could bowl at cricket. I certainly had no idea whether she'd be a fast or spin bowler. I was about to find out.

Shirl said something to Isobel. Isobel waved her arms about a bit. Called in the fielders to closer catching positions.

At the wicket, Scarlett watched this. Tapped the bat on the ground impatiently.

Shirl paced out her run-up. A short run-up. So, Shirl was a spin bowler. She turned round and marked the spot for the start of her run-in. Waited for Scarlett to take her guard at the wicket. Began her run. Shirl's hair bounced around her face as she picked up speed.

One, two, three, four big paces to the wicket.

Then over with the arm.

A cunning twist of the wrist as she released the ball.

It moved through the air like it was flying through treacle.

Scarlett shifted on to her front foot. The ball pitched a yard over length on middle stump. Scarlett moved forward. An over-pitched ball. A gift to the batter. Scarlett lifted the bat into her back-swing, ready to come forward and hit the ball for six.

At the far end of the pitch, Shirl stood, arms akimbo, watching the ball like it was a guided missile.

Scarlett moved into her stroke, a vicious cover-drive that would lift the ball far over the boundary. Even out of the ground.

But as the ball had pitched, it swung to off and rose sharply, like a bouncer from a fast bowler.

Scarlett stepped back to adjust her stroke. But the ball caught the shoulder of her bat and flew high into the air.

Up, up it went, like it had been launched into orbit.

The fielders stood around mesmerised. They'd never seen anything like this before. It had captured their imaginations. And made them forget that they should catch the ball before it landed.

All but one. Shirley spring-heeled into action.

Up, further up, the ball flew.

And then it started to fall, seemingly slow at first. But then faster.

Shirl raced down the wicket.

But the ball gathered pace.

It was going to hit the pitch just in front of Scarlett's wicket. She stood her ground.

The ball was six feet from the pitch.

Shirl was six feet from the spot it would land.

She dived forward. Cannoned into Scarlett's thigh. Scarlett stepped back on the stumps and crashed over them. She tumbled to the ground in a confusion of legs and stumps and arms and bails.

Shirl hit the ground as her arm stretched forward – and grabbed the ball in her right hand.

"Owzat!" she yelled.

With one voice, the other ten Ladies of Eastbourne, screamed: "Owzat!"

Scarlett scrambled to her feet. Her face was pink with effort. Her eyes were black with hatred.

"Not out," she yelled at the umpire.

But this time Winifred Purcell wasn't looking the other way. She raised her index finger.

Scarlett stomped down the wicket and fronted up to Winifred. "You can't be serious," she screamed.

Winfred said nothing. She stood with her right arm raised. Her index finger extended.

Suddenly, Scarlett realised the ground had gone silent. Not exactly a "breathless hush in the Close" – but not far off.

And, then, from the far corner of the ground a woman's voice – haughty, fruity - rang out: "Play up! Play up! and play the game."

Not everyone in the ground would have known Henry Newbolt's poem *Vitai Lampada*. But they all recognised the sentiment. And burst into laughter.

A gale of hilarity swept round the ground.

Scarlett glared once more at Winifred, turned and stomped from the field.

She stepped over the boundary rope and clumped up the steps into the pavilion.

I sprang from my chair and hurried after her. She was marching down the corridor to the dressing room by the time I caught up with her.

"Really bad luck," I called out.

"What?" she said over her shoulder.

"Damn hard cheese you getting a duck. And a golden one," I said, trying to summon up the stiff-upper-lip of Newbolt.

Scarlett swung round. "Cheese doesn't come into it. Cheating does. You could tell I wasn't out after that bowler crashed into me."

"She also caught the ball and you broke your wicket while playing a shot. Mind you, I've often wondered why the Marylebone Cricket Club even considered including those as reasons to be out in the Laws of Cricket."

"Are you trying to be funny?"

"Not on this occasion. I'm wondering what Hobart Birtwhistle would have made of it all."

I had to give her credit. She allowed only the tiniest of pauses before she said. "Who?"

A tiny pause but it was all I needed.

"Hobart Birtwhistle of Muddles Green."

"I don't know a Puddles Green."

The deliberate mistake. Another giveaway.

"You visited Hobart at his home," I said.

"No, I did not."

"Hobart was murdered shortly after your visit."

"I hope you're not suggesting what I think you are."

"Hobart was killed by person or persons unknown."

"Well, bad luck to Hobart – and you can go and bother the persons unknown."

"Happy to do that, if you can answer one more question. Where were you on the evening of the second of July or the early morning of the third?"

"Not killing Birtwhistle. No, wait. That was the evening I was at the women's cricket dinner at the Oval. It's a cricket ground in London."

"I know the Oval."

"Two hundred people were there – and I made a short speech. If you don't believe me, you can check."

I nodded. I would check, but Scarlett would be telling the truth about that. And, if she was at the Oval, she wouldn't have killed Hobart.

"I wouldn't dream of doubting your word," I said.

"Yeah! That's what I thought." Scarlett turned and stomped off to the dressing room.

I mooched back to the front of the pavilion wondering what I should do next. One point was hammering away in my brain like a woodpecker giving an elm tree a hard time. If Scarlett knew she was going to be at the Oval dinner, why had she arranged to visit Hobart at the same time? Could the dinner engagement have come up after she'd fixed the meet with Hobart? She was a booked speaker at the dinner, so that didn't seem likely.

Perhaps Hobart had made a mistake in noting the date and time of the meeting. Maybe he'd written the second but meant the third. He'd taken the trouble to save the slip of paper on his spike which suggested he thought it was important. Or perhaps there was another S Ballantyne, but that didn't seem likely, either.

By the time I reached the front of the pavilion I felt I hadn't made any progress at all.

But the Eleven Ladies of Eastbourne certainly had.

There'd been a collapse in the Aussie batting while I'd been bearding Scarlett. With just 87 runs on the board, the visitors had lost nine wickets. And as I moved towards an empty deckchair, the final wicket fell.

Shirley raced off the field grinning like she was bewitched. She threw her arms around me and gave me a big fat kiss. The kind that's worth a gold medal.

She said: "Take a look at the scoreboard, big boy."

I turned towards it. Shirley had taken five of the Aussie wickets for just 32 runs.

"I sure gave that Scarlett Ballantyne a hard time," Shirley said.

"Me, too. Trouble is she returned the compliment."

I explained how Scarlett couldn't have murdered Hobart because she was attending a fund-raising dinner.

Shirley was about to say something. But Major Urquhart appeared at the top of the pavilion steps. He scanned the crowd, spotted us and hurried over.

"Mr Crampton, I've an urgent telephone message for you from your paper – a Mr Piggis."

"Figgis."

"Really? Anyway, it appears there's been a murder."

"In the office?"

"No, in Kemp Town. Mr Piggis insisted I write down the address. Here it is." Urquhart handed me a slip of paper. "Terrible business. Terrible."

Urquhart turned and hurried back up the pavilion steps like a man who's just stepped in something unpleasant.

I looked at the address on the paper.

"Looks like I'm gonna miss my lap of honour," Shirl said.

I parked my MGB a hundred yards from the murder victim's house.

It was little more than an hour after receiving the note from Urquhart.

Shirl had missed her lap of honour at the Saffrons. Before I dropped her at her flat, I'd told her we'd find another way to celebrate. She'd made a disappointed little pout with her lips. But I could tell she was fizzing with excitement after reaping her revenge on Scarlett – with interest.

The murder victim lived – and, it turned out, died - in the ground floor flat of a house in one of those streets of Victorian terraces just off Edward Street, near Brighton College. The place looked well kept. The outside had been whitewashed recently. The windows were clean. The steps leading up to the front door had been swept.

There was a separate flat upstairs with its own set of stairs at the side of the building.

As I approached, a plod, who'd been leaning on the railings at the front of the house, came to life.

He couldn't hide a sneer as he said: "It's you."

I said: "It's either my being or a nothingness, as Jean-Paul Sartre might say."

"Yeah! I've often thought I feel free but, you know, like free in a prison."

"Hell is other people, especially Alec Tomkins."

"Tomkins has been and gone. He's left Ted Wilson to clear up the detail."

"In that case I better catch time by the tail and go inside."

"Yeah! Do that before my head explodes," the plod said.

I pushed on the door. It opened and I stepped into a hallway lit by a weak bulb behind a pink lampshade. There was brown embossed wallpaper on the walls and a green dado rail. A half-moon table up against the wall held some old newspapers and a pile of leaflets for the Royal Society for the Prevention of Cruelty to Animals. Two brown coats, like the kind worn by hospital porters, hung from a coat hook. There was a black telephone on a small shelf screwed to the wall by wooden brackets. Just above the shelf, a frame held a graduation photo. A dozen grads in mortar boards and black gowns stood in a row grinning at the camera. Their names were listed along the foot of the photo. Further along the hall, a picture in a gilt frame showed Francis of Assisi holding a new-born baby in a farmyard. A group of pigs, ducks, goats and horses had gathered round to welcome the nipper into the world. The air smelt of furniture polish and disinfectant. (In the hall, that is. I can't speak for the farmyard.)

Ted came out of door further down the hall just as I stepped towards it.

He said: "It's you."

I said: "Don't say we've got to go through all that Sartre nonsense again."

Ted scratched his head. "Who's Sartre?"

"French bloke. Philosopher. Couldn't quite work out which way up the world was." I nodded to the door Ted had just come out of. "Is that where it happened?"

Ted nodded. "I suppose you'll be wanting a look."

"Off the record, of course."

"Where have I heard that before?"

"First things first – name of the victim."

"Tom Ryan. Veterinary surgeon. Died by a blow to the head. But that's off the record until we've contacted next of kin."

"No strangulation?"

"Not that we could see. Why do you ask?"

I put on my bored look. Dead eyes. Half-open mouth. "No reason."

"Yeah! That's what I thought." Ted sounded unconvinced.

"What about suspects and motive?"

Ted shuffled about. Looked at his feet.

"You won't find any suspects round your size elevens," I said.

"It's a question of discretion. Ryan lived with a flat mate, Mungo Brown. He was a vet, too."

"Nothing wrong with that."

"We think Ryan and Brown may have been a little more than flat-mates."

"Working colleagues?"

"Not that, exactly."

I knew why Ted wanted to dodge the issue. Like hundreds of men living in Kemptown, Ryan and Brown were gay. I could understand the discretion.

Homosexual acts between men were illegal. Prison sentences were counted in years. But reformers hoped that was all going to change if a new law got through parliament.

I said: "The only evidence of crime concerns Tom's murder. Has his body been identified by Mungo?"

Ted shook his head. "We can't find him. We've called his surgery, but the receptionist said he left early this afternoon."

I thought about that for a bit. "Could Mungo be a suspect?" I asked.

Ted looked at his size elevens again. "The pair lived together and neighbours say they appeared to get on well. Too well for some of the cavemen types who live in parts of the town."

"You think the fact they were gay could have been a motive?"

Ted shrugged. "Don't know yet."

"Can I see in the room now?"

"You know the rules. You wear gloves. You don't report who gave you access."

"Forgotten already."

"I'll get you some gloves."

I reached into my jacket's inside pocket and whipped out the surgeon's gloves. "Always carry my own."

Ted raised his eyebrows. "Just in case you're called on to conduct a life-saving operation, presumably."

I ignored that.

Ted led the way down the hall and into a neat sitting room. The room was decorated with a yellow and white wallpaper in an oriental design. There were a couple of deep leather armchairs, complete with lacy antimacassars, either side of a handsome walnut coffee table. A pair of basketwork coasters had been placed on the table precisely in front of the chairs. A small television set lurked behind doors in its own cabinet, like it had been told to stand in the corner of the room. There was a fire laid with pine logs in a neat criss-cross pattern, but not lit. Above it, a broad mantelpiece held two handsome silver photo frames, one at each end. The light glinted off the frames and caught my eye.

Opposite the fireplace, there was a desk. It was loaded with bulging files. It looked like Tom and Mungo hadn't been great at paperwork.

I strolled over and took a closer look at the photos.

One showed a tall man with fair hair, cut short, and a handsome open face. His eyes were shaded by prominent eyelids. His thin lips were slightly parted and there was a small dimple in his chin. A nameplate at the foot of the frame read: Mungo Brown.

The other photo was crooked in the frame. It showed a man with dark wavy hair cut below his ears. His eyes were close together under heavy eyebrows which almost met above the bridge of his nose. He had a broad chest and the beginnings of a middle-aged paunch even though I wouldn't have put his age much above thirty. The nameplate read: Tom Ryan.

I looked again at the first photo. Then peered at the back of the Tom Ryan photo frame. There were four clips which held the back of the frame in place. Only two of them were closed.

Ted was looking over my shoulder.

I said: "Did you use these photos to make an initial identification?"

"Tomkins did. He insisted that photographs never lie. Of course, there'll be a formal identification when we locate Mungo Brown. Failing that, we'll ask a neighbour to do the honours. The old girl upstairs seems to know them well."

I said: "Come with me. I need to show you something."

We trooped into the hall and stood before the grad student photo.

I said: "Look at the first person from the left. Dark hair, pudgy frame, thick eyebrows. Mungo Brown, according to the caption below. The same guy in the mantelpiece photo is labelled Tom Ryan."

Ted put on his glasses. His nose was almost touching the frame as he stared at the picture.

"Now look at the person third from right. Tall, fair hair, slim figure. Tom Ryan. But in the Mungo Brown frame on the mantelpiece."

Ted switched his gaze. Stood up straight. Took off his glasses slowly. Made a performance of stuffing them into their case.

"Must be a mistake in the caption of this photo," he said.

"I don't think so. For starters, these university graduation photos are always captioned very carefully – people wouldn't buy them if they were wrong. And would Tom and Mungo really have a picture that misidentified them on the wall. I don't think so."

"But that means..." Ted began.

"That the pictures on the mantelpiece are in the wrong frames.

I think they've been switched. And done recently, in a hurry."

"You can't possibly know that."

"You must have seen how everything in that room was in apple-pie order. A place for everything and everything in its place, as my old mother used to say. Mungo Brown's photo was crooked in the Tom Ryan frame. And two of the hooks on the back hadn't been closed. The dead man is not Tom Ryan. It's Mungo Brown."

Ted looked down at his boots.

I said: "You won't find the answer down there."

He said: "The answer to what?"

"Either Mungo Brown wanted his killer to believe he was Tom Ryan. Or Tom Ryan found Mungo's body and wants us to believe that it's him who is dead."

Chapter 11

There was one of those awkward moments of silence.

Like when you look at your feet. Or shuffle around nervously. Or clear your throat. Or wish you were somewhere else.

Ted and I looked at one another wondering who would be first to speak.

Ted said: "Damn him! I knew Tomkins shouldn't have relied on those photos for identification."

I said: "Anything for an easy life. That's Tomkins."

Ted slumped into one of the leather chairs. The poor bloke looked like he wanted to find a hole and crawl down it. "Now I've got to sort out the mess."

I let that idea sink into Ted's mind before I said: "There needn't be any mess."

Ted looked up. Like a prisoner who realises the hangman has run out of rope. "How do you mean?"

"There hasn't been a formal identification yet. Any names that Tomkins has bandied around have been off-the-record. Any come-back is only going to land in his porridge. I'll make sure that you come out of this as the hero who discovered the truth."

The muscles round Ted's mouth relaxed. "You'd do that?"

I said nothing.

Another silence lengthened until it became embarrassing.

"I get it," Ted said at last. "You want something. What is it?"

"Ten minutes while you turn your back and I look around the place."

"Why?"

"I want to see if I can find the answer to those questions."

"Which questions?"

"Whether Mungo wanted his killer to believe he was Tom or whether Tom wanted us to believe he was dead."

Ted scratched at his beard. A clear sign he was engaging all his brain cells while he thought that one out.

"Just ten minutes?"

"Yes."

"And you'll make me the hero?"

"Order your laurel crown."

"As it happens, I need to speak to the officer outside the door," Ted lied. "Ten minutes. Not a second more."

He stomped out of the room. Seconds later, I heard the front door open and close.

I swung round and looked at the picture frames on the mantelpiece again. The frames were handsome items. Hand-tooled silver plate. Not a bargain buy from Woolworth's. Perhaps, I wondered, a gift to each other. A love gift, even.

There was no doubt the pictures had been swapped between frames – and done in a hurry. But who had done it – Mungo or Tom? Mungo was the dead man, but Tom's picture was in Mungo's frame.

Could Mungo have feared for his life for some reason? Did vets make enemies? Suppose a clumsy slip with a scalpel had sent a pet peke to the animal's graveyard. Could the distraught owner seek the ultimate revenge? It seemed unlikely, but people could be passionate about their pets. And when passion rears its ugly head, reason flies out of the window.

But if someone wanted to kill Mungo because of a grudge, they'd already know what he looked like. Switching photos wouldn't put them off the scent. It would just make the pursuer angrier.

So that left me wondering why Tom would want to swap the photos. I couldn't think of any reason – other than a bizarre practical joke that Tom wanted to play on Mungo. But could there be a reason why Tom was panicked into the action when he knew that Mungo had died?

I played out a scene in my mind.

Tom comes back to the house and finds Mungo lying dead

on the carpet in the sitting room. His initial reaction is horror. Followed by grief. But, perhaps, also a concern for his personal self-preservation. Maybe Tom worries that the cops will think he's killed Mungo. Or perhaps Tom knows the killer had got the wrong victim. Perhaps Tom has good reason to suspect there is a threat to his own life. And decides to vanish for his own safety. He changes the photos to make whoever investigates think that he's the dead man. To give him more time to flee to a hiding place.

Of course, that's a crude ploy that wouldn't hold for more than five minutes. Except that Tom got lucky. Tomkins, the cops' equivalent of a fairground huckster, was in charge of the case.

My ten minutes were running out.

I crossed to the desk opposite the fireplace. The one with the bulging files. I lifted a couple of heavy buff jobs and a business card fell out of one of them.

Sam Ballard, keeper of wallabies at Leonardslee Gardens, presented his compliments.

I flipped inside the file. There were learned papers on the health, welfare and diseases of the Aussie marsupials. Most of them included Tom Ryan as one of the authors. Looked like Tom was top banana when it came to wallabies. Well, somebody has to be.

I replaced the file but made a note of the name and contact details on the card.

I glanced at my watch. I had four minutes left.

And a theory about Tom's disappearance that would be laughed out of court.

I walked into the hall. Stopped by the shelf that held the telephone. There was a notepad and pencil beside the phone. The top page of the notepad had a scribbled message. It read:

"1.30pm: Mungo, you had urgent call-out to sick puppy. Asked for you personally, but not a previous client. After I put the phone down, decided to go myself, as you were at lunch. See you later. Love, Tom."

I thought about that. Why should someone with a sick puppy want a specific vet they'd never used before? Perhaps they'd heard that Mungo was top banana on sick puppies. But I wasn't convinced. If you had a sick animal, any vet would do.

A black thought ran through my mind. The unknown caller wanted Mungo out of the way while they croaked Tom. But Tom had taken the call-out and Mungo had returned for lunch to find he had an unexpected appointment with death. Perhaps only minutes later Tom had returned to find Mungo dead. He would've discovered that the sick puppy call-out was a hoax. That would have heightened his fears that the killer had really come for him.

I'd used up my ten minutes. I had a theory, but no hard evidence to support it. But it was all I was going to get.

I walked up to the front door and opened it.

Ted was leaning on the railings at the front of the place. He had the stub of a Capstan Navy Cut between his lips.

I said: "If you let that dogend burn any further, you'll singe your beard."

"Saves me having to trim it. Anyway, you're the one who likes to live dangerously."

"Not today," I said.

Ted gave me a dirty look and went back inside with the plod who'd been guarding the door.

I walked up and down outside the house a couple of times while I thought about Tom. I needed to know more about him - and about Mungo. I slipped up the staircase at the side of the house. I'd spotted the door to the top flat up there.

Neighbours. Sometimes they know everybody's business. Sometimes nothing. Ted had said the old girl upstairs was friendly with Tom and Mungo. If Tom fled because his life was in danger, I needed a line on where he might go.

I knocked on the door.

It was opened by an elderly lady with silver grey hair that straggled around her face and down her back to her waist. She had a warm face where every wrinkle seemed to speak of kindness. She was wearing a floral kaftan over faded jeans. A battered pair of sandals flip-flopped on her feet when she moved. She'd hung a dangly string of coloured beads around her neck. Bangles on her wrist jangled as she opened the door. The whiff of something more exotic than Capstan Navy Cut wafted up the hall. Powerful enough to catch in your throat outside the place. I wouldn't have been surprised to see a queue taking turns to open her letterbox and have a good sniff.

It looked like I was meeting the only hippy in Brighton with a pension book.

She said: "If you're the rozzers, I've told your fellow filth, I've nothing to say."

She had a calm confident voice – the sort of person you'd want giving the orders in a shipwreck.

I said: "I'm not the old Bill. But thanks for asking."

I pulled a card from my pocket and handed it to her.

She looked at the front. Turned it over and looked at the back. Sniffed it. Decided it didn't hold a candle to what she'd obviously been burning in the back room.

She said: "So, you're Colin Crampton. I'm Twilight."

"Even in the morning?"

"It's what my friends at the commune call me. On account of I'm past the first flush of youth - in body."

"But not in mind."

Twilight grinned. "It says Agnes Barnes on my birth certificate."

"But not in your heart. I prefer Twilight."

She said: "You're a newspaper reporter. Have you been corrupted by the capitalist system?"

"Only on pay days. The rest of the time I'm one of the workers and a proud member of the National Union of Journalists."

"You've not come to vilify those nice boys downstairs?"

"You know them?"

"They're my neighbours."

"And the police have asked you about them in the past?"

"Sticking their noses in where they're not wanted. They bring bad karma."

"Especially bad today," I said. "One of the nice boys – Mungo Brown – is a dead boy."

The bangles on Twilight's wrists jangled as her hands flew to her face.

"How?" she stammered.

"Murdered."

She threw out an arm to steady herself on the wall.

I stepped forward. "You should sit down."

She nodded. "Come inside."

I held Twilight's arm as I guided her along a short passage into a room at the back of the flat. Big fat cushions were spread around the walls. A basket chair hung by a chain from the ceiling. The place was lit by a reluctant bulb inside a yellow paper shade shaped like a full moon. The walls were decorated with Indian prints. Over the fireplace there was a photo of the Maharishi Mahesh Yogi. It was flanked by pictures of John Lennon and Yoko Ono. In the centre of the room, a low table held a teapot and some small cups. Beside the cups, a plate held a glowing spliff. A wraith of smoke rose towards a ceiling studded with painted stars.

Twilight collapsed on one of the cushions and reached for the spliff. She took a deep draw on it and relaxed a little. She exhaled the smoke in a long stream.

She said: "The rozzers killed him."

"They didn't deliver the blow that split his skull."

"They brought the bad karma that foretold his doom. There were always cops here asking me about Mungo and Tom.

Whether I heard anything. Whether they had callers, especially other men. Whether they did things they shouldn't. And when I asked them what things they had in mind, they went all coy on me. I know what their grubby little minds were thinking. I'm not doing their dirty work for them. I knew Tom and Mungo lived together, you know, like man and wife. They lived in love. The best way. Who am I to question that? Start making judgements on how other people live and soon they'll start on you. Live and let live is my motto. And the cops can go and swivel on their own truncheons. Some of them might even enjoy it."

"How did you know Tom and Mungo were gay? Did they tell you?"

"No. They were both like old-fashioned young guys. It was that contradiction I liked in them. They'd worry about embarrassing an old biddy like me. I knew they were gay when I saw their laundry hanging on the washing line. Double sheets for their bed. The giveaway is always in the details. If I had my way, I'd change the law to stop the cops making life a misery for them. I saw the old Bill down there today."

"The cops are investigating the murder. They may want to question you." I nodded towards the spliff. "May be wise to be ready for them."

Twilight had a final giant suck on the spliff. Then pinched it out.

I said: "Tom wasn't at the flat. I wonder whether he's been spooked by the killing. Taken off for somewhere safe. Any ideas where that might be?"

Twilight leant back on the cushions and exhaled smoke slowly. She shook her head. "I was friendly with them – and they responded. I think they liked the fact they had a neighbour who wasn't tutting over the garden fence at them. Not that I have a garden fence. They even gave me a key so I could take in parcels while they were out at work. Don't tell the cops about that. They'll try and pin the killing on me."

"When you talked to them, did any particular subjects come up?"

Twilight thought about that for a moment. "Tom talked about his love of wallabies sometimes. There are nine different species, apparently. Suppose that doesn't matter. Except to other wallabies. But Tom never talked about his love for Mungo."

I yawned. My eyelids drooped. The smoky atmosphere was getting to me. Much more, and I'd think I could float on air.

"Some people like to keep themselves private," I said.

Twilight said: "But I wouldn't be surprised if Mungo's death doesn't hit him hard. Tom was telling me only a few weeks back that his uncle and cousin back in Australia both died violent deaths on the same day."

My eyelids snapped up. I was wide awake. Not floating at all. Hobart Birtwhistle had a press cutting about a father and son who were murdered on the same day. I'd spoken to Henry Truelove, crime reporter on the Melbourne *Herald Sun* about it.

"Two relatives died on the same day," I said. "Did Tom mention their names?"

Twilight sat up straight. Wide-awake herself, now. "I think he called one Fletcher. Can't remember whether that was the uncle or the cousin."

It was the uncle. My mind was racing now. Fletcher isn't common as a given name. The Fletcher Tom mentioned to Twilight had to be the Fletcher murdered on the same day as his son Jake. And Tom was Fletcher's nephew.

I sat there thinking about what it all meant. Downstairs, I'd wondered whether Mungo had been murdered by mistake for Tom. I'd had no evidence to support my theory. Now, I was sure. I was certain that Tom knew only too clearly that a killer was on his tail.

And another demon was gnawing at the back of my mind. Hobart Birtwhistle had connections to Australia – and he was dead, too. Could he have been a victim of the same assassin that now stalked Tom?

Twilight said: "You look worried. I can sense when a soul is not at ease. Shall I put on a record of some great psychedelic sounds and we'll light the joint and puff 'til our souls ascend to nirvana?"

"It sounds tempting, but I have to go on another journey."

The trouble was, I didn't know where. Or whether I could reach Tom before his assassin completed his work.

Half an hour later, I parked the MGB in front of the impressive house which sits at the heart of Leonardslee Gardens.

The gardens were a big tourist attraction twenty miles from Brighton. Sam Ballard, keeper of wallabies at the gardens, was the only other person I could think of who might have some idea where Tom had gone.

After a bit of confusion – no, I didn't want a tour of the gardens; no, I didn't want a cream tea – I got to meet Sam. He was a plump jovial type with reddish brown hair finished off with bushy sideburns that could have provided nesting places for a flock of sparrows. He was wearing a checked shirt, rolled up at the sleeves, and brown corduroy trousers. He had a sturdy pair of green wellington boots on his feet.

He said: "Not often we get any interest from the newspapers. But the wallabies have been here since 1889, so I suppose it's old news. By the way, they roam free so watch where you tread. The piles can be quite big. It's not very nice if it comes over your shoes and sticks to your socks."

I kept my gaze on the ground as I followed Fred into a shed that served as his office.

The place had a small desk strewn with papers and several upright chairs. There was a pin board covered with scribbled notes. Over one wall was a collection of photos of wallabies in different poses.

Sam said: "Take a pew."

I sat on one of the chairs. Sam walked over to the wall and gestured at the wallaby porn.

He said: "The cute creatures are my whole life, you know. Not forgetting Hilda."

"She's one of the wallabies?"

"No, my wife. Never forget a birthday."

"Hilda's?"

"No, the wallabies. I was present at the birth of each one. You can count on me to come up with a bouquet of blooms on the special day."

"On a wallaby's birthday?"

"No, Hilda's."

I took a breath and said: "I understand Tom Ryan is your vet of choice when it comes to the wallabies."

"Well, I'd hardly trouble him on Hilda's account."

"When did you last see him?"

Sam crossed the room and sat on the other chair.

"Must've been a couple of weeks ago now. One of the wallabies had a thorn in its pad. Had turned a bit septic. Tom sorted the problem. Best wallaby vet in the country. Of course, they'll have others in Oz."

"Did Tom mention anything about a problem he had on his mind?"

Sam gave me a sharp look. "Should he have? Is the lad in trouble?"

I told Sam the tale. About Mungo's murder and Tom's disappearance.

He said: "That's serious. I rely on Tom to keep the wallabies healthy. There are other vets, but they're used to dogs and cats. Don't jump about so much."

"I'd like to keep Tom healthy, too."

Sam nodded. "Yeah! I can see that."

"Do you have any idea where he might have gone?"

"We passed the time of day. Chatted about this and that. But

I wasn't his social secretary."

"Point taken."

Looked like I'd reached the end of the road.

Sam swivelled round and stared at his wallaby pin-ups. Scratched his sideburns. Turned back to me.

"Course, when you're a wallaby specialist, you'll likely be called in by other wallaby owners."

"Are there many?"

"No. I've heard there are some wallabies loose in the Peak District – up in Derbyshire. Escaped from a zoo during the war and bred in the wild. But I don't know that they'd call in a vet to treat them."

"So that's it?"

"Not entirely. There's a well-kept colony of red-necked wallabies in Scotland. Tom has told me quite a bit about them. Guess he must've been there several times."

"Whereabouts in Scotland?" I asked.

"On Inchconnachan. It's a private island in Loch Lomond. I believe it's owned by that Earl of Arran who's been in the news lately."

That had my attention. Arran had certainly hit the headlines in the last few weeks. He was promoting the bill in parliament which would change the law to make legal homosexual acts between consenting men over the age of twenty-one. The bill had faced a lot of controversy, but there was a strong body of opinion that the reform was long overdue.

If Tom wanted a safe haven, I just knew the island in the loch would be the place he'd make for.

"'On the bonnie, bonnie banks of Loch Lomond.'" I said.

"What about it?" Sam said.

"It's the place I'll find Tom Ryan," I said.

I broke into song. "You'll take the high road and I'll take the low road, And I'll be in Scotland afore you.'"

"Don't drag me into it," Sam said.

Chapter 12

I had much to think about as I drove back to the *Chronicle*.

It had been something of a long-shot to expect Tom Ryan's veterinary knowledge of wallabies to lead me to him. But when I learnt that Inchconnachan was owned by the Earl of Arran, I rated my chances had become odds-on. I'd definitely put fifty quid on it.

As Tom had treated Arran's wallabies in the past, the two would know one another. Perhaps they'd even struck up a platonic friendship. I knew a bit about Arran. One of those eccentrics the British upper-classes breed. His full name was Arthur Kattendyke Strange David Archibald Gore, eighth Earl of Arran. Try fitting that lot on your library ticket.

But Arran hated the fact he'd inherited the earldom because his elder brother – the seventh earl – had committed suicide. It was said he took his life because he couldn't handle the fact that he was a homosexual in a society which made it a criminal offence. No wonder his younger brother felt so strongly about the issue. But then, Arran – the eighth one – was a man of strong opinions. He wrote a weekly column in the London *Evening Standard* under the heading "The outrageous Arran, the earl you love to hate". He plumbed the depths of the dictionary for insults to hurl at his enemies. But his loyalty to his friends and the causes he held dear was even more passionate.

The more I thought about it, the more I was certain I'd find Tom in the care of Lord Arran.

But there were still plenty of unanswered questions.

To begin with, did the Mungo killing mean that Tom had been targeted by a killer simply because he was gay? The fact that parliament was debating a change in the law had stirred up strong feelings. But I'd not yet heard them lead to murder.

Besides, that motive for the killing would only make sense

if there were such a link with the murders of Fletcher and Jake Woodburn. And I couldn't see any evidence of that. There'd been no hint in the press cuttings I'd read that Fletcher and Jake were gay. Henry Truelove hadn't mentioned it either when we'd spoken.

Nor had there been anything in Hobart Birtwhistle's papers to suggest the same. So, I concluded, the theory was a non-starter.

But if that was the case, what was the motive? The more I thought about it, I couldn't help feeling the secret lay in the fact Tom was related to the dead Fletcher and Jake. But they were killed in Australia – and Tom was now fleeing his nemesis in Britain. Did that mean there were two killers? One in Australia. Another in Britain. Or did it mean a killer had come from Australia and was now on the prowl here?

If either were the case, they'd need a strong motive for so many murderous attacks. There'd been talk of a gold nugget worth more than £100,000. A lump of cash that big could cause a lot of trouble. But would it lead to murder? And, if so, where was the nugget?

I had no answer to that question. But perhaps Tom Ryan did. Perhaps that was why he was targeted by a serial killer.

I had no choice. If I was to get to the bottom of this mystery, I had to go to Inchconnachan.

But to do that, I'd need to win backing from Frank Figgis. And that could be a more fearsome prospect than facing the killer.

Frank Figgis lifted an anonymous brown manila file from his desk.

He said: "I'll bet you don't know what's in here."

I said: "Is this a panel game like *What's My Line?* on television? I'd wager that Barbara Kelly and Gilbert Harding between them wouldn't be able to puzzle this one out."

Figgis took out a couple of sheets of blue-tinted paper which I recognised immediately.

"Yes," he said, like an executioner about to swing his axe. "It's your swindle sheets. Your expenses."

This wasn't good news. I'd just asked Figgis if he'd fund my air fare to Scotland. The flight from Gatwick to Glasgow, nearest city to Loch Lomond, left in two hours. I wanted to be on it.

"Were you aware," Figgis said, "that your expenses regularly come to almost as much as the rest of the newsroom together?"

I knew for a fact that was an exaggeration.

So I said: "And when I get to Glasgow, I'll need to hire a car. I'll have to spend at least one night in a hotel. I was thinking somewhere AA-recommended in Sauchiehall Street. Then there'll be restaurant meals – probably haggis and neeps. And, of course, there are the inevitable tips and gratuities."

Figgis held up a nicotine-stained hand. "Just a minute. Before we talk about that, we need to deal with your expenses - and the task I gave you a couple of days ago."

My heart flopped. The Figgis memoirs. I needed to divert his attention.

So I said: "As far as possible, I've got receipts for most of those expenses."

"Don't take me for a sucker. I know there are bars and restaurants in this town that'll issue a false receipt in return for a small commission."

Wide-eyed, I said: "Is that true? But that would be dishonest."

"And as a crime reporter, you mix with some very dishonest people."

"From whom I pick up circulation-boosting stories," I said.

Figgis ran his hand speculatively over his chin. "I'll grant you that. But don't think I'm going to fund the cost of a wild goose chase to Scotland."

"In Scotland, it's usually a wild grouse chase."

"Makes no difference to my decision. Besides, you have work still to do for me personally."

This was bad news. I couldn't get him off the subject of his damn memoirs.

I said: "If it's the manuscript, I'm on the case."

"Really. You seem to have been out of the newsroom a lot."

"Making enquiries."

"Where?"

"Here and there. Building a picture."

"And your conclusion?"

"I think you may have taken the manuscript home. Or left it on the bus. Chances are, if you go down to Southdown's lost property, you'll find them leafing through it and laughing themselves silly."

The furrows on Figgis' brow darkened like slow-setting cement.

"I did not leave it on the bus because it never left this office."

"If it never left, it would still be here. Have you checked everywhere?"

Figgis thumped the desk with his fist. "This is something I take very seriously. Let me make that clear: very seriously."

I'd misjudged the mood. Figgis was angry. His eyes were little spots of black. His chin jutted forward.

I said: "I've questioned some of the prime suspects in the newsroom already. No dice. When I get back from Scotland, I'll give the rest of them the old thumbscrew treatment."

"You won't be getting back from Scotland."

"I don't plan to stay there. I wouldn't look good in a kilt. And I've got nothing to put in a sporran."

Figgis leaned forward, like he wanted to climb over his desk and throttle me. "I evidently didn't make myself clear. You won't be coming back from Scotland, because you won't be going."

"But this could be a big story for us."

"You will remain in this office and follow-up the Hobart Birtwhistle murder. And the personal matter we've just mentioned."

To be fair, Figgis looked embarrassed when he said that last bit.

"So you won't fund the trip?"

"No."

"And you won't let me go on it?"

"No."

"Even if I find your manuscript as soon as I get back?"

"No."

"Then there's only one thing I can do."

"That's what I'd hoped you'd say."

"I'm taking some of the back holiday the paper owes me."

"That's not what I'd hoped you say. But delay it a couple of weeks and we'll see if we can come to a compromise."

"I've just decided what the compromise is going to be. I'm leaving now. I'll return when my back holiday allowance has expired."

Figgis was purple with fury. His jaw clenched and a vein on the side of his forehead throbbed.

"There's only one thing to say to that," he growled.

"I agree. Goodbye."

I stood up, headed for the door and reached for the handle.

Figgis was on his feet, too. He was shaking a fist at me.

"If you open that door you're finished here," he yelled.

I turned the handle, opened the door, and stepped into the newsroom.

"Don't expect me to welcome you back with open arms," Figgis shouted after me.

"I won't be looking for a cuddle," I said over my shoulder.

Sally Martin looked up as I passed her desk. She grinned: "Good meeting?"

"The best," I said.

I strode across the newsroom and pushed through the doors without looking back.

Shirley handed me a steaming mug of black coffee.

She said: "You're the craziest bastard I know. And I've known a few – here and back in Oz."

I said: "Thanks."

"For calling you a crazy bastard?"

"No, for making me the coffee. I'll need it to keep me awake on the long drive."

"That means you really are crazy. No one can drive that distance in one session. And at night."

"Best time. The traffic will be lighter. It's 490 miles to Loch Lomond. Now the new extension of the M6 motorway is open, I reckon I can do the trip in eight hours. Perhaps nine."

"Or perhaps never if you end up in that MGB of yours wrapped around the crash barrier."

We were sitting side-by-side on the busted sofa in Shirley's flat. It was half an hour after I'd stormed out of Figgis' office. I told her how Figgis had refused to allow me to go to Scotland. I told her I was going anyway. And why.

Shirl said: "This is all getting out of hand."

I said: "It got out of hand when person or persons unknown murdered Hobart Birtwhistle. In fact, probably when Fletcher and Jake Woodburn were killed."

Shirl snuggled closer to me. "I wanted to know what it was that Hobart was going to tell me. Now I'm not so sure."

I put down my coffee mug and put my arm around Shirley.

"What's changed your mind?"

"There's been too much killing. I don't want any more."

"But you're not the cause of the killing. You're an innocent bystander."

Shirl had a sip of her own coffee. "I'm not so sure. The way you've discovered that Tom Ryan and the Woodburns were related has spooked me. I just wonder whether there are any more connections we don't know about."

I thought about that for a moment.

"You said your Ma was the daughter from her mother's

second marriage to Eddie Green. And the mother's name at the time of that marriage was Bella Birtwhistle."

Shirl nodded.

"Do you know what her maiden name was?"

Shirl shook her head. "My Ma never got on with her. Found her too high and mighty."

"So you didn't really know your grandmother Bella?"

"No."

"And you never knew who her mother and father were?"

"Nope. It never came up at home."

I thought about that some more. Wondered whether it was among the information Hobart had planned to tell Shirley.

"You think her maiden name could be important?" Shirl asked.

"I don't know. There's a lot we don't know yet. Which is the reason I'm going to Scotland."

Shirl rolled her eyes. "You sure I can't persuade you to stay?"

She leaned even closer and kissed my ear. Then my cheek. Then planted a gold medal plonker on my lips."

I hugged her close and we kissed some more. I came close to deciding I'd stay the night.

We broke our clinch and I said: "I'd better get ready to leave."

"Says the man who can go one better than Oscar Wilde."

"And resist everything – as well as temptation," I finished the misquotation.

"Yeah! Well, big boy, just remember what it's like to be next to the most desirable woman in the world when you're on those lonely miles north. Colder up there, too."

I stood up. "I've got your love to keep me warm."

Shirl grinned. "Don't you forget it."

I pulled the MGB into a service station north of Birmingham just before one in the morning.

I parked up next to a trailer lorry carrying steel girders. I

122

switched off the engine and exercised my shoulders. They felt like they'd been strapped to a board. I opened the car door and climbed out. Each joint creaked. Each muscle protested. I felt like I'd been stored in a cardboard box and only let out on Christmas morning.

The night air was warm. An acrid stink of petrol fumes drifted across from the nearby road.

I had to admit that Shirl was right. The miles had proved lonely. I'd tired of the car radio by the time I'd left London's North Circular Road and made it on to the M1 motorway. And for three hours, the same stories about Hobart Birtwhistle, Fletcher and Jake Woodburn, and Scarlett Ballantyne had been whirling around in my mind.

I made my way towards the cafeteria determined to have a late supper. Or would that be an early breakfast?

I pushed through a pair of swing doors. I screwed up my eyes at the glare of the fluorescent light. Bang went my night vision.

I was surprised the place was crowded. Mostly by men. Mostly with mugs of tea. Many with plates of chips. Close by a heavy man, with a three-hamburger stomach hanging over his belt, inserted sixpence in a juke box. He selected Sandie Shaw singing *Puppet on a String*.

I pushed my way between the tables to a metal-topped counter and ordered egg and chips and a black coffee. The order came promptly with a side-serving of grease.

I carried my plate and mug into the sitting area and looked for a table. They were all taken. It was that awkward moment when you have to ask someone whether you can share.

I scanned round the place looking for my victim. Over the other side of the room, there was a middle-aged man with brown hair that straggled over his ears. He munched a sandwich while he read the *Daily Mirror*.

I walked over and said: "Mind if I join you?"

The man looked up. He had sad brown eyes and a long nose.

He said: "Why not? Welcome a bit of company, to tell you the truth."

I put my plate and cup on the table and sat down opposite him.

He extended a hand across the table. "Percival Spooner."

"Colin Crampton."

He nodded at my plate. "I usually avoid the chips here. Indigestion, you know. The eggs make me feel nauseous."

I said: "I really came in for the coffee."

"Gives me a headache."

"Keeps me awake on a long drive."

"Going far?"

"Scotland."

"Try and avoid the place myself. Brings me out in blisters."

I sipped my coffee. "What do you do?"

"I travel in foot creams."

"Don't you find that a bit slippery when coming downstairs?"

Percival frowned. "Not a bit of it. I sell them. Foot creams – it's the business of the future. Did you know that nine out of ten people don't pay enough attention to their feet? I've got a lemon-scented verruca lotion in the car. Happy to give you a free sample if you're interested."

"I usually save the lemons for my gin and tonics."

Percival's long nose vibrated a little as he sniffed. There I go again – I'd annoyed a harmless bystander with a smart remark.

To soften my put-down, I asked: "How did you get into the foot cream business?"

"Teapots."

"I don't understand."

Percival let out a long sigh. "It all goes back to my great grandfather Heptinstall Spooner. Known to his friends as Stan. He was a young potter, down in Stoke on Trent. You know, the Five Towns. Best pottery in the world, but there was one problem they hadn't cracked – and Stan was determined to make his name by solving it."

"What was that?"

"How to make a teapot that didn't drip when you poured it. In those day, they all did. The British empire was an expanse of dripping teapots. From Dundee to Darjeeling – drip, drip, drip. Stan intended to do something about it. He studied at night school, worked as an apprentice potter for three years, and then branched out on his own. He finally worked out that stopping the drip was all a question of geometry. It was the angle of the spout and what happened inside it when you stopped pouring the tea."

I pushed my egg and chips away untasted.

Percival ploughed on. "He worked out that teapots dripped when you stopped pouring because there was still some tea left in the tip of the spout. But if you cut a little groove on the inside of the spout, the surplus tea would run back down it into the pot. Drip misery solved. But that was when Stan made his big mistake."

"Which was?" I asked.

"He shared his secret with someone else. Endecott Hardcastle. Known as Casey."

"To his friends?"

"He didn't have any friends. He was a hard-faced twister who ran a small pottery. But he had his eye on the main chance more than his kilns. He promised Stan a partnership in the dripless teapot business. Stan would create the designs. Casey would fire the pots. But Hardcastle double-crossed Stan. He stole his secrets and cut him out of the business. Stan was furious. He scraped together the last of his savings and hired a lawyer to sue Hardcastle. Lawyer said Stan's case was bound to succeed. But then tragedy struck. Stan was found dead in his design studio. Knocked out, apparently. Could have been an accident. But the family reckoned it was murder."

"And the finger of suspicion pointed at Hardcastle?" I asked.

"Not for long. He wriggled out of it. Even went on in later life to be made a lord. Our family have hated them ever since. I could have been a teapot magnate. Instead, I'm selling foot cream. Still, it could be worse. And there's a big new opportunity. I may diversify into corn plasters."

I finished the last of my coffee and left Percival flipping the pages of the *Daily Mirror* and nursing his dreams of what might have been.

Trust. Greed. Betrayal. A story for many down the years. The prospect of wealth – whether it's a gold nugget or a dripless teapot – brings out the worst in people. And in some, it sparks the urge to kill.

Percival's story gave me plenty to think about as I climbed back into the MGB, fired the starting button, and swung the car northwards.

Chapter 13

I was awakened by a sharp knocking on my car window.

I raised my eyelids like I was hauling up heavy shutters. I'd slept in my clothes. So this is what it felt like to doss down in a doorway.

I stared through the windscreen. Ahead I could see a stand of trees running down a narrow lane. Beyond the lane, the water of a lake shimmered blue in the early morning sun. In the distance, grey mountains rose towards the sky.

The knocking came again.

I didn't know where it was coming from. My mind was befuddled by heavy sleep. I'd been slumped over the steering wheel of the car.

I half remembered turning off a road and seeing a light. I was exhausted. I'd stopped the car, turned off the ignition, and leant on the wheel.

Knock, knock.

This time I realised where the sound was coming from. I turned my head. A young woman was stooped over the car's side window. She had fair hair tied under a scarf, brown eyes and a big smile. She wore a kitchen apron in a yellow and black tartan tied over a pair of jeans.

She'd raised her fist to knock again, but when she saw me turn my head, she lowered her arm.

I wound down the window. A draught of cool air blasted into the car.

The woman said: "Yer lookin' a bit peely wally."

I said: "What?"

"Peely wally. Not well. Have ye taken a dram too many? If so, you need to watch for the polis. They can be awful severe on that around here. Even though I ken the sergeant keeps a bottle in his desk at the station."

I levered myself up in the seat and ran a hand over my chin. It felt stubbly. And worse. A bit sticky.

I said: "I haven't been drinking. Where am I?"

"You dinnae ken?"

"That's why I asked."

"This is Luss. You've parked in Pier Road."

"On the banks of Loch Lomond?"

"Aye. There's only one Luss."

"Do you have a hotel?"

"Och, we have a bar – Jock's Bar. It's run by that Jock Cameron. And he serves his customers in a string vest. I wouldn't touch the place, even wearing a pair of those Marigold gloves."

I shifted uncomfortably in the car seat. My shirt was sticking to my back. I smelt of long hours on the road.

I said: "I've had a hard journey. I need to find somewhere to freshen up and have some breakfast."

She smiled like she'd just had an idea. She pointed down the street. "I'm Helen McInnes. I live in yonder house. If you've got the bawbees, I can cook you the best breakfast in Scotland."

"And could I have a bath?"

"Aye. But you'll pay for the soap - and not ask me to scrub your back."

As it happened, Helen McInnes' bath came with a rubber duck.

No extra charge. I named it Daffy.

I gave him a little push and he sailed off towards the taps.

I leant back in the bath scented with a few of Helen's lily-of-the-valley bath crystals.

I pushed myself under like I was Lloyd Bridges in *Sea Hunt*. I came up with soapy water in my nose but the comforting thought that I no longer smelt like a pig bin in a heatwave.

I ran in some more hot water and lay back to think.

Percival Spooner's story about how his great-grandfather Stan had been swindled by Endecott Hardcastle had played on my mind. I'd turned it over and over as I'd covered the long miles north from Birmingham.

Two themes hammered away in my brain. How greed can transform ambitious men into monsters. Perhaps even murderers. And how, as old Mark Antony put it, "the evil that men do lives after them". Percival still resented the fact he'd not had the opportunity to inherit a non-drip teapot empire. I wondered whether the killer of Hobart, Fletcher, Jake and Mungo also harboured an historic grudge.

If that was the case, what was the grudge? Not much argument about that. It was the gold nugget, last seen in the possession of Ned Hambrook. And who could hold the grudge? Anyone without a gold nugget. But especially the descendants of Roderick Tuff, the prospector who died in the mine shaft.

But no one had put their hand up as a chip off the Tuff block.

Daffy floated towards me.

"Got any ideas?" I asked him.

He looked at me with his painted blue eyes and said nothing.

Helen had cooked me eggs, bacon, sausage and tattie scones – served with a steaming mug of coffee.

I sat at her kitchen table and tucked in.

She sat opposite me and sipped her own coffee.

The coffee pot simmered on top of an Aga cooker.

"Not often I find a young man asleep in a car outside my house first thing in the morning," Helen said.

I stuffed some sausage into my mouth and said: "I'll try and do it more often."

"I guess you did it for a reason," she said.

"My reason? I was tired."

"It was more than that." She had the kind of eyes that made you feel you had to answer her questions. She'd have made a great prosecuting lawyer. Would have looked good in a wig and gown, too.

"I'm chasing a story," I said.

"Makes a change from a woman."

"Actually, I want to speak to a man."

"Anyone in particular?" Helen raised her coffee cup to her lips.

"The Earl of Arran."

She put down her cup. "I hear say his lordship doesn't welcome visitors. If you have a mind to visit him on Inchconnachan, that is."

"That's what I plan to do."

"I'll not pry into the reasons why you need to speak to his lordship," Helen said. "Everyone is entitled to his secrets."

I said nothing.

The silence hung in the air while I finished off the tattie scones. Clunked my knife and fork down on the plate. Wiped my mouth with a linen napkin.

"How do you plan to get to Inchconnachan?" Helen asked.

"I've ruled out swimming," I said.

"Wise. The water's still cold at this time of year."

"I guess I assumed there'd be a ferry service."

Helen stood up and walked over to the Aga. She took out some slices of toast, put them on a plate with a small mountain of home-made marmalade, and handed it to me.

"There's no ferry service," Helen said. "Inchconnachan is a privately-owned island. Fiona Colquhoun, the speedboat racer, bought the place way back in 1920. Later, she married Arthur Gore. His friends call him Boofy."

"And does he have many friends around here?"

"There's plenty who are undecided about that. He and his wife built a bungalow on the island – a bit like those the English built in India in the days of the Raj. Not that it would suit a Scot like me. There are wallabies on the veranda and I've heard badgers wander the rooms."

"Makes a change from a pet dog," I said.

"Harder to house train a badger, so I've heard. They're one animal that does bite the hand that feeds them."

I took another sip of my coffee.

"Is there anywhere near here where I could hire a boat? I'd like to take a look at Loch Lomond from the water."

Helen grinned. "And before you know it, run aground on Inchconnachan."

"My navigation skills are certainly untested." I winked.

"But you're no eejit, I ken."

"I'll take that as a compliment. But what I'd really like is some advice on how to get to Inchconnachan."

"Well..."

"I can pay," I added.

Helen raised an eyebrow. "If you're a man of means, that's different. I can ask my brother Rory. He has a small motor boat. He's been known to take the tourists on their trips."

Helen was as good as her word – even though I couldn't understand all of them.

She called Rory, who ran a small motor repair business, on the other side of the village. I met him at the public pier, a wooden job which jutted twenty or thirty yards out into the loch.

Rory was a well-built man with a bushy head of ginger hair. He had the kind of shrewd dark eyes that forewarned me I'd probably end up paying handsomely for the trip. He had a pair of big muscle-bound arms that reminded me of Bluto, the character who ended up being roundly beaten by Popeye in the cartoons. Happily, Rory didn't have Bluto's aggressive manner.

He greeted me with a firm handshake. He had the broad grin of a man who knows he's just about to fleece a mug who has no choice but to pay up. But I'd misjudged him. The three pounds Rory demanded for the trip seemed reasonable enough to me.

Rory's motorboat was moored halfway down the pier. It was a modest craft, open to the skies. It had a couple of seats up front and a couple behind. It was painted blue. It looked shipshape and Bristol fashion, which was just as well. There didn't seem to be any radio aerial – which meant if anything went wrong, we wouldn't be able to make a distress call.

Rory invited me to climb aboard first. I settled myself in the passenger seat up front while he took his own place. He began to run through a series of checks.

He gave me a shrewd glance and said: "Are you a strong swimmer?"

I said: "Do I need to be?"

"Hope not."

"I would come in last in any Olympic competition. But I can swim between the two piers in Brighton without the aid of water-wings."

"That sounds good enough."

"I agree – especially as there are no women or children to go first if we have to abandon ship."

He tapped a couple of dials and checked the wind speed and direction.

I waited until Rory had finished his checks, then asked: "Do you often ferry people across the lake?"

"Loch," Rory said sharply.

"Sorry, loch."

"Might do."

"Do it recently?"

"Why do you ask?"

"Just idle curiosity."

Rory turned sideways. "There's nothing idle about your curiosity."

I grinned. "You got me banged to rights, guv. I'll come clean."

Rory smiled. "It's the best way. As it happens, I haven't been out on the lake for several days. Too much work at the garage."

"Just thought I'd ask," I said.

Rory leaned forward and pushed a button. The boat's

outboard motor coughed a couple of times, then settled into a growl.

Rory unhooked a rope which held us to the pier. He turned up a throttle and we edged out into the loch.

The boat settled into a steady pace. The outboard sputtered away behind.

Rory said: "Friend of mine, Alister McIver, had a strange experience a couple of nights ago. Late in the evening, he saw a guy walking along the pier looking at the boats. Thought no more about it at the time. Tourists often do it. Sometimes take photographs of themselves."

"One for the album."

"Maybe. Anyway, the following morning, Alister came down to the pier and his boat was missing."

"What kind of boat?"

"Just a rowing boat. No outboard, like this one. Alister likes to travel the loch the old-fashioned way. Anyway, he was just about to report the loss to the constabulary when he spied Richie Baillie's fishing boat coming in. Towing his rowboat. When Richie came ashore, he explained he'd found the boat drifting about a hundred yards off the east coast of Inchconnachan."

"No sign of anyone who might have been in the boat?" I asked.

"Richie said not. They searched the immediate area for a body - but found nothing. Richie accused Alister of not mooring his rowboat securely. There was a right row over that. Alister said if the boat had floated away from the pier, it would have drifted on the current south of the island. Richie knew he was right and they settled the argument over a dram or two in Jock's Bar."

"So, someone took the boat to row out into the loch?" I asked.

"And at night."

"And then disappeared Did Alister get a good look at the man on the pier?"

"He was young. Dressed in light-coloured blouson and jeans.

That was all. We'll never know who the guy was or whether he took the boat. Or what happened to him."

"Look at it this way," I said. "At least you've got your own mystery."

"How do you mean?"

"To rival the Loch Ness Monster. You can call yours the ghostly rower."

Of course, I didn't believe a word of it. There was no mystery in my book.

Tom Ryan had rowed himself. He didn't want anyone to know he was holed up on Inchconnachan.

Rory put me ashore at Inchconnachan on a small pier connected to a wooden platform on the land.

The platform led up a sloping path to a stand of trees, mostly firs. Beyond the trees I could see part of the roof of a wooden building. There was a fresh peaty smell to the place.

I turned to thank Rory for the trip. But he had already put the motorboat about and was speeding back to the mainland.

There were no people around to greet me. No wallabies either. I made my way up the path towards the stand of trees hoping that the Earl of Arran was at home. If not, I was going to look a fool.

I didn't even know whether there was a telephone on the island. If so, I wasn't sure how I would alert Rory that it was time to collect me. Perhaps I'd try smoke signals.

I was musing on this as I reached the stand of trees. A man stepped out from behind a large Douglas fir. It had thick crusty bark, sharp pine needles, and some fancy cones. They always look good at Christmas when they're used as a table decoration.

The man didn't look like he'd come to collect cones. He was wearing a brown tweedy jacket with a lot of buttons and a kilt. The kilt was finished with a sporran. It looked a bit like the spiders' webs you find under the bed when you haven't swept there for months. He had brown ankle-length boots and thick socks with a skene knife stuck in one of them.

He carried a two-barrelled shotgun which was open at the breech.

I said: "What's with the shotgun? I'd hoped you'd greet me with a chorus of Scotland the Brave on your bagpipes."

The man said: "I'm James Stuart, Lord Arran's ghillie. The shotgun repels unwelcome visitors."

"I'm the kind you'll want to greet when you know why I'm here."

"Not before I've emptied one of these barrels in your direction."

"You don't want to shoot me."

"Why not?"

"You can't eat me. Save the buckshot for some hapless grouse that fly by."

"His lordship doesn't want people on his island."

"He should have thought of that before he built a landing stage."

Stuart took a step forward and snapped shut the breach on the shotgun.

He said: "State your business and then leave."

I said: "I'm here to discuss a confidential matter with Lord Arran."

"What confidential matter?"

"If I told you, it wouldn't be confidential."

Stuart shouldered the shotgun and took aim.

I said: "I bet you didn't threaten to shoot the visitor who came two nights ago."

Stuart relaxed his grip on the shotgun. "There was no visitor two nights ago."

"You must remember. He came in a rowboat he'd, er, borrowed from Luss. After he stepped ashore, he forgot to secure the boat to the mooring. It floated offshore where it was spotted by a fisherman. He towed it back to Luss, where the mystery of its occupant is currently the talk of the town."

"Folk may blether about it, but there was no visitor here."

"His name is Tom Ryan – and he would be an especially welcome visitor for Lord Arran for reasons I won't go into now."

"We have had no visitor with that name."

I said: "The only thing I don't know about Tom Ryan is whether he is still here or has left the island."

A man's voice behind me said: "He has left the island."

I whirled around. The man had a compact open face with high cheekbones. He had a mouth that smiled a lot but could also look determined. His white hair parted to one side. He was wearing a double-breasted brown tweed suit.

He looked towards Stuart and said: "I'm afraid I must disappoint you on this occasion, James. You will have to refrain from shooting this visitor. Perhaps next time."

He turned to me: "I'm Boofy Arran. You better come up to the house and tell me how much you know. If you know too much, I may decide to shoot you."

Chapter 14

Silently, Lord Arran led the way along a path through the trees.

We came out in a glen, flanked by more firs. The house I'd first spied from the landing stage occupied a plot of level ground. It was a squat bungalow with a corrugated iron roof. The architect had done his best to make the building more imposing with a sort of green-painted gable in the middle. Otherwise, the place could have passed for a cricket pavilion at one of the poorer county grounds. There was a veranda which stretched the length of the front. As we approached something moved. A couple of wallabies that had been snoozing, roused themselves and hopped away.

I said: "Do the wallabies often drop by?"

Arran said: "They have as much right to occupy the island as we do."

"I bet they don't get greeted by a ghillie with a gun."

"Why should they? Unlike others, they pose no threat."

Having put me firmly in my place, Arran led the way into the house.

Inside, the central area was kitted out as a sitting room with a kind of dining annex at one end. The walls had been wallpapered and painted a pale green. The floor was strewn with a few worn rugs. Half a dozen easy chairs occupied the centre of the room. A bookcase held a few well-creased paperbacks and some photo frames with what I imagined were family pictures. In the dining area, a circular table held a four-branch candelabra complete with stubby candles.

The room smelt musty and heavy with the stench of unwashed animals. It wasn't the kind of place you'd choose for a rest cure.

Arran, however, seemed perfectly at home.

He turned towards me and said: "I assume you'd like a glass of whisky before you leave."

I said: "As I'm hoping to stay for a bit, better make it a large one."

Arran moved across to a drinks table in the corner I'd not noticed before. He busied himself pouring the drinks.

It looked like he wanted me off the island as fast as he could arrange it. And without a chorus of Auld Lang Syne to see me on my way.

Arran returned with the drinks and handed me a cut-glass tumbler with enough scotch to fell a wallaby.

I raised my glass and said: "*Slàinte Mhath.*"

Arran raised his glass but didn't drink. "Cheers, yes. But to your health? Well, we shall see what you have to say for yourself."

Then he brought the tumbler to his lips and took a long pull at the scotch.

He flopped into one of the chairs and waved me to another.

He fixed me with a hard stare and said: "You evidently know that Tom Ryan came to this island. I want to know two things. First, who you are. And, next, how you came by the knowledge of Tom's movements."

He took another good pull at his whisky.

I reached into my jacket pocket, took out a card, crossed the room and handed it to him.

Arran gave it a brief glance. "Colin Crampton. A newspaperman."

"Yes."

"We have something in common."

"I hope that includes not shooting reporters."

"We shall see."

"I have often read your column in the London *Evening Standard.*"

"I have never read the Brighton *Evening Chronicle.*"

"I doubt we sell any copies on Inchconnachan."

"Certainly. But how did you know Tom Ryan had come

here?"

Arran sat silently and sipped his whisky as I told him how I'd worked out why Tom might come to the island. How I'd verified that from information from Rory. How the mystery of the abandoned rowing boat confirmed my suspicions. And how I'd arranged to come to the island to meet Ryan.

"And now that you've confirmed your suspicions, what do you propose to do?" Arran asked.

"I would like to know where Tom Ryan is."

"That I cannot – will not – tell you."

"In that case, can you tell me why Tom fled here?"

Arran stood up, crossed to the drinks table, and poured himself another knock-out measure.

"Fear," Arran said. He sat down again.

"Fear of what?"

"Of the worst that can happen to a human being. Of being accused of committing a crime of which he is innocent."

"I'm also sure he didn't kill Mungo Brown." I told Arran what I'd learnt from Ted Wilson and from visiting the scene of the crime.

"But, because of the kind of man he is, Tom faces prejudice," Arran said. "Especially from the police. He told me of their raids on the basis of trumped-up tip-offs. Of the constant harassment by, I think, a man called Tomcat."

"Detective chief superintendent Tomkins," I corrected.

"Tomkins, then. The police are not above planting the evidence they want."

"We're on the same side here," I said.

"Are we? I want to keep Tom's ordeal confidential. You want to splash it in headlines."

"That's my job as a newspaperman."

"But I won't permit it."

"You can't stop me."

Arran cocked his head to one side.

"Can't I? You are on an island. You don't have access to my boat. And there are no telephones. I shall keep you here until such time as I am certain Tom will be safe."

"But that's kidnapping."

"Let us call it enforced hospitality."

"Is that any way to speak to a guest?" said a woman's voice.

I swivelled round. The woman standing in the doorway had a bronzed face, a strong chin, deep-set eyes and a broad nose. She had a head of dark curly hair and a mischievous grin hovering on her lips.

"I was about to offer Mr Crampton another whisky, Fiona," Arran said in a voice I imagined would be the nearest he ever came to contrite.

"Then you had better do so," Lady Arran said.

Arran crossed to the drinks table to refresh my glass while Lady Arran entered the room and walked towards me.

I stood up and shook the hand she extended.

"Did I hear Arthur call you Mr Crampton?" she asked.

"At your service, my lady."

"The Colin Crampton who exposed that affair over the World Cup last year?"

"My fingerprints are on that."

"And saved those young gentlemen, the Rolling Stones, from a certain death the year before?"

"The same, my lady."

"It's a privilege to meet you, Mr Crampton. And please drop that 'my lady' tosh. I'm Fiona. Arthur is Boofy - when he's not in trouble."

Arran crossed the room and handed me another whisky.

He turned to Lady Arran. "Can I get you a snorter, Fiona?"

"Perhaps later. In the meantime, perhaps we will have a little talk, Arthur."

"Oh, one of your little talks, is it?"

"Yes, sit down. And, Mr Crampton, it's a lovely morning.

Why don't you enjoy your whisky outside?"

"It would be a pleasure," I said.

I made for the door. Glanced back as I was about to close it.

Arran had sat down in his chair with an anxious expression on his face. Like a naughty boy caught scrumping apples.

Fiona, Countess of Arran, to give her full title, had been right.

It was a glorious morning. The sun peeped out from behind a flotilla of cotton wool clouds that floated in from the west. I found the trunk of a long-felled tree, sat on it, and sipped my whisky. In front of me, the fir trees swayed gently in the breeze. Between the trees, sunlight sparkled on the loch throwing up little pinpricks of light. Away in the distance, the mast of a small yacht cut the horizon.

I'd been flattered when Lady Arran had recognised my name. And I sat there speculating about what she would say to her husband. Arran was a good man – it took moral courage to sponsor the gay sex bill through parliament. But he was impulsive. He was a man who saw every issue as black or white. At least, that was the impression I'd got from reading his *Evening Standard* column. Good for a journalist with a need to entertain his readers. Bad for a legislator who needed to formulate a law that had to balance freedom with responsibility.

I suspected that Fiona Arran was giving her husband a short lecture on the true meaning of hospitality.

I was so lost in my thoughts I hadn't noticed that James Stuart was making his way towards me. He wasn't carrying the shotgun. But he still had the cutlery stuffed into the top of his sock. And the knife wasn't for peeling the skin off an apple.

Stuart sat next to me on the tree trunk, nodded at my glass and said: "Twenty-five-year-old Macallan. His lordship only serves the best."

I said: "Does that apply to ghillies, too?"

Stuart shot me a questioning look. His face relaxed. He'd

decided I wanted to be friendly.

"Aye. I've served my time. Pleased to be in the service of an earl who's a good man. And woe betide any who try to cross him."

"And you now think I pass the test?" I asked.

"Wouldn't be drinking his lordship's twenty-five-year-old malt if you hadn't."

Stuart sighed and leaned forward as he stared out across the loch. Or perhaps he had just looked into the future and didn't like what he saw.

I said: "You're worried about Lord Arran, aren't you? Is it the bill? Is he working too hard?"

"His lordship always works too hard. But that's not what worries him. The problem is that he's made enemies. Bad enemies."

"When you write a column for a newspaper, you make some people angry. They work off the anger by writing a letter to the editor. But when you introduce a new law which upends a hundred years' conventions about how people live their lives, the angriest don't write letters."

"They come to kill you," Stuart said. "How did you know?"

"I assume you don't always carry a double-barrelled shotgun when you greet unarmed visitors."

Stuart nodded.

"Has anyone tried to kill Lord Arran?"

"Not yet. But there have been some serious threats. When Tom Ryan appeared on the island, we were worried. His lordship understood why Tom had fled, but was concerned that others would follow his trail."

"Have they?"

"Only you, so far. But how can we know who may be coming down the track?"

"Do you know of any who might?"

"Some, who've made their threats public. But his lordship

has been brooding these past days. There's something he won't tell me."

"About a threat?"

Stuart shrugged. "Aye. Could be. But perhaps he's just worried about turning his bill into law."

I was about to ask whether Stuart had any theories on that when Lady Arran stepped out of the bungalow.

She walked over to us and said: "Stuart, bring the boat round to the landing stage. Mr Crampton will be returning to Luss."

"You're throwing me off the island?" I asked.

"Not yet. Boofy wants to see you first. About a matter of life and death. In private."

I found Lord Arran standing by the fireplace.

He gazed into an empty grate. He turned as I entered the room. He nodded an embarrassed welcome.

He said: "I think we may have got off on the wrong foot. You'll have another whisky?"

He took my glass, went to the drinks table, and poured in two fingers.

I said: "Your wife tells me you face a life-or-death threat."

"That is so. And I believe you can help me. Fiona has told me much about you. She is a keen follower of your work. We take *The Times* but I know she secretly buys the *Daily Mirror*."

Since my first murder mystery, when I'd exposed the disappeared golf man who'd left his balls behind, the *Mirror* had covered my exploits.

"Have you told the police about these threats?" I asked.

Arran moved to his chair and sat down. "No."

I sat down and asked: "Why not?"

"In the first instance, because it involves our friend Tom Ryan. His case is already being investigated by the police – and they are drawing the wrong conclusions."

"Where is Tom?"

"He is in London. At a place where he will be safe."

"So you think he still faces a threat?"

"I do – and so does Tom. He has told me about it. But he understands the ramifications of it better. He will explain it to you when you meet."

"You can arrange that soon?"

"Maybe as soon as tomorrow. But, first, I need your help in connection with a deadly threat I face."

"Which is?"

Arran leaned back in his chair and sipped at his whisky.

"When I undertook to try and change the law on gay sex, I understood, only too clearly, I would be met with vociferous opposition from some quarters. That is something I expected and, you may not be surprised to learn, relished. What I did not expect was that there would be some who threatened me with violence. Many of these threats are mere words – the bombast of empty vessels."

"But not all?" I asked.

"No, not all. There have been some threats against me, against Fiona, and against my property. I have reported them to the police. But they have taken little action."

"Because those who write threatening letters rarely sign them. 'Dear Sir, I plan to kill you. I remain your humble and obedient servant. Yours sincerely, John Smith.' Not likely, is it?"

Arran smiled but the smile never reached his eyes.

"There is one threat which has come from a powerful group of men who have been careful not to draw attention to themselves. They are men who are resolutely opposed to the changes I wish to make. They will take any action – any action – to stop me. They mean to see me in my coffin. And they have commissioned a deadly killer to ensure it happens."

"A contract killing?"

Arran nodded.

"Let me guess," I said. "Frank 'the Chopper' Hitchcock."

Arran's eyes widened in surprise. "How did you know?"

"I didn't. It was a guess. But if I wanted to see a victim dead – job done with a money-back guarantee – he's the man I'd hire."

Hitchcock was a notorious career killer who'd served several prison sentences – but none for murder. His speciality was cutting victims up with an axe. The kind a woodcutter wields. It was a bloody death. Especially as Hitchcock completed his assassinations one limb at a time.

Then he would go to his local pub, the Crooked Servant, and have his fan club rolling in the aisles with his tasteless one-liners. "I left him legless." "He won't be so handy in future." "The long arm of the law just got two feet shorter." And his favourite: "He won't twist me round his little finger any more. I've got it." At which he'd produce the digit from his pocket.

Arran shifted uneasily in his seat.

He said: "I have reason to believe the threat from Hitchcock is close at hand. We reach a critical point in the passage of the bill through the House of Lords in two days. If Hitchcock could kill me before then, it would undermine the support we have carefully built, peer by peer. I cannot let that happen."

I swallowed a slug of the twenty-five-year-old Macallan. The prospect of tackling Hitchcock aged me twenty-five years in a minute, just by thinking about it.

Arran sensed my unease. "I'm not suggesting you make a frontal attack. But there is one man more deadly than Hitchcock. One man who could persuade him to call off his contract killing. I use the word 'persuade' loosely."

"Ronnie Kray," I said.

Ronnie was the most lethal of the Kray twins. Even more vicious than his brother Reggie. The two dominated the crime life of London's east end.

I said: "Ronnie is a hardened criminal. But why should he want to kill Hitchcock? I don't think he'd do it, even for a million pounds."

Arran smiled. "I don't propose to offer him a million pounds. Indeed, I don't have that sum of money. But I do have something that will make him want to persuade Hitchcock to call off his plan to murder me."

"What?"

"A photograph."

"A snapshot." I laughed.

"Not any photograph. Would you like to see it?"

Arran crossed the room to the bureau and picked up an envelope. He came over to me. Took a black-and-white print out of the envelope and handed it to me.

I gasped. I couldn't help it. I'd never seen a photo like it.

It was a photo of two men. Neither was dressed for a royal appearance at Buckingham Palace. Or for anything, as it happens. And it definitely wasn't a picture of them shaking hands. The picture was slightly blurred. I wasn't surprised the photographer had been trembling as he took it. And a black smudge in the top right-hand corner looked like he'd had part of his thumb over the lens.

Arran said: "That photo is a copy. The original is in a bank safe."

I gave the photo back. Arran took it, slipped it back in the envelope. Handed the envelope to me.

He said: "Now you know why Ronnie Kray will use his very best offices to stop Frank Hitchcock killing me. Neither of the men in the picture would want it falling into the wrong hands. Neither of their reputations would ever recover."

"Where did you get this picture?"

"When I agreed to promote the bill in the House of Lords, many people approached me offering help. The photo came from one of them."

"Why have you given the photo to me?" I asked. I was sweating slightly. I pulled out my handkerchief and mopped my forehead.

"You will use the photo to persuade Ronnie to lean on Frank Hitchcock. Fiona speaks highly of your resourcefulness. You will be able to do it."

"I don't know…" I began. "But what has this to do with Tom?"

"It clears the way to make Tom safe again. And…" He winked. "…and, at your newspaper, it will give you the chance to make a bigger splash than Niagara."

I gulped a couple of times. My heart was beating like a steam-hammer. My mouth was dry. I'd never taken on such a difficult challenge.

"You'd better be on your way," Arran said.

Chapter 15

James Stuart ferried me back to Luss in Arran's motorboat.

We didn't speak on the journey. He could sense I had some serious thinking to do.

I sat at the back and watched the wake recede into the distance. I tried to comprehend the scale of what Arran had asked me to do. I had never taken on such a difficult job.

Stuart moored the boat at the far end of Luss Pier. He left the wheel with the outboard idling and climbed into the back of the boat. He gave me a knowing nod and extended his hand. I shook it.

He said: "You've had a short visit."

I said: "Not short enough."

"I don't know what task his lordship has given you. But I ken it's dangerous."

I nodded.

"Then lang may yer lum reek," he said.

My brow creased in a puzzled frown.

Stuart grinned. "Good luck and good fortune."

I climbed out of the motorboat onto the pier. I watched as Stuart turned the boat around and pulled away into the loch.

He shouted something over his shoulder. It was hard to hear over the roar of the outboard. I'm no Bonnie Prince Charlie but I think I caught the refrain: "Will ye no come back again?"

I stood for a while and watched the boat disappear towards Inchconnachan.

Then I turned away and hunted for a telephone box.

I called Shirley and asked her to meet me in London at eight o'clock.

Shirl asked what she should wear.

"Come dressed to kill," I said.

She wanted to know what it was all about. I couldn't go into the detail over the phone. Too much to take in when we were hundreds of miles apart. So, I pretended there was a fault on the line and rang off.

Then I climbed into the MGB and settled myself comfortably. I had much to think about on the long drive south.

I parked the MGB in a small garage under London's Charing Cross railway bridge.

I'd arranged to meet Shirley in the Coal Hole, a pub in the Strand. I'd used the place when I needed to meet a contact from nearby Fleet Street.

I found Shirley sitting on a banquette in the corner, well away from the bar. Shrewd girl. She'd have known we needed a quiet spot for our talk.

Shirl stood up and greeted me with such a hot kiss that I could have pasted it into an album and looked at it on long winter evenings. We broke our clinch. Shirl stepped back, and did a twirl.

"You said 'dress to kill'. What do you think, big boy?"

She was wearing a black top with a plunging V-neckline that pushed her breasts upwards. A tight black skirt ended reluctantly three inches below her bum. She had seamed stockings and a pair of sparkly four-inch stilettos. They clacked on the floor when she walked.

I said: "Wow! Is this what the well-dressed Pirelli calendar girl is wearing this year?"

Shirl said: "I'm over-dressed for the Pirelli calendar. As I'm finding out. But this outfit makes me hot enough to take on anything you can come up with. Call it my good-time girl kit."

I wasn't so sure about that. But I ordered the drinks – gin and tonic for me, Campari soda for Shirl – and we sat down.

I said: "Pin back your ears for the most extraordinary story you've ever heard."

So between sips of my G&T, I told Shirl about my overnight

drive to Luss, my boat trip to Inchconnachan, and my meeting with the Earl of Arran.

Shirl soaked it up – eyes wide with astonishment.

She said: "Let me get this right. You're going to get one gangster to stop another gangster from killing Lord Arran by showing the first gangster a photograph?"

"That's the plan."

"It'll never work."

"You haven't seen the photo yet."

"Where is it?"

"In my inside pocket."

"Show it to me."

"It's not the kind of thing you'd see on a Pirelli calendar."

"I can handle it."

I scanned around the pub to make sure nobody was watching. Then I reached into my pocket and took out the photo.

I passed it furtively across the table face down. Shirl took it and turned it over.

"Jeez! Are those two guys doing what I think they're doing?"

"Yes."

"Who are they?"

"The thinner guy standing up with his trousers round his ankles is Ronnie Kray. The fat guy down on his knees is Lord Boothby, a Conservative peer of the realm and member of the House of Lords. He was a former private secretary to Winston Churchill."

"Does anyone know about this?"

"That's the point. A lot of people have been told that Ronnie and Boothby are, shall we say, close friends. But nobody has seen this picture."

"I don't get it. If the world and his wife know the pair are gay, why is Ronnie going to be spooked by a picture showing it's true?"

"To begin with neither Kray nor Boothby have ever admitted

they swing that way. When the *Sunday Mirror* published a front-page story three years ago about an improper relationship between a peer and a gangster, Boothby sued the paper. The *Mirror* settled out of court and paid him £40,000 in libel damages."

"Phew! That's some serious cabbage." Shirl had a swig at her Campari.

"Boothby won't want all this dragged up again – and he certainly won't want the picture circulated. It proves that he's a liar. Worse, that he committed perjury in the claims he made under oath to win his libel settlement. And that means he could spend time as a guest of Her Majesty."

"Peering at the world through a barred window."

"Right. Ronnie Kray knows that as well. Boothby has used his influence corruptly to take the heat off the Krays' criminal operations. Scotland Yard picked one of its finest, detective inspector Leonard Read, Nipper of the Yard, to nail them. He's not managed it yet, but if this photo became public, you can be sure Nipper would soon be knocking on their door."

"Real drongos like the pair of them should have been jailed years ago."

"Not easy, because the Kray twins rule the east end through fear. Witnesses won't come forward. Last year, Ronnie walked into the Blind Beggar pub, where George Cornell, a member of a rival gang, was drinking, and shot him dead."

"In cold blood?"

"While the juke box played *The Sun Ain't Gonna Shine Anymore*."

"The Walker Brothers' number."

"I heard that one of the bullets ricocheted off the juke box and the needle got stuck – repeating anymore... anymore... until someone switched it off. Thing is, half a dozen people saw Ronnie pull the trigger on his Luger and leave the pub. But they were all too scared to give evidence."

Shirl pushed her glass around the table for a bit. She was thinking. I sipped my gin and tonic.

She gave me a flinty look and said: "So, let's get this straight. We're going to front up to the east end's most dangerous gangster. And we're going to blackmail a guy who shoots people he doesn't like in cold blood. And then gets away with it."

I drained the last of my drink. "That's about the size of it."

Shirl looked around the pub while she thought about that. Put her hand to her face and gave her thumb a little suck. Relaxed back on the banquette and gave me a look that could have gone either way.

"Couldn't let a dumbo like you try it on your own. Jeez, Ronnie would pull out that Luger and would probably pot you before you'd even started."

"Not with a doll like you on my arm," I said.

Shirl grinned. "When you asked me to dress to kill, I wondered who our victim was going to be."

"We're not going to shoot Ronnie."

"But we're going to screw him," Shirley laughed.

"We need a plan," I said.

"First, we need another drink."

I took the hint and walked up to the bar.

The Blind Beggar pub occupied a smart three-storey building in the Whitechapel Road.

The ground floor had a pair of high arches, like the kind you might see in a stable. The upper storeys were built in mellowed red brick. There was a swinging signboard which featured a painting of the original blind beggar. He was an aristocrat called Henry de Montfort who'd lost his sight in a thirteenth-century battle. A passing baroness nursed him back to health. He thanked her by fathering her child. Good of him. Anyway, back in those far-off days, life didn't hold much for a bloke with a white stick. So, he spent his days begging at the crossroads.

Didn't even get a pay-off when they named the pub after him.

Shirley and I took a taxi round there and got it to drop us a hundred yards up the street. There was a blue police box – fast telephone contact to the cops – nearby. I imagined it got a lot of use in this area.

A summer's day was turning to dusk. The street lights had flickered on. A red London bus roared by. Black taxis swarmed up and down the road like flies. Blokes with flat caps cycled home with their fish suppers wrapped in newspaper under their arms.

We loitered on the corner, while we put the finishing touches to our plan.

Plan? More a hypothesis based on improbable assumptions supported by unlikely facts. But you have to start somewhere.

We knew that the Blind Beggar was the local pub for the Kray twins and their hangers-on. But the chance of finding Ronnie at the bar when we called was remote. Besides, I needed to talk to him in private, not with a bunch of heavies touting pint beer glasses nearby. And I certainly couldn't bring out the photo Arran had given me and flash it around. The black fact at the back of my mind was that Ronnie might be carrying - the Luger he'd used to top George Cornell. Loaded guns make me nervous.

But even if Ronnie wasn't at the bar, it was probable that some of his gang would be. They'd take refreshment after a heavy day of running protection rackets, extorting blackmail, and pimping prostitutes. Our bet was that Shirl in her good-time girl role could get them talking and reveal where Ronnie was spending the evening. So, she'd go into the pub alone – and if she wasn't out in fifteen minutes, I'd appear like the Seventh Cavalry. And then I remembered it was the Seventh Cavalry and Lieutenant-Colonel George Custer who'd been at the battle of the Little Bighorn.

And that didn't end well.

A couple of lads on bikes rode by, saw Shirley, and let out a piercing wolf-whistle. She ignored them, while I waved cheerily and shouted: "Thank you."

They exchanged confused looks and cycled on.

An old boy with a straggly moustache rounded the corner. He gave Shirl the eye as he shuffled up.

Winked and said: "You remind me of my missus. She's also got two feet. Unfortunately, the resemblance ends there."

He tottered on, laughing to himself.

"The East End of London," I said. "Every guy a comedian."

"Yeah! I can't wait for the show to begin."

We turned and looked towards the Blind Beggar. No one was hanging around the doors. No drunks lurched out. I wondered how many customers there were inside – and who they were. The Blind Beggar wasn't going to be first choice for honest citizens who wanted a quiet drink without the danger of being shot.

"Looks just like a typical neighbourhood boozer," I said.

"Yeah! The dead bodies are piled up behind the bar."

"Do you want to go? Not too late to pull out."

Shirley gave me a sharp look. "Do I look like a quitter?"

I pulled her to me and kissed her.

"That's what I thought you'd say," I said.

She turned and sashayed towards the pub. An east end good-time girl looking for a lively night out.

I watched her push through the pub's door. My insides tightened up. It felt like a lizard had just slithered down my spine.

This wasn't going to be easy.

Every second seemed like a minute. Every minute seemed like an hour.

I paced around the police box and looked at my watch so often if felt like I'd got a twitch in my arm.

My gaze fixed on the doors of the Blind Beggar. An old bloke with a trilby hat came out. He looked up and down the street like he was checking for cops. Walked briskly away.

No one went in.

I wondered who else was in there. Suppose we'd miscalculated and Ronnie Kray was inside. Perhaps with brother Reggie. The pair meant more than double trouble.

Shirl was the most resourceful woman I'd ever met. But could she take on the Krays?

I glanced again at my watch.

Fifteen minutes were up.

I took a deep breath and headed for the door.

I pushed through the door of the Blind Beggar into the public bar.

The place was dimly lit and sparsely furnished. Perhaps too many tables and chairs had been broken in fights. The walls were lined with oak panels. I didn't see any bullet holes, but perhaps they'd been repaired. A row of stools lined a long bar.

I stood just inside the door and surveyed the place. Three punters sat on the stools with pint glasses in front of them. They looked round as I walked in. Decided they didn't need to kill me and went back to their beer.

I couldn't see Shirley anywhere.

I walked up to the bar and signalled to the barman. He was at the other end of the bar drying a glass with a tea towel. He had weightlifter's shoulders and big hands. There was a scar on his cheek that ran from the edge of his mouth to his left nostril. He probably needed it to get a job in a place like this.

He took his time to finish his drying. Put down the glass and the towel. Sauntered over to me like it was the one thing in the world he least wanted to do.

I said: "Have you seen a young woman come in?"

He said: "What does she look like?"

"An inch under my height. Wearing a top with a neckline

that plunges deeper than the Grand Canyon. Short black skirt, seamed stockings, stiletto heels. Blonde hair. Totally gorgeous."

"No."

I said: "Are you sure?"

He said: "What's your interest?"

"I'm her stalker."

"Get much satisfaction from the work?"

"Not much."

"Yeah! It's a dead-end job."

"Sometimes I turn to drink."

"We get a lot like that in here."

"I'll have a gin and tonic. One ice cube, two slices of lemon."

He scowled like I'd just asked him to burn the place down, and poured the drink.

I paid him and took my drink to a table as far away as possible.

I waited until the barman had gone back to his glass drying. Then got up and made like a guy looking for the lavvies.

I walked out through a door into a passage. It was also oak panelled. Perhaps they'd got a discount on a job lot of the panels.

The floor was covered with cheap lino which squeaked when I walked on it. At least it would stop anyone sneaking up on me from behind.

There were two doors on the right. Both open. I walked up to the first. Stuck my head inside. It was a kitchen. There was a cooker covered in grease. There was a Welsh dresser loaded with cheap crocks. There was a Formica-covered table with a bottle of HP sauce. The place smelt like the milk had gone off.

I stepped outside and headed for the second door. Before I reached it, I caught the smell of scented soap flakes. This was the laundry room. There was an old-fashioned boiler and a large double sink. One of them held a washboard. The last time I'd seen one of them, Lonnie Donegan was pounding it with thimbles on his fingers as he belted out *Does Your Chewing Gum Lose its Flavour on the Bedpost Overnight?* There was no sign of

Donegan. But someone had been doing the laundry. A drying rack, with vests and knickers, hung from the ceiling.

There was only one door on the left. It was shut. A notice on the door read: Strictly no admittance to patrons.

I walked over to the door, opened it, and stepped into the room.

The place had a high ceiling with fancy Victorian mouldings. A single lamp hung from a long wire over a green baize card table.

Shirley was sitting on the far side of the table. To her left was a thin man. He had slicked back hair and a pointy face like a demented weasel.

The weasel turned to me and said: "The notice on the door says: Strictly no admittance to patrons. Can't you read?"

I said: "I'm dyslexic."

The weasel looked confused. "Does that mean you don't put sugar in your tea?"

"You're thinking of diabetic."

A stocky man sitting to Shirl's left stirred irritably. He had a paunch you could pitch a tent on. He had a bald head and so many jowly chins he probably had to count them before he went to bed to make sure they were all there.

He said: "What is this? Visiting hour?"

Shirley grinned at me, indicated baldy, and said: "Rufus here is going to tell me where I can find Ronnie Kray this evening. But first I have to beat him at poker."

Rufus seized a pack of cards, shuffled and cut them like a pro.

He turned towards me and leered. "Strip poker. And when the little lady loses, we get a great show."

Chapter 16

I tried to speak but only a dry croak came out.

I swallowed hard and said to Shirley: "Let me get this right. You've agreed to play strip poker so we can meet Ronnie Kray?"

Rufus growled: "You got a problem about that?"

"It's a great deal," Shirley said before I could speak. "Not only do we get face-to-face with Ronnie, I also get to see whether Rufus is fat everywhere."

The weasel snickered.

Rufus said: "Only if you beat me, honey. Some hope!"

He picked up a pack of cards from the table. Did that trick where you cut the pack and swivel the cards from underneath to the top of the deck – all with one hand.

I said: "I'm not happy about this."

Shirley winked. "It'll be fine."

She stood up and headed for the door.

Rufus said: "Hey, the game is here. Where are you going?"

Shirley wiggled her hips to make sure she had everybody's attention. "The ladies' room. If a gal's gonna put her goods in the shop window, they need to look their finest. Give me five."

The weasel snickered and a bead of saliva dribbled down his chin.

Rufus swallowed heavily and a sweat broke out on his forehead.

Shirley opened the door and flounced into the passage.

I crossed the room and closed the door after her. Sat down in the chair opposite Rufus and surveyed the room. The walls were covered with – guess what? - oak panels. Some of them looked black. They would have darkened when they'd been polished as the years rolled by. A metaphor for the Krays perhaps. The wall behind Rufus held one of those old-fashioned brewer's mirrors you used to see behind bars. "Guinness is good for you" and all that. This mirror had a picture etched into it. Dray horses pulling a cart.

I turned back to Rufus and said: "This better not be a double-cross. Do you definitely know where we can find Ronnie Kray tonight?"

"I know where you can find the boss every night."

The weasel snickered.

It looked as though we had no choice. Strip poker. I sat there and thought of the odds. Shirley was wearing two shoes, two stockings, a suspender belt, a pair of panties, a skirt, a bra, and the top with the plunging neckline. Nine items. As far as I could tell, Rufus was wearing two shoes, two socks, a pair of pants (presumably), a pair of trousers, a belt, a shirt, a singlet (visible through his open collar), a waistcoat, and a jacket. Eleven items.

He had a two-item advantage over Shirley that could be vital if the game came down to a tight finish. But I doubted it would. Shirl knew how to play poker, but she wasn't a regular in a nightly card school like Rufus. He did that one-handed trick of cutting the pack again. A show-off. But designed to put less experienced players on the back foot.

Shirley came back flashing a smile that lit up the room and reflected off the ancient mirror.

She said: "Hi, guys."

She crossed the room walking a little awkwardly and sat down in the free chair opposite the weasel.

The weasel leered at Shirl like he'd just been fitted with x-ray eyes.

Rufus said: "Eric can be the dealer unless he makes the cards all sticky."

The weasel – Eric, apparently, to his mother – reached for the pack and snickered. He didn't try the one-handed trick. Which was something to be grateful for.

I said: "This better be a fair game or there'll be trouble."

"We know all about trouble here," Rufus said.

"Let's play," Shirl said. "I gotta get a guy naked."

Rufus growled and swivelled his eyeballs.

I could feel my insides tightening up. This wasn't going to end well. And there was nothing I could do about it.

Or could I?

The weasel flipped two cards across the table to Rufus and two to Shirl.

They picked up their cards and looked at them while the weasel dealt each of them their two bonus cards face down.

I peered at the brewery mirror. I could see the wart on the back of Rufus' neck and the dirt behind his ears. And the face of the cards he was holding not close enough to his chest.

Rufus stared at his cards and made little grunting sounds.

The weasel's gaze was fixed on Shirl's cleavage. He was making like a pig on heat, too.

Shirl shot me a glance.

I held out both hands with fingers and thumbs extended and then used my left fist to touch my chest where my heart was.

Shirl blinked. She'd got the message. Rufus held the ten of hearts.

I made the index finger and thumb of my left hand touch the index finger and thumb of my right and pressed them to make a diamond shape. Then I held out the fingers and thumb of my right hand and two fingers from my left.

The seven of diamonds.

Shirl blinked again. Message received and understood.

Rufus looked up from his cards, turned to the weasel and said: "Deal the flop, stupid."

The weasel didn't snicker.

Instead, he dealt three cards face up – jack of clubs, queen of spades, two of hearts - in the centre of the table.

The weasel asked Shirley if she'd like to exchange her bonus cards. Shirl lifted the edges of each and decided she would. Two more cards flipped face down across the baize.

Next Rufus had the opportunity to change. He chose one new card.

Rufus and Shirley both looked pensive.

The weasel dealt the last two cards to the centre of the table – the nine of clubs and eight of diamonds.

Shirl looked confident. She showed her cards.

"Two pairs," she said. "Threes and Jacks."

Rufus leered. "Too bad, honey. Three of a kind – he laid down the sevens of diamonds, hearts and spades."

Shirl looked unfazed.

She leant down and took off her left shoe.

"That's as far as you'll get tonight, Rufus."

Rufus' grey tongue licked his top lip. "Honey, I can already smell your bare flesh."

One hour later Shirley was wearing her bra, her skirt and her panties.

The shoes had gone. So had the stockings. And the suspender belt. And the plunging top. Only three items left before she'd be back to her birthday suit.

But Rufus was also feeling the heat. Or perhaps that should be the draught. He was down to his trousers, pants and singlet.

Three items each to go.

Shirl lost the next round.

Rufus drooled. "Guess that pretty lacy bra has got to hit the floor."

Shirley shook her head. She stood up and began to wiggle her tight skirt down her legs.

Rufus' eyes looked like they were spinning.

The weasel snickered.

My jaw dropped.

Shirl was wearing a pair of knickers made from thick flannelette. You could have made a tent out of it. They were tho kind of knickers that used to be known as harvest festivals – "all is safely gathered in".

I, *ahem*, knew Shirl's taste in underwear well. It was for something silky and slinky. She wouldn't step into a pair of harvest festivals even if she had a date with the Archbishop of Canterbury.

She looked at me and grinned.

And now I knew why she'd taken that five-minute break earlier. It wasn't so she could visit the ladies. It was so she could raid the laundry room on the other side of the passage. There had been plenty of knickers hanging on the washing line.

The tight skirt slid to the floor. Shirl stepped out of it. Pirouetted around the garment and sat down again.

But she'd been standing long enough for me to spot what she'd done. Shirl's slim figure was bulked out with several pairs of extra panties. Buttock busters on the outer layers. Slinkier numbers closer to her skin. As they came off, it would be like digging down through geological layers of knicker fabric.

Rufus would be furious, but what could he do? The rules were that you wore what you had on when the game started. When the first card was dealt.

Right now, Rufus and the weasel were too busy ogling Shirl in her bra. And in her panties. They just didn't know how many.

I thought I spotted something in bottle green under the harvest festivals. I reckoned Shirl must have had at least seven pairs around her hips. With the bra, that gave her an eight-three advantage.

I didn't think Rufus and the weasel realised what Shirl had done. They didn't look like the kind of guys who'd have had much active campaign experience of women's underwear. If Shirl could win the next three rounds, they'd never find out.

And if she didn't, she'd have thought of a clever way to explain it all away.

Shirl grinned: "What's the matter, boys? Never seen a girl in her smalls? Deal the next round, Eric."

***

Half an hour later, Shirley and I were in a black cab in the Whitechapel Road.

We were heading towards a joint called the Secret Pleasures nightclub. If Rufus was right, it was where Ronnie Kray spent most evenings.

I said: "I felt like giving you three cheers when I saw all those panties."

Shirl grinned. "Just borrowed them from the laundry room I spotted off the passage. Thought I might need a little extra help when I saw how Rufus cut that deck of cards. Pleased to have taken the extra panties off now, though. Itched like hell. I think one pair was made out of sacking."

In fact, Shirl had only had to take off one more garment. She'd won the next two rounds. With ill-grace, Rufus had taken off his singlet and his trousers. Which meant he was down to his boxer shorts.

Shirl had then lost the next round. The harvest festivals came off to reveal the bottle-green number. For a moment, it looked like Rufus might cut up rough when he realised Shirl was wearing multiple pairs of knickers. But she explained it. She said she had a boil on her bum. Needed the extra layers of knicker to provide softer support.

Rufus had growled something about bad sportsmanship. A great sentiment coming from a gangster's assistant.

The weasel had just snickered.

Shirl said: "Rufus didn't exactly give us the low-down on this Secret Pleasures joint easily."

When he'd lost the final round, he'd refused to take off his boxer shorts.

He became angry as Shirley taunted him. "Will I need a magnifying glass to see it?"

He refused to agree that he'd lost. He protested he'd never agreed to tell us where we'd find Ronnie. He said even if he had, he wouldn't do it because Ronnie would kill him.

In the end, Shirl grabbed his clothes and threatened to throw them out of the window. The prospect of leaving the Blind Beggar wearing only boxer shorts changed his tune.

"Ronnie will want to know how we tracked him down. He won't be pleased Rufus told us."

"What is this pleasure that's supposed to be so secret, anyway?"

"Probably murder," I said.

After that, there didn't seem much more to say. We finished the journey in silence.

The Secret Pleasures nightclub occupied a converted cinema not far from Stepney High Street.

The old cinema had had a neon sign in the days when it showed flicks. Now only the first letter – an R – remained. I wondered whether the place had been a Regal, a Roxy or a Regent.

The cab driver pulled open his window. He peered with wary eyes at us in the back.

He said: "Are you sure this is the place you want to go? I could take you to a nice pub, not half a mile from here. They have no trouble. Lovely pint of bitter on draught. Even get a bowl of jellied eels, if that's your fancy."

I said: "Do you drop many fares here?"

"Some - but never had a pick-up. I believe they normally send a hearse for the pick-ups."

Shirley and I exchanged worried glances.

But I paid the fare and we scrambled out of the cab.

We walked up to the door. It was a heavy-duty item made out of teak and reinforced with metal plates on the jambs.

A notice on the door read: "Members only".

There was a peephole below the notice and a bell-push on the jamb. I couldn't see any bullet holes.

I pressed the bell and waited.

The glass in the peephole darkened and a lock clicked back. The door swung open.

A bouncer type with a wobbly belly and a sagging bum gave us an unfriendly look. His name badge read Mort.

I said: "We've come to see Ronnie Kray. Recommendation of Rufus at the Blind Beggar."

Mort grinned and turned his attention to Shirley. Looked her up and down in her good-time girl kit. Then looked her down and up, just to be sure. Licked his lips, like he could taste her.

He said: "You the doll who beat Rufus at strip poker?"

"You're looking at her, sweetheart."

"Heard from Eric that you had him stark-bollock naked."

"Rufus didn't like to go the whole way in case I got overcome with desire."

"Wouldn't mind taking you on myself some time."

"Can't wait, sweetheart. But we gotta meet the boss first."

"Ronnie? I mean, Mr Kray?" Mort said. "He told me he's not to be disturbed."

I said: "That's because he's meeting with us. We'll ask him to give you a gold star when we meet him."

Mort opened the door wider and we walked in.

He said: "Be great if the doll could pin it on me."

Shirley leaned forward and gave him a peck on the cheek. "Hold the dream, sweetheart."

We left him gawping like a lovelorn teenager and pushed on into the club.

The club had a shiny mahogany floor and red velvet wallpaper that would have looked tasteless in a tart's boudoir.

The place was lit by a couple of baroque chandeliers. Half a dozen couples shuffled around a small dance floor to the song *Call Me Irresponsible*. Seemed an appropriate choice for a club full of gangsters. The music was provided by a three-man combo of piano, trumpet and drums.

There were circular tables for two. Each covered with a white tablecloth. Each with a gold candlestick and flickering candle. Each with an ice bucket holding a bottle of champagne. And each with an older guy who talked too much and younger woman who looked bored.

Along the back wall, there was a series of booths. Subtler lighting. More privacy.

I nudged Shirl and pointed. "That's where the favoured clients take their secret pleasures."

We skirted round the dance floor while the band ended its number and the dancers gave a little ripple of applause.

Ronnie Kray was in the first booth we came to. He was sitting with two bulky types who looked like they'd been carved out of granite. One had a full head of red hair. The other was bald.

Kray looked up as we came round the side of the booth and said: "Who the hell are you? This is private. Get out before I have you thrown out. In several different pieces."

I said: "I come with important news of your favourite peer of the realm. No front-page story in the *Sunday Mirror* this time. Just a discreet enquiry. And, yes, this is private."

The band struck up *Boogie Woogie Bugle Boy*.

I said to the granite guys: "Sounds like a quickstep. You can take to the floor and each pretend to be one of the Andrews Sisters. Red hair can be the one who dances backwards."

The granite guys gave one another puzzled looks.

Ronnie smirked. Said to the red-haired guy: "Piss off, Mallory."

Nodded to the bald guy: "You, too, Dumbbell."

The pair shuffled to their feet like they'd never been so insulted in their lives. They stomped off to the bar.

Ronnie turned to me and said: "You've got some balls to come in here. I've shot people for less."

Shirl said: "We've both got balls."

Ronnie smirked. "In your case, that I would certainly like to see."

Without waiting for an invitation, I sat down on one of the chairs occupied by the granite guys. Shirl took the other.

Ronnie said: "Who are you?"

I said: "That doesn't matter at this stage."

Ronnie nodded thoughtfully. "Okay. We'll leave that for now. You mentioned my favourite peer. What's Bob Boothby been up to this time? Is it girls or boys?"

I said: "In this case, Lord Boothby might end up as collateral damage. Or maybe not. We'll come back to that if we need to. It depends on how willing you are to help with a difficult situation."

"How difficult?"

"Frank, the Chopper, Hitchcock difficult," I said.

Ronnie frowned. "That is difficult. Frank is a dangerous man. Unpredictable. Wrong in the head. Vindictive. Deaf to reason."

"I've heard he speaks highly of you, too. The point is, he's been commissioned to apply the strong-arm tactics, as only he can, to a friend of mine."

I know. I was stretching a point to call Lord Arran a friend. But I was running an errand it would take courage for even a best friend to perform.

Ronnie said: "Tell me what Frankie's been asked to do this time."

So I laid out the story. How Arran was piloting the gay sex bill through parliament. How this had made him some powerful enemies. How some of those enemies were prepared to stop at nothing to kill the bill. And how Hitchcock had been commissioned by a dark cartel of them to kill Arran if he didn't drop his campaign.

Ronnie's eyebrows beetled together as I told the tale. A couple of times, the shadow of a smile passed across his lips. He said nothing.

I finished: "Lord Arran believes there is only one man in the Kingdom who can persuade Hitchcock to drop his death threat."

Ronnie sat back in his chair. His eyes were wide with surprise. "Me?"

Then he laughed. A raucous rollicking laugh which made the *Boogie Woogie Bugle Boy* seem like a funeral dirge.

He said: "Yeah! I can just see Frankie saying 'Yes, Ronnie. Anything you say, Ronnie. Three bags full, Ronnie.' Frankie should be in the mad house. You should join him if you think he can be stopped."

"I believe he respects you."

"Everyone respects me. Even Frankie. But he respects himself more. What would it do to his reputation if he knew he could be talked out of a job? He'll understand that."

"You could explain the consequences to him."

"Frankie's built his name on handing out consequences. They never touch him. Can't."

"But you could."

"The answer's no. I admire your spunk in coming here." He nodded to Shirley. "You, too, miss. But you'll take a drink at the bar – on the house – and then leave."

He paused. Gave us a hard look.

"If you know what's good for you," he added.

I looked at Shirley. Telegraphed the question in my eyes. She made a tiny nod.

I said: "There is one thing that could change your mind, Ronnie."

"What thing?"

I reached into my pocket and pulled out the photo. The one of Ronnie and Boothby together. Two men enjoying secret pleasures.

I offered the picture to Ronnie. He snatched it from my hand. Stared at it. Glanced at me, then back to the photo. His eyes turned to fire. His body tensed. A twitch started in his right leg

His neck swivelled from side to side as he shook his head.

"How dare you come into my club and try to blackmail me," he said softly. "Nobody does that and gets to come back."

He raised his hand. Mallory and Dumbbell appeared beside the table. Not doing the quickstep. Without Mallory dancing backwards.

"Take these two outside and shoot them," he said.

The pair drew guns from shoulder holsters. They grabbed our arms and hauled us to our feet.

"Get your hands off me, you ape," Shirley screamed.

But they had their guns rammed in our backs.

Dumbbell pointed at a door marked "Private" and said: "Walk."

We walked. Every step closer to death.

The club had gone silent. You could have heard a bullet cartridge drop.

Then the band struck up. Mendelssohn's *Funeral March*. It sounded a bit ragged played by a three-man combo.

But thoughtful of them.

Chapter 17

Mallory and Dumbbell pushed us through the door with their guns in our backs.

We were in a corridor lit by bulkhead lights fixed to the wall every ten yards. The walls were painted the kind of green you used to see in hospitals. The place smelt like a rugby club changing room after a team bath.

I reached for Shirley's hand. She took mine in a firm grasp.

Dumbbell said: "Where do you think we should do it, then?"

Mallory said: "Not here. We'll get blood on the floor. The boss doesn't like that. He'll make us get on our knees and mop it up. Besides, they'll hear the gunshots in the club and some busybody will call the cops."

I said: "We could always come back later when the place is empty."

Dumbbell said: "Shut it. Or you're dead meat."

Mallory said: "That's the answer. We'll shoot them in the meat locker. Thick walls to sound proof the gunshots and a reinforced door to keep the cold air in. Perfect. The refrigeration will keep the bodies from going off before the undertaker arrives. That could be some time."

Shirley and I exchanged an anxious glance. We trudged on down the corridor.

The meat locker was near the end. It had a thick white door with a large handle. There were long scratches on the paintwork. Like some previous victim had used his fingernails to cling on and avoid his fate.

Mallory grabbed the handle and heaved the door open. The airlock sighed as it was released. The putrid stench of aged animal carcasses crept into the corridor. If we got out of this, I certainly wouldn't be ordering a steak here.

Mallory gestured at me with his gun: "Get in there!"

I said: "After you."

Shirley said: "It's ladies first, Sir Galahad."

She barged past me, stepped sideways. And stamped on Mallory's foot. I heard Shirl's four-inch stiletto crunch his toes. There was a sharp snap as a bone cracked. Mallory screamed, a high-pitched shriek that ricocheted off the walls.

Shirl shoved Mallory backwards. He bounced off the meat locker door. She grabbed his gun as it slipped from his hand.

Dumbbell's jaw dropped and his gun hand fell to his side. I grabbed his arm and twisted it behind his back. The gun clattered to the floor. I bent down and snatched it.

Mallory was hopping around on one foot. He squealed like a whistling kettle. Shirl shoved him in the back and he stumbled into the meat locker.

I had Dumbbell in an armlock. I pushed him into the locker after Mallory and slammed the door.

At that moment, we heard running feet at the other end of the corridor. Mort raced towards us. He stopped a yard away. He was panting so hard he couldn't speak. Beads of sweat ran down his forehead. His legs wobbled from the effort.

He caught a breath and yelled: "Don't kill them. The boss wants them alive."

"Wants who alive?" I asked.

"The busybodies, he says. Wants to see them in his office."

"He means us," I said to Shirley.

Mort looked confused. "Wait a minute. You are the busybodies. Where are Mallory and Dumbbell?"

I thumbed casually at the meat locker. "They wanted time to cool down," I said.

Two minutes later Shirley and I walked into Ronnie Kray's office

The place had a padded door, regency stripe wallpaper, and some framed photographs of boxers on the wall. There was a red carpet with a pile so thick we felt we were walking on air.

Or perhaps we were walking on air because we were still alive.

There was a group of leather armchairs gathered round a glass-topped drinks table.

Ronnie Kray was sitting in one of the chairs facing a thick-set character with his back to us.

He turned as we advanced into the room. My heart went binkety-bonk as I recognised him. The thinning hair swept back from a broad forehead. The deep-set eyes constantly on the move. The insincere grin of the crafty politician. The triple chins of the sybarite for whom enough is never enough.

I said: "Good evening, Lord Boothby."

Boothby stood up and advanced to shake our hands. He was wearing a tweed suit and a waistcoat with a gold watch chain strung across his belly. He had a show handkerchief in his breast pocket and a white carnation in his buttonhole. His black polka-dot bow-tie had slipped to an angle as though it'd had one too many. Which Boothby's puffy eyelids suggested he had.

I said: "What brings you here? Not to discuss another libel writ against the *Sunday Mirror*, surely?"

Boothby said: "I had hoped we might speak calmly about matters of mutual interest."

"Sure, like you, we all have a mutual interest in not being dead," Shirl piped up.

Boothby made a suave gesture with his hand, like there was some servant in the room he wanted out of the way.

He said: "Shall we accept Ronnie's hospitality and sit down?"

I glanced at Shirl and she nodded. It seemed a better prospect than being banged up in a meat locker.

We sat down and Boothby took time to settle his bulk near to us. Ronnie sat on the other side of the drinks table. He had a petulant look on his face, like a child who's had his favourite toy snatched away.

Boothby said: "I understand that you were discussing ways in which a threat to a fellow peer of the realm could be removed."

"Lord Arran is being threatened by a shadowy group who have hired Frank Hitchcock to make their case with extreme violence," I said.

"Most regrettable," Boothby said. "I understand Boofy feels that Ronnie here is in a unique position to remove that threat – or at least cauterise it. We have discussed the matter and I think I have persuaded Ronnie to undertake the task. Isn't that so, Ronnie?"

Ronnie shot Boothby a dirty look, but nodded.

"Excellent. I do hope this matter can be settled without any more unpleasantness."

Boothby turned towards us. "If that is the case, I understand Boofy will provide you with important information on an unconnected matter. Am I correct?"

"You are," I said.

Boothby drew a gold hunter watch from his waistcoat pocket, sprang the lid, and consulted the time.

He said: "The hour is late. As some recompense for the inconvenience you've experienced, Mr Crampton and Miss Goldsmith, I would like to offer you a night's accommodation at the Ritz hotel. At my expense, of course."

I was thinking of a tactful way to refuse when Shirley said: "Bonzer! We can get a taste of what those rich dudes have. Can't wait to slide my bum between the silk sheets."

"I'm sure the silk sheets will also look forward to that experience," Boothby said.

I gave Shirl a sharp look, but the decision was made.

Besides, it had been a long day. And it hadn't ended yet.

"What was that dirty look all about?" Shirley asked

We were in a black cab barrelling down the Whitechapel Road on our way to the Ritz in Piccadilly.

I glanced out of the window as shop fronts flashed by. I felt tired. Make that exhausted. The trip to Scotland. The race back to London. The strip poker game. The adventures at the Secret Pleasures Club. All of them had finally caught up with me.

I glanced at Shirley. She was giving me a concerned look. She reached out and stroked my cheek.

I said: "I don't like taking favours. Especially favours that come from a cunning operator like Boothby. He expects something in return."

"What can he want from us?"

"It's from me. He wants to make sure I don't mention that he's still involved with Ronnie Kray."

"Will you?"

"If it comes up in the story and it's relevant, yes. But I've got involved with Ronnie Kray as a favour for Boofy Arran. In return Boofy will tell us where Tom Ryan is hiding out. When we speak to Tom, I hope we can get to the bottom of what the series of murders that started with Hobart Birtwhistle is all about. At least, I hope so. I suppose, accepting Boothby's hospitality is a price we have to pay."

Shirl snuggled closer. "I guess I shouldn't have spoken up so quickly. But a free night at the Ritz! It was just too tempting. Besides, if Boothby hadn't turned up and talked Ronnie out of killing us…"

"Yes, Boothby's unexpected appearance was convenient. Perhaps too convenient."

The cab slowed as we drew up outside the Ritz.

The driver lowered his window and said over his shoulder: "Last fare I dropped here was that Julie Christie. She gave me the biggest tip I ever had."

"I asked her to save me the trouble," I said.

Our room at the Ritz looked like something out of an eighteenth-century French chateau.

There were armchairs that could double up as thrones, tables with gilt edges and bowed legs, fancy curtains with swags and flounces. There were Baroque mouldings on the walls and doors picked out in gold paint.

And a bed large enough for Louis the sixteenth to share with the fifteen Louis that came before him.

You half expected to see Marie Antoinette lean out of the window and tell the peasants below to eat cake.

Shirley said: "I love hotel bathrooms." She disappeared through a door. I heard a lavatory flush and a tap run.

She came out excited. "They've got cuddly bathrobes and little bottles of shampoo and moisturiser. They've got fluffy bath towels you could wrap a polar bear in. And little bars of soap I could eat."

"Instead, why don't we order some smoked salmon sandwiches and champagne on room service? We can afford it as Boothby's paying."

I needed a drink. I had to telephone Frank Figgis. He would be pleased to hear from me, but not inclined to show it. Like you get all huffy when you were expecting an important call - but about twenty hours earlier.

There was a telephone on a fancy bureau with a roll top lid. I lifted the receiver and dialled Figgis' home number. The bureau came with hotel notepaper and blue, black and red pens. I selected the red – for danger – pen in case Figgis was especially angry and I needed to take notes.

When Figgis came on the line I skipped the pleasantries – like an apology for calling him late.

Instead, I said: "I have a strong lead on the Mungo Brown murder. Tomorrow, I expect to find Tom Ryan's hidey-hole and get an exclusive interview."

Figgis said: "Oh, it's you. I thought you'd fallen down a sink hole or been kidnapped by bandits. And you're a touch late on Tom Ryan. The world and his wife seem to be after him."

I didn't like the sound of that one bit. "What do you mean?"

"We've been getting messages for you in the newsroom. Agnes Barnes…"

"…the elderly woman who lives upstairs. Otherwise known as Twilight."

"Anyway, she left a message. Apparently, Tom had called her. He sent a courier to pick up some personal effects from his flat. He'd asked Agnes… Twilight… who has a spare key, to let the courier in."

"Did Twilight say where the courier was taking the stuff?"

"She wouldn't say, but she did call a couple of hours later to say she'd had another caller – from Ryan's victim welfare counsellor. He wanted to visit Tom to provide a healing session of treatment – to combat post-violence trauma, he said."

"Did Twilight provide Tom's address this time?"

"The idiot in the newsroom who took the message forgot to ask that. But Twilight did say she'd be away from her flat this evening. The murder downstairs has unsettled her. So she's spending the night at her sister's place in Hove. We don't know where that is, either. But she'll be back in the morning."

"I'll call her first thing tomorrow."

"Do that. And call through some copy immediately afterwards. That is, if you still want to work here."

The line went dead.

There was a gentle tap at the door. I opened it.

A waiter pushed a hospitality cart into the room. There was a bottle of champagne in an ice bucket, and a large plate of smoked salmon sandwiches.

But I'd lost my appetite.

After the champagne and sandwiches, Shirley had slipped naked between the silk sheets of the vast bed.

She was soon in dreamland.

I spent a restless night. I was worried about what Figgis had told me. I couldn't figure out what the call by the so-called victim welfare counsellor was all about. It was the first time I'd heard of such a character operating in Brighton. The town's cops worked on the principle of hard knocks. You became a victim, you had to learn to live with it. The tough way.

I didn't like the idea that Twilight might have given this shadowy character Tom's hideaway address.

At seven o'clock, I heaved myself out of bed. I felt ravenously hungry. I rang room service and ordered porridge, devilled kidneys, toast and marmalade (Cooper's Oxford, of course) and coffee.

As soon as I'd finished my breakfast, I called Twilight's number. I hadn't really expected her to have returned from her sister's place so soon. But she answered after three rings.

"I was really worried about giving Tom's address to the victim support man, but he was insistent," Twilight said. "He told me of the terrible things that happen to people who've had trauma. Migraines. Stomach cramps. High blood pressure. Asthma attacks. Strokes. He said Tom could suffer some or all of them. I didn't know what to do, but I didn't want Tom to suffer."

"You did what any good neighbour would. I'll visit Tom this morning to make sure he's well."

Twilight gave me the address.

I assured her again that she'd done nothing wrong and rang off.

Shirley woke just as I'd finished dressing. I went over and sat on the edge of the bed. Leant over and gave Shirl a good morning kiss.

She reached up, put her arms around my neck, pulled me towards her, and returned the compliment with generous interest.

She winked. "I'm already stripped for action, big boy."

It was tempting. So tempting. But, after talking to Twilight, I was worried about Tom.

I explained to Shirl.

Her eyes clouded with concern. "You must go. Let's meet later."

I kissed her again, then headed for the door.

The address Twilight had given me turned out to be a quiet street in Hampstead.

I asked the cab driver to drop me at the end of the street. I wanted to approach the house where Tom was staying on foot. No noise. No fuss. Nothing to disturb the neighbours.

The house was a handsome property designed in the Arts and Crafts style. It had mellowed red bricks and a slate roof that sagged with age. There were two gables at the front and some exposed oak beams on the side. I guessed this was a discreet place Arran kept for his visits to London.

The front door was at the top of three stone steps. I rang the bell and heard it make a dignified ding-dong inside the house. No answer.

I tried again. Nothing.

Another flight of steps ran down to a basement flat. A faded notice pinned to the railings at the top said: All enquiries to caretaker's flat. An arrow pointed down below.

I beetled down the steps to a blue door set under an awning. I rang the bell.

The door was opened by a middle-aged man. He had a thatch of grey hair and a pair of intelligent eyes behind tortoise-shell framed glasses. Those eyes were giving me a wary look.

I came straight to the point: "Lord Arran has told me that a friend, Tom Ryan, is staying upstairs."

It was a lie, of course. But Arran was going to tell me in his own good time.

The man's eyes narrowed. "I'm Maurice Page. My wife Zeta and I are caretakers here. Would you mind telling me who you are?"

I pulled out a card and handed it to Page.

He studied it. "You're a newspaperman."

"As is Lord Arran. I'm here because I believe, like Lord Arran, that Tom Ryan's life may be in danger."

"Tom's quite safe here."

"Have you spoken to him this morning?"

Page looked at the floor. Didn't answer.

I said: "I rang the bell. There was no answer."

Page's eyes now registered concern.

"Why do you think Tom is in danger?" he asked.

I told him about my suspicions about the victim welfare counsellor.

Page said: "Come in."

We walked through a short entrance hall and turned a corner. Another door barred a set of stairs to the upper floors. Page opened the door and we went up.

We found Tom in the sitting room. He lay on his back spread-eagled across a fancy Persian rug. The skin on his forehead had been broken by a vicious blow so that bone showed through. There was a red bruise around his neck. His eyes bulged horribly in their sockets.

Page knelt down by the body and gently closed his eyelids.

He looked up at me and said: "I never heard a thing."

Chapter 18

There was no doubt in my mind who the killer was.

He was the so-called victim support counsellor who'd conned Tom's whereabouts from a tricked Twilight.

I felt a flush of anger around my neck and on my cheeks. The killer had been one step ahead again. I should have contacted Boofy last night after Figgis had told me about Twilight's calls.

Another black thought flashed into my mind. Would Twilight now be in danger? She'd been fine when I'd spoken to her on the phone less than an hour ago. She hadn't seen the killer and could only recognise him by his voice. Weak evidence at the best of times. So, I reckoned the murderer would work out there was more risk in killing Twilight than letting her be. But I'd warn the cops to keep their eyes open.

I turned to Maurice. His face was pale and he was shaking.

I said: "You're in shock. You should go back downstairs and sit down. I'll take a look round to make sure the killer isn't still hiding on the premises."

His scared eyes and gawping mouth told me he'd not considered the possibility.

I thought it was unlikely. Killers don't hang around afterwards to see what happens. Usually, they can't get away fast enough. But I wanted an opportunity to take a shufti with Maurice out of the way.

He descended the stairs like a man making an unwelcome trip to Hades.

I called after him: "I'll be down in a minute to make you a strong cup of tea and call the cops."

And, I didn't add, Frank Figgis. He'd make a front-page splash out of this.

I heard Maurice close a door behind him.

With him safely out of the way, I darted into the hall and took a good look at the front door. When we'd come upstairs, we'd done so through an internal door which separated the rooms on the upper floors from the basement flat. But there was also a direct door from the ground floor on to the street. I wanted to see whether it had been forced.

It hadn't been. Which left two possibilities. Either the killer had been skilled enough to pick the lock silently. Or Tom would have let him, or her, in. But wait a minute…

The walls in the hall were painted cream, I guess to make the most of the light which filtered through the window in the front door. It looked a pretty fresh paint job, too. But here on the wall barely six feet in from the door were three spots. They ran in a line up the wall like an ellipsis…

I knelt down and took a closer look. It would take a forensic scientist to confirm, but they looked to me suspiciously like dried blood.

So I formed another theory. The killer rang the doorbell. Tom answered and was immediately pushed back into the hall. He was hit with the object which had caused the slash in his skull. The blood spots on the wall were collateral damage. Tom would have fallen, perhaps unconscious. The killer would have either dragged Tom's body into the sitting room and strangled him. Or strangled him in the hall and then dragged the body through. I thought the first. There would be no point moving Tom if he was already dead.

I walked back down the hall into the sitting room. I took a quick look round without touching too much. There were no notes, no papers, no hints that Tom lived in the place. But, then, why should there be? He had stayed for barely a day.

I heard Maurice open the basement door. He shouted up the stairs: "Everything okay?"

Well, no. Everything was not okay. Tom was dead – and he should be alive.

With this dark thought, I beetled down the stairs to the

basement flat.

I found Maurice in his kitchen making the tea. Handy for me. It would take him a few minutes and give me time to make a couple of telephone calls before we alerted the cops.

I put my head around the kitchen door and said: "Make sure you put plenty of sugar in yours. Helps the shock. I'll have a biscuit with mine if you can rustle one up. Don't mind if I use your phone?"

Maurice looked at me with vacant eyes – the shock had set in badly – and nodded.

I slipped into the sitting room and called Boofy. He seemed to take the news calmly. But I detected a suppressed anger as he spoke. He was brief. He planned to take the morning plane from Glasgow to London. He would meet Shirley and me at the House of Lords at three o'clock.

Then I called the *Chronicle* and asked for a copy-taker. I dictated a hundred words of holding copy. It was not much more than a few notes. They'd help others on the paper plan for the splash coverage we'd eventually give a full story when I had all the facts.

I didn't call Figgis. He would only have wanted to know everything and make impossible demands.

I just had time to call Shirley at the Ritz. She was horrified by the news. But I told her Boofy was coming to London in the afternoon. We arranged to meet later.

Then I dialled nine, nine, nine.

I was making the call when Maurice came in with the tea and biscuits.

I heard the first police siren as I bit into my custard cream.

As a result of Tom's murder, there was one person I urgently wanted to speak to.

And face-to-face. No phone call for Ronnie Kray. He had promised to persuade Frank Hitchcock to call off his threat to

Lord Arran. I needed him to tell me to my face that he'd done so.

Tom's murder complicated the issue. Tom had been under Arran's protection. So could Hitchcock have been Tom's killer? I didn't think so. The *modus operandi* of the killing – a heavy blow to knock out the victim, then strangulation – fitted earlier killings. We could be certain Hitchcock hadn't committed those, so it was unlikely he had murdered Tom.

But I needed to be sure. Besides, as Arran was coming to London, he would be more vulnerable than if he'd remained sequestered on his Scottish isle.

I finally ran Ronnie to ground at the Blind Beggar shortly after midday. He was sitting in the private bar at the back of the pub. He was eating a steak sandwich and drinking an orange squash. A couple of hard man types – bulky bodies, stony faces, heavily gelled swept-back hair – were jawing with him. He saw me and nodded at the pair. They stood up and swaggered off, like they'd just knocked out Muhammad Ali.

I sat down opposite Ronnie and helped myself to one of his steak sandwiches.

He said: "If you take one more of my sandwiches, I'll stuff it up your arse."

I said: "I better make sure I choose one with no mustard, then."

Ronnie took a bite of his sandwich and said: "You're not here for a free lunch."

I bit into my sandwich and said: "There was a murder this morning. A friend of Lord Arran. And at his lordship's London home. I hope you weren't involved."

"Yeah! I heard about that. Not one of my guys. Thought it might be one of the Richardsons. But they thought it was one of us. So blanks all round."

"The name I had in mind was Frank Hitchcock."

"No. We warned him against anything to do with Arran last night."

"Hitchcock is reputedly a man who's difficult to convince."

"Tell me about it! Our guys had to hang him from a warehouse girder by his feet and threaten to cut his throat before he'd even think about it."

"But he agreed?"

"Eventually. We had to offer him a sweetener to make up for the fee he'll lose from the consortium what hired him."

"Sweetener?"

"Some debt collecting bunce."

"Isn't that a bit humiliating for a league one gangster like Hitchcock."

"Normally, yes. But if he gets to beat up some snotty type in a pin-striped suit, it makes his day. Good exercise, too. Frank was never one for this new jogging craze."

"So Arran can walk the streets of London in perfect safety?"

"As far as Frank is concerned. Of course, we ain't got a clue whether there's some other geezer out there waiting round the corner."

I finished the steak sandwich and stood up to leave. "Thanks for the sandwich."

"Bollocks."

"What?"

"What'll be in your next sandwich if I see you around here again. And they'll be yours."

I reached the door and turned to face Ronnie

"In that case, I will ask you to pass the mustard."

I met Shirley in the ABC café in Parliament Street, opposite the Palace of Westminster.

Shirl had just come from another meeting with the Pirelli calendar people.

She bounced into the place, sat down opposite me, and said: "An ABC café would be a great place to serve alphabet soup."

I said: "The ABC stands for Aerated Bread Company and

there are so many of these cafés all over London that George Orwell called them the 'sinister strand in English catering'."

Shirley said: "This new murder just makes me feel like we're living in 1984."

I reached across the table and squeezed her hand. "Perhaps Boofy will be able to throw some new light on Tom's killing."

Shirl didn't look convinced.

A few minutes later, Shirley held my hand as we walked to the House of Lords.

We gave our names at the Lords' entrance and were told we were expected.

A footman in a braided tailcoat led the way along a corridor. Our footsteps echoed off the stone floor. The corridor was hung with paintings of smug types with self-satisfied expressions on their faces. No wonder they were wrapped in red robes and ermine.

The footman showed us into a small room with no windows. It was furnished as a sitting room with two sofas covered in red leather on either side of a coffee table. The room was lit by a gilt chandelier.

Boofy was sitting on one of the sofas reading a large document which looked like a mediaeval parchment. He put the parchment on the table, stood up, and crossed the room to greet us.

He shook Shirley's hand and said: "'Man's inhumanity to man makes countless thousands mourn!'"

Shirl shook her head and said: "That's so sad, your lordship."

"Robbie Burns," Arran said. "And please call me Boofy. Everyone else does."

I shook Boofy's hand and said: "Despite the inhumanity of Tom's murder, I may have some good news for you."

"And I some surprising news for you. But you must speak first."

Boofy waved at the sofas and we sat, Shirley and I on one side of the table, Boofy on the other.

I said: "I've had a steak sandwich lunch with Ronnie Kray. He assured me that Frank Hitchcock has been left in no doubt about what will happen to him should he continue to persecute you."

"Did you believe him?"

"Yes. Ronnie's initial reluctance to help changed when Lord Boothby appeared on the scene by chance."

"Not by chance. I have known Bob for many years. He is a complex character with an exotic private life which he would prefer to keep to himself. That life includes a long friendship with the Kray twins. I persuaded Bob that he might make himself useful in achieving our ends."

So, I thought, it was no accident that Boothby had appeared at the Secret Pleasures club just at the moment we needed help.

"He certainly did that," I said. "But Ronnie has made it clear that if I have to go back to him, it won't be steak in my sandwich."

Boofy grinned. "In that case, let us hope our dealings with the Krays are closed."

Shirley pointed at the parchment on the table. "'Scuse me for asking, but what's with the ancient flapdoodle?"

"We'll come to that in a moment," Boofy said. "But first I wanted to remember our late friend Tom Ryan. I deeply regret his death and feel I have let him down. My actions now must ensure that justice is done to Tom's memory. I hope, also, to provide a measure of redemption for my own failings."

"I've failed Tom, too," I said. "I should have called you last night when I suspected the victim welfare counsellor was a threat."

Boofy shook his head. "I should never have used Tom's life as currency in a deal to save my own skin. It was wrong of me not to tell you where Tom was. Or to share with you the secrets he'd shared with me."

I leaned closer to Boofy across the coffee table. "Secrets?"

"I have known Tom for a few years," Boofy said. "I first made his acquaintance when I needed his veterinary skills for my wallabies. A professional association led to friendship. So I was not surprised when Tom turned to me in his moment of crisis. When he arrived at Inchconnachan, he was out of his mind with worry. He knew that the murder of Mungo Brown had been a mistake – and that he was the real target. He also knew that the Brighton police, with whom he'd had previous dealings, would write off the killing as a gay murder. I am sorry to put the matter so bluntly. But the police's attitude meant they would not make much effort to seek out the killer. And that killer still had Tom in his sights."

I said: "Once detective chief superintendent Tomkins gets an idea in his mind, it's set in concrete."

Boofy nodded. "Exactly. Tom took a different view because he had learnt some troubling facts. And here I must tell you a little of Tom's family background, as he told it to me. He was the only child of Alec and Fleur Ryan. Both his parents are now sadly deceased. But his mother Fleur had a brother, Fletcher."

"Who would have been Tom's uncle," I said.

"Yes. Fletcher and his wife Grace had one child – Jake."

"Tom's cousin," Shirley said.

I said: "And both were murdered earlier this year. It's a double killing that's had the Aussie cops baffled. They can't find a motive. And without a motive, it's near impossible to go looking for the killer."

Boofy said: "Tom heard of the murders from friends in Australia. He was sad at the loss of his uncle and cousin, but like the police, baffled for the motive of the killings. So he decided to do some digging himself. He had been close to his paternal grandfather and grandmother – Alec's parents. But his mother – Fleur – had never spoken of her mother and father."

"Tom's maternal grandparents," Shirley said.

Boofy nodded. "Tom assumed they must be dead. But he was surprised to find that his maternal grandmother was a lady he knew as Francesca Woodburn – and that she had been alive until early this year. But she was killed by a shark while swimming off Bondi beach."

Shirley said: "Nothing suspicious about that."

I said: "Perhaps not. But very strange that her son Fletcher and grandson Jake were both murdered just weeks after. No shark bites there."

Boofy said: "I knew little of this until Tom arrived on my island a few days ago. He poured out his story to me. He asked me what he should do. I said I would look into the matter. I contacted one of the clerks at the House of Lords. I knew her to be a keen genealogist. I asked her to discover what she could about an Australian citizen called Francesca Woodburn. She came back to me the following day and I could tell by the urgency in her voice that she had found something important. Francesca Woodburn had a title."

"You mean like missus?" Shirley asked.

"No. I mean like baroness. Her title was Baroness Poynings."

Shirl shot me a confused look. "Why did Tom think her name was Francesca Woodburn?" she asked Boofy.

"Because it was. Your name and your title are different. Your name is what is on your birth certificate. Your title is what you inherit or acquire later in life. But if you inherit a title from a forebear, you don't have to use it. It seems that Francesca Woodburn preferred not to."

"We're leery about titles in Oz," Shirl chimed in. "If you're a lord or a lady a lot of guys are gonna think you've got a gold bar rammed up your bum."

Boofy laughed.

"Not you, of course, your earlship," she added.

Boofy said: "It's lordship. But no matter. Anyway, I asked my friend, the clerk, to trace the Poynings peerage to its source."

"To the first person to receive it?" I asked.

"Yes. It appears to have been granted in 1920 to one Sydney Fortescue by David Lloyd George, the then prime minister. Fortescue took the title Baron Poynings because he owned a house – Poynings Old Place - with his wife Adelaide in the Sussex village. Although I gather the house has long since fallen into disrepair."

"Poynings is just a few miles from Brighton," I said. "But who was this Fortescue?"

Boofy reached inside his jacket pocket and pulled out a piece of paper. "Sydney Fortescue was a banker in the City of London. Not unusual for someone like that to get a peerage if they'd made the right donations to the right political party. Anyway, years earlier Fortescue had bought into an ailing private bank called Carruthers & Stoat as a silent partner. His money revitalised the operation and he did well out of it – without having to get his hands dirty in the cut-throat world of banking. As it turned out, the peerage seemed little more than an honour he never put to use. My friend, the clerk, researched his record. He hardly ever turned up to the House of Lords and never made a speech in it."

Shirley chipped in. "What happened when this guy fell off the perch?"

Boofy smiled. "I asked the clerk to obtain a copy of the letters patent."

"Letters what?" Shirl asked.

"The document which sets out how a peerage is created and what happens to it when the holder dies. You must remember that until 1958 all peerages were hereditary. They passed down the generations, sometimes for hundreds of years. In the case of the Poynings peerage, the letters patent set out how the peerage would be inherited – through precedence."

Boofy reached forward and picked up the parchment from the table.

"This is the letters patent for the Poynings peerage," he said.

"Usually, peerages pass down the male line. The eldest son would inherit – as my late elder brother did the Arran earldom. It was only when my brother died, that I inherited as the second oldest. But in the case of the Poynings peerage, the title would pass to a son or a daughter."

Shirley said: "I get that. But what happens if the sons or daughters are dead?"

"Then there's an order of precedence."

"Whoever gets first dibs at the title," I chipped in.

Boofy frowned. "First dibs if you must. In fact, if the title holder's sons or daughters have died, the peerage passes to his or her grandsons or granddaughters. Then to the title holder's brothers or sisters. Next to uncles or aunts. After that, to nephews or nieces. And finally, to cousins – first cousins, second cousins, and so on. In each case, precedence moves from the oldest to the youngest."

"Jeez, it sounds really complicated," Shirl said.

"Normally, not," Boofy said. "But it can become confusing when a peerage passes to a distant relative. Indeed, there are cases where people were not even aware they stood to inherit a title."

I leaned across the table and pointed at the parchment.

"What does all this mean for the Poynings peerage?" I asked.

"With the help of the clerk, I have traced its progress. It seems that Sydney Fortescue, the first Baron Poynings, and his wife Adelaide, had four children. In order of birth, Francesca, Charles, Bella and Dorothy. In the case of the Poynings peerage, the title passes first to the male heirs and then to the female. So, when the first Baron Poynings died, the title passed to Charles. He died without children so the title then passed to the elder of the first Baron Poynings' daughters – Charles' sister."

"Francesca," Shirley said.

Boofy grinned. "Glad to see you're keeping up. She became the third Baroness Poynings. As we know, she died after a shark attack. She had a son, Fletcher, and a daughter, Fleur, who died two years ago. Fletcher became the fourth Baron Poynings but was soon murdered. His son, Jake, was the fifth Baron Poynings for a matter of hours before he was killed. The clerk believes that neither of them were aware that they'd inherited a title. But, of course, when one holder of the title dies, it passes on to the next in line according to the rules of precedence. And in this case that was Tom Ryan, Jake's cousin, who became the sixth Baron Poynings. He, too, is now sadly dead."

Shirley and I stared at one another. We struggled to take it all in. A death threat hung over the Poynings title. It spelt doom for whoever held it.

Shirl turned to Boofy. "So, now poor Tom has gone, who's the mug who's become the seventh Poynings?"

Boofy turned his wise old eyes on Shirley. They seemed tinged with sadness.

"You are," he said.

Chapter 19

Shirley looked like her face had been slapped.

Her eyes popped like they were on springs and her mouth gawped.

Her gaze flashed from me to Boofy and back again in a panic.

Then she threw back her head and laughed. The kind of laughter sparked by fear. Nervous and edgy.

She slumped towards me. Her head flopped on to my shoulder. And her laughter turned to tears.

I put my arms around her and gently stroked the back of her head.

Boofy lowered his eyes, embarrassed. He picked up the parchment. Took it to a table on the other side of the room. Tactfully rummaged through a pile of papers stacked there.

I whispered in Shirley's ear. "It will be all right. We'll find out what's going on."

But I was not sure how we could. Or whether we would.

Shirl sat up straight. She looked at me with a tear-streaked face.

She said: "Fancy, me a baroness. What would my old Ma and Pa have to say about that?"

Boofy returned to his sofa and sat down. Gently, he spoke to Shirley. "You've inherited the title because you're the closest relative in the line of succession – Tom Ryan's second cousin. You shared the same great-grandparents."

Shirl pulled a handkerchief out of her handbag. Wiped her eyes. Blew her nose.

She said: "The last three Poynings were murdered. Am I next?"

I said: "We have to make sure that you're safe until we can find whether there is a threat against you. And, if so, where it comes from."

Shirl said: "Someone is killing off the Poynings' peers one by one. What's behind it?"

I looked at Boofy. "Did your research go beyond Shirley?"

He shook his head. "I've not had time to look into the future. You must remember I'm currently pushing a controversial new law through the House of Lords."

"I'm sorry…"

Boofy held up a hand. "But, of course, I'll do what I can to help."

"If only we knew why these murders have happened," Shirl said.

I said: "We need to find a motive. That will lead us to the killer."

Boofy rose from his sofa. His signal the meeting was over.

He crossed the room and shook Shirley's hand. "I welcome you as a new peer of the realm. I hope your elevation to the peerage will not prove to be a curse."

By the time we'd found our seats on the train home, Shirley had recovered her old spirit.

As the Brighton Belle pulled out of Victoria Station, we ordered a half-bottle of champagne and some Welsh rarebit.

"There you are, miss," the steward said as he put the rarebit in front of Shirl.

"That should be 'your ladyship' now," I said, after he'd returned to the galley.

"Me? Your ladyship? You gotta be kidding me. My friends will think I've gone all snooty."

"The guys at the Pirelli calendar will be impressed. I bet they don't get to photograph any other scantily clad baronesses."

Shirl cut a piece of rarebit and popped it into her mouth. "I'm not sure. I don't think it will go down well with the other girls. They're a jealous crowd. Stop at nothing to get into the limelight. I've already got one killer after me."

I took a sip of the champagne. "We don't know that for sure. But you should certainly be cautious. I don't think you should stay at your flat for the time being. You can come and kip with me."

Shirl grinned. "Only kip?"

"And any matters arising."

Shirl raised her eyebrows in mock surprise. "A man and a woman sleeping in the same bed in the Widow's house. The roof may fall in."

She laughed. And this time there was genuine merriment in the sound. It was good to hear.

It was dark by the time we reached the Widow's house on the east side of Regency Square.

The place had a solid oak front door with a small pane of frosted glass. The key hole was in the middle of a brass plate covered with a tracery of scratch marks.

I inserted my key in the lock and opened the door. We crept silently into the hall.

From the hall, a corridor led to the kitchen at the back of the house. To the left, a door opened into the holy of holies, the Widow's parlour. There was a small hat-stand near the stairs. It held a bowler, a trilby and a busted umbrella, all left behind by former tenants.

The place was lit by a dim bulb hung from a ceiling light. The light fell on the only picture – the *Light of the World* by that hopeless old Victorian romantic Holman Hunt. It showed a figure holding a lamp and dressed like he was on his way to a fancy-dress party as the Ghost of Christmas Past.

Shirl said: "Creepy."

I said: "Let's sneak up the stairs quietly. The Widow may be asleep."

We held hands and took the first step on the stairs together.

Somewhere at the back of the house a door opened.

The Widow said: "If that's you Mr Crampton, may I advise that Chanel Number 22 is not a suitable perfume for a man?"

Steps clickety-clacked up the corridor and the Widow appeared at the foot of the stairs. Her nose was still twitching at Shirl's perfume.

The Widow was wearing a tartan dressing gown, which came down to her ankles, and a hairnet. She had pom-pom slippers. She'd taken off her face, as I've noticed women like to call the night-time ritual of make-up removal. I believe most women use cotton wool balls. The Widow looked as though she'd done it with a trowel. She had powder tramlines on her left cheek and some spots of black stuff around her eyes.

She said: "I now deduce the fragrance I detected, even at the far end of the corridor, comes from a person of the female sex."

Shirley turned round sharply. "Watch your language, sister."

"I am not your sister."

"It's a relief to meet someone I'm not related to."

"I'm sure I don't know what you mean."

The situation was getting off on the wrong foot. We needed a favour from the Widow.

I said: "Shirley Goldsmith is the well-known photographers' model, seen in a glossy magazine near you."

The Widow sniffed. "I'm sure I've never seen her in the Reader's Digest."

"That's because they leave out the interesting bits," I said.

"Anyway, Miss Goldsmith, the way out is behind you. Not at the top of the stairs."

This wasn't working out at all well.

I said: "Shirley and I hoped to spend a little time to discuss our meeting with the Earl of Arran this afternoon."

The Widow's eyes widened at that. She was an Olympic-class snob.

"You had a meeting with an earl?"

"Of Arran," I said.

"Where did this meeting take place?" the Widow asked.

"The House of Lords."

"The dear old boy asked us to call him Boofy. All his friends do," Shirley said.

I could see the clockwork turning in the Widow's head. She knew tenants looked for a place with a bit of class. If she could boast that one of her tenants was on Boofy terms with an earl, she could add another ten bob a week to the rent.

The Widow said: "If his lordship ever plans to visit Brighton, perhaps you would recommend this establishment."

I said: "He usually spends time on his Scottish island with a few wallabies."

The Widow pulled her disappointed face. "In that case, Mr Crampton, perhaps you would reconsider your earlier hasty response," she said.

"What response?" I asked. I didn't let on I knew which response the Widow was talking about. She was miffed I'd refused to write a letter for her.

"I refer to the picture by John Singer Sargent which I wish to acquire."

"Under certain circumstances I could put pen to paper."

The Widow shifted irritably so the pom-poms on her slippers bounced around.

"In that case, a short visit by your lady friend might be in order."

Shirley chimed in: "And don't worry, Beatrice. We'll put in a good word with Boofy. If he stays, you'll sure find he's a big spender."

The Widow sighed. "I could do with one. Only last week, one of my previous tenants changed his name to avoid paying three months' rent he owed. Fully eighteen pounds seventeen shillings, too. What kind of person alters their whole identity to avoid honouring their commitments?"

What kind of person would change their identity?

I felt like lightning had zigzagged across my brain. It was like that moment when a rainbow lights up the sky. If I'd had a lamp on the top of my head it would've flashed red.

I should have thought of this before.

Because, if I was right, it could provide the vital clue that would solve the mystery of the murders.

Up in my rooms, Shirley and I lie side by side on the bed.

Shirl nudged me in the ribs and said: "I bet I know what you're thinking about, big boy."

I said: "You're wrong. I'm not thinking about sex."

"Jeez. Has the Widow been putting bromide in your tea?"

I grinned. "They haven't used that since the First World War. I'm thinking about something the Widow said."

"I thought you normally tried to forget that."

"Not this time. It was that anecdote about her former tenant who changed his name to avoid paying the rent."

"What about it?"

"Remember that Boofy told us you got your name at birth and your title later. But your title doesn't change your name. But suppose you'd changed your birth name *before* you gained your title. Anyone can do that by a process known as deed poll."

"What's your point?"

"We know that the first Lord and Lady Poynings were Sydney and Adelaide Fortescue."

"What about it?"

"Suppose they weren't. Suppose they'd changed their name by deed poll years before their title was granted. Then we wouldn't know who this Lord and Lady Poynings really were. Or where they'd come from."

I sat up on the bed. "And if we knew that, we might be able to discover why an unknown killer has murdered some of their descendants."

Shirley snuggled closer, leant over and kissed me. A million-pound note of a smacker. But it was also a plea for help.

She pulled away. Her lips quivered. And not just from the kiss.

"I can't get out of my mind that a killer could be stalking me," she said.

"Be strong. Tomorrow I'm going to find out who these Sydney and Adelaide Fortescue really were."

Shirley put her arms around me. Hugged me tight and whispered in my ear: "A little love might help."

I arrived at the *Chronicle* early the next morning.

I'd left Shirley munching toast and marmalade at the Widow's kitchen table. Shirl's easy-going ways had knocked the rough edges off the Widow. I was confident she would be safe in the Widow's not-so-tender care. (The Widow had taken to carrying a poker around the house in case an intruder appeared.)

I'd lain awake most of the night thinking about the names of the first Lord and Lady Poynings – Sydney and Adelaide Fortescue.

Sydney and Adelaide!

What were the odds of a married couple both having given names the same as big cities in Australia? True, Sydney and Adelaide were both popular given names in Victorian times. Even so, the combination of both in a married couple must shorten the odds considerably that they might be false.

That thought made me wonder where the Fortescues had come from. If you wanted to choose a family name to impress, it wouldn't be a Smith, a Jones or a Brown. It would be something like a Marjoribanks, a Carrington – or a Fortescue.

As the first light of dawn appeared behind the Widow's threadbare curtains, I was certain. Sydney and Adelaide Fortescue weren't the birth names of the first Lord and Lady Poynings.

If I could trace their original names, I might be able to throw a whole new light on the killing of Poynings' descendants.

When I reached the *Chronicle,* I headed straight for the morgue. The person who would know all about tracking deed polls was Henrietta Houndstooth.

When I walked in, Henrietta was pinning notes on a wall calendar. She turned towards me as I crossed the room.

"How I hate holidays," she said.

"I thought you always looked forward to your fortnight on the Italian Riviera."

"I was speaking of other people's holidays. Elsie is at a boarding house in Margate. Mabel has taken her nephew to Chessington Zoo, and Freda's at the dentist."

"That's not a holiday."

"It is for Freda. She'll take the afternoon off to get over it."

Henrietta was speaking of her three assistants who snipped the newspapers into cuttings and filed them. They were known around the paper as the Clipping Cousins.

I said: "I'm pleased I've got you to myself."

Henrietta treated me to a big fat wink. "I've heard single women need a chaperone when you're around."

"A rumour put about by Shirley. But, to come to the point, what do you know about deed polls?"

Henrietta's eyebrows beetled together, her lips screwed tight, and she stared into the air. Like she expected to see the answer written on the ceiling.

She said: "The first deed poll in Britain was recorded in 1851, although people had been changing their names long before that. George Eliot's real name was Mary Evans."

"And, later, king of the western movies, John Wayne, was Marion Morrison – although you can see why he wanted a change," I said.

Henrietta huffed. "To continue, the deed part refers to a legal document. The poll part was the word they used to describe how they cut the edges off the document so that no-one could add extra writing to it. But, in Britain, anyone can change their name and they don't need to use a deed poll to do it. You can just let your friends know you want to be called something else."

"So if someone has changed their name, it might be impossible to find out what they were called originally?" I asked.

Henrietta nodded. "But even if you change your name by deed poll, you don't have to register the fact. You can enrol your name in the Chase Rolls of Chancery at the Royal Courts of Justice. But it's complicated and expensive and most people don't do it."

"But that would be the first place to look?" I asked.

"Yes. Chances are you wouldn't find what you were looking for. So your next port of call would be the National Archives. When do you think your targets changed their names?"

"Hard to say. But it could be in the early years of the Edwardian period – at the beginning of the twentieth century."

"If the name change is from 1903 onwards, the National Archives hold enrolment books containing both the original and new name of everyone who used a deed poll."

I thought about that for a minute. To flip through books containing thousands of names could be a long job.

Henrietta said: "You're wondering how you could spare the time to do it. You can hire people to do the job for you."

I smiled. "I dare not ask whether you know anyone who does that work."

"What are the names?"

"The new names are Sydney Fortescue and Adelaide Fortescue. I need to know their previous names."

"When do you need to know?"

"When do you think?"

Henrietta said she'd make some calls and hope to have a researcher on the job within a couple of hours.

How long it would take after that, she couldn't say. Could be hours. Could be days.

I sat at my desk in the newsroom feeling tense and frustrated. I changed the ribbon on my typewriter. Filed my notebooks in the right order. Counted my paper clips.

This was no good. While Henrietta's minions did their work, I needed to find a way to take the story forward. Boofy Arran had mentioned that Lord Poynings had his family seat in the village of Poynings. The place was only ten miles from Brighton, on the other side of the range of gentle hills we call the Downs.

I stood up, grabbed my notebook, and headed for the door.

Poynings was a village built around a winding lane that twisted in the shadow of the Downs' north escarpment.

There were little Tudor cottages with ancient oak beams behind crumbling flint walls. There were spartan Victorian town houses in fading red brick. There was a row of tenements with doors whose lintels would decapitate anyone over average height. Everywhere gardens bloomed with lupins and foxgloves and sweet peas. There was a village pub – the Royal Oak – named after the tree in which Charles the Second hid before he escaped to France after the Battle of Worcester in 1651.

I imagined that people born in a village like this would never leave.

The thought brought my mind back to Lord Poynings. Obviously, he had left. And never returned.

I found Poynings Old Place on the outskirts of the village. The house was surrounded by a long stone wall which had been breached in several places. Two tall brick pillars stood on either side of the entrance. They had once supported large oak gates, but one of these had long since fallen from its hinges. It lay at the side of its pillar, like a wounded soldier.

I pulled the MGB up on a grass verge and turned off the engine. Silence. Except for the starlings which twittered noisily in a nearby bush. And the cows which lowed in a meadow behind the house. And the village church's clock which struck twelve.

I climbed out of the car and walked into the grounds like I owned the place.

(Crampton, lord of the manor.)

As I came round a bend in the drive, I got my first glimpse of the house. It was a once solid structure built out of Sussex flints faced off with red brick at the corners and footings. I'm no architectural historian, but I'd say it was a Queen Anne property. That would make it around 250 years old. And it looked it. Queen Anne would not have been pleased. But, then, by all accounts, she was rarely pleased about anything.

Paint had flaked off the doors and window frames. Guttering dangled from broken brackets. Cement had worn away so that flints from the walls had tumbled to the ground.

As I stood and looked at the ruin of a fine house, a man emerged from around the side. He had a stocky frame and a rubicund face, like someone who spends most of his time out of doors. He was wearing a grey overall, flat cap, and brown boots.

He strode towards me. As he came closer, I saw he had a wart on his chin and a forest of hairs sprouting from his ears.

He walked up and said: "This is private property."

I said: "In that case, what are you doing here?"

"I'm Hector Pilbeam. Everybody in this village knows me."

"I'm here and I don't"

Pilbeam sniffed like he didn't believe me. "The parish council has asked me to keep an eye on the big house. We wouldn't want squatters moving in."

I took another look at the ruin. "In my experience, squatters are usually particular about where they park their bums."

Pilbeam looked a bit put out by that. So I said: "Actually, you may be able to help me. My name's Colin Crampton, *Evening Chronicle*. We're running a series on famous old Sussex houses and I was wondering whether you could tell me something about Poynings Old Place."

Pilbeam shot me a crafty look. A look I've seen before. The look that warns that information is going to cost money.

He said: "I was just on my way to the Royal Oak. Hoped I might see a mate who'd buy me a pint."

I reached into my pocket. Pulled out half-a-crown. Handed it to Pilbeam.

He said: "I might fancy a bite of bread and cheese, too."

I added a florin to the half-crown in Pilbeam's fist.

He said: "Nothing like a couple of pickled onions to spice up the bread and cheese."

A shilling joined the other coins.

I said: "Are you ready to talk now or were you also hoping for pudding?"

Half an hour later, Pilbeam and I were sitting on a hard bench outside Poynings' village hall.

It turned out he was also the caretaker.

I said: "What you've told me about the history of the house is interesting. But I'd really like to know why Lord Poynings left the place."

"Because he found another house," Pilbeam said.

"Which house?"

"The house of God."

That had my attention. "You mean he got religion?"

"In a big way. Soon after his wife died. Could have been the trigger. Anyway, this preacher, Norbert Carr, came to Brighton. Big noise in the soul saving business. Fire and brimstone. He held a huge revivalist meeting at the Dome. Two thousand souls to be saved. Find God and book your ticket to Heaven. Seems Poynings took the bait. Went forward, signed the pledge, grasped the hand that heals all souls, or whatever they called it. By all accounts, he was never the same man again."

"When was this?"

"I was just a nipper at the time, which would make it early nineteen-thirties. Hard times. The great depression. Millions out of work. Worst up north, but we had trouble here, too. I remember one month when I never had a bite of meat for dinner at all. Anyway, Carr was a cunning basket. He used the misery to recruit new souls. And the rich were his targets. He played on their guilt like he was Paderewski on his fiddle. Poynings sacked his servants and moved out. Don't ask me where. But he died a few months later. Helped on his way, if you ask me."

"By Carr?"

"Well, if you're in the soul saving game, you need a regular supply. Anyway, Poynings' son, Charles, inherited the house and estate. But what's the use of a house and estate if you don't have the folding stuff to support it? Charles handed the house to the parish council. Not much has happened since then – except the council hired workmen to demolish the house's old barn about ten years back."

That had my attention.

Hadn't Professor Victoria Nettlebed said she'd bought a trunk when an old barn was demolished? The contents had fired her enthusiasm for Australian history. Could this be the site of the barn?

"Find anything of interest when the barn was pulled down?" I asked.

Pilbeam shot me a crafty glance."

"What kind of anything?" he said.

"At a random guess, a cabin trunk."

Pilbeam thought about that for a bit as he worked out how to play it.

"Yeah! I remember now. There was some lady egghead staying at the Royal Oak. The trunk was full with old documents. No interest to anyone, I would have thought. But she paid a few quid for it. If she'd stayed on a bit longer, she could have the other one."

"What other one?"

"Couple of days later, we found a second trunk when we demolished the west wing of the barn."

"What happened to that?"

Pilbeam scratched his head.

"It was stored in the basement at the village hall. Might still be here."

I said: "How would it suit, Hector, if I picked up your drinks bill at the Royal Oak for the next month?"

Hector grinned. "I'll get the key," he said.

Chapter 20

Frank Figgis rummaged for the last Woodbine in his packet and lit up.

He said: "I've sat in this chair for nigh on thirty years and it's the most remarkable story I've ever heard. Go through it again."

I was in Figgis' office at the *Chronicle*. It was two hours after Hector Pilbeam had led me into the village hall's basement. He'd shown me the cabin trunk stored behind a pile of folding chairs, dusty old curtains, and a broken lamp shade. He'd lifted up the lid of the trunk and stood back while I rummaged inside.

Figgis took a long drag on his fag and let the smoke drift down his nose. "Well?"

I said: "The trunk held the remnants of Poynings' life. Sad remnants, too. There were accounts books for the Poynings Old Place house and estate – wages paid to staff, costs of food supplied, and so on. There was a collection of random parliamentary papers – the kind he'd have routinely received as a member of the House of Lords. There was an album of old photographs, mostly views of the countryside and villages around Sussex. There was an Ordnance Survey map of Sussex with some pencil markings – I guess places he'd visited. There was a collection of press cuttings about Norbert Carr, the self-styled preacher who described himself as the 'Messenger of the Lord'. And, finally, there was a new verse to the song *Waltzing Matilda*. It had been written neatly in script on some fancy parchment to make it look like a scroll. It had been rolled up and put in a box. The kind a woman would use for her jewellery. I've copied the verse in my notebook."

I handed the notebook to Figgis open at the page.

He read:

Once a lucky hunter searched for a cross of gold,
Hid where it's safe – as safe as a tree.

When you find the cross, you'll understand about your life,
And not go a-Waltzing Matilda, you'll see.
Waltzing Matilda, Waltzing Matilda,
And no more a-Waltzing Matilda, you'll see.
When you find the cross, you'll understand about your life,
And not go a-Waltzing Matilda, you'll see.

Figgis' brow furrowed like a freshly ploughed field as he read the verse.

He looked up, handed the notebook back to me.

"What does it mean?" he asked.

I said: "I've been thinking about that for the past couple of hours. There are three possibilities. One, it is just a frivolous piece of fun Poynings indulged himself in. In which case, we can ignore it, save for one point – it suggests Poynings had some affinity with Australia. Two, it has some kind of religious meaning, perhaps linked to his conversion by the so-called Messenger of the Lord. In which case, we can note it and move on. Three, that it is not a frivolous piece of fun, but a specific set of instructions on how to find some gold. In which case, we have three more questions. Why has Poynings apparently hidden some gold? Where is the gold? And who is supposed to find it?"

Figgis scratched his brow. "Four questions. Exactly who is Poynings?"

I filled Figgis in on what Boofy Arran had told us about Poynings' background in banking and never making a speech in the House of Lords.

I said: "It's difficult to understand why Poynings' descendants should have been targeted by a killer. It's unlikely to be anything to do with the bank and even less likely that it's connected to him finding God. My theory is that Sydney Fortescue might not be his original name. Henrietta has someone searching the deed poll records in the National Archives."

Figgis groused: "And how much is that going to cost us?"

"Less than the circulation revenue we'll pocket from the extra copies sold with the sensational story we'll publish."

"Except, at the moment, we don't have a sensational story."

I was thinking hard for a riposte to that when there was a knock at the door. It opened and Henrietta walked in. She had a grin on her face that would have made the Cheshire Cat envious.

She said: "Guess what, boys? We've hit pay dirt, as the Americans like to say. Although, personally, I'm not sure how pay dirt differs from ordinary dirt."

"Get to the point," Figgis growled.

"Sorry, Mr Grumpy," Henrietta said. "My contact at the National Archives has found a match for both the Fortescues. They were respectively named Ned Hambrook and Shamrock O'Reilly."

I felt like a searchlight had just switched on. It was like we were stumbling around in the dark and suddenly the road ahead was lit up.

"Ned Hambrook," I said. "The prospector who found the Teetulpa gold nugget with his partner Roderick Tuff. Tuff died and Hambrook disappeared. Never to be heard of again. Until now."

Henrietta said: "Hambrook and O'Reilly changed their names by deed poll in January 1904. We know about Hambrook. O'Reilly has not crossed our path before, but I think we can safely assume she's not a princess travelling in disguise."

"More likely a common-law wife," I said. "Great work, Henrietta. Now we know Lord Poynings, Sydney Fortescue and Ned Hambrook were one and the same person, a whole new range of possibilities opens up. Hambrook must have somehow made his way to England, almost certainly with the nugget. How else would he have had the wealth to buy into one of the City's private banks? And a man in possession of a gold nugget must be in want of a wife. I'm guessing that Hambrook met Shamrock O'Reilly on his travels in the years between discovering the nugget in South Australia and buying into a private bank in London as Sydney Fortescue."

"That accounts for Hambrook," Figgis said. "But what about his partner?"

"Roderick Tuff," I said. "After discovering the nugget, he also disappeared. Which was a surprise at the time because he had a wife and child. At first, the Australian cops suspected Hambrook had murdered Tuff so he could keep the whole nugget. Violence between prospectors wasn't uncommon. But later, the remains of Tuff's body were found at the foot of a mine shaft. It was near the place where Tuff and Hambrook found the Teetulpa nugget. According to reports, the shaft was unsafe and Tuff could have fallen in by accident. But Tuff's wife never accepted that. To her dying day, she maintained that Hambrook had murdered Tuff – and deprived her and her child of his fair share of the wealth."

"Hatred can roll down the generations," Henrietta said.

"I can vouch for that," Figgis said. "The wife's sister has never been able to stand me."

Henrietta and I exchanged glances. She was doing her best to keep a straight face.

I said: "On the face of it, a Tuff descendant could be stalking the Poynings' line – killing them off one by one. But there are three problems about that. One, we don't know whether the Tuffs found out about Hambrook's change of name. Two, even if they did, we don't know who currently carries the torch for the Tuffs' vendetta. And, three, a claim on the Poynings' fortune would be the obvious motive. But since the first Lord Poynings found God, there doesn't seem to be one. A fortune, that is, not God."

"Could be hidden away somewhere," Figgis said. "That verse even hints that it is."

"I don't see many hints in the text which would point us in the right direction."

"What about that reference to a tree?"

"Do you know how many trees there are in Sussex? And the tree in the verse may not even be in the county."

Figgis reached for his ciggies.

Henrietta said: "You won't find inspiration in a packet of Woodbines."

I said: "There is one hope."

Figgis looked up. Put the fag back in the packet. "Well, go on. Don't keep us in suspense."

"Lord Arran helped us research the Poynings family tree. But we don't know where the title will pass after Shirley. I could call Boofy and ask whether he's been able to get any information on that."

"Do it," Figgis said.

I stepped back into Figgis' office twenty minutes later feeling a bit sick.

"What's wrong?" Figgis asked.

"You've turned very pale," Henrietta said. "Would you like a glass of water?"

"A large gin and tonic," I said. "I spoke to Boofy. His clerk has managed to trace the next heir in line to the Poynings title. It's Rod Ballantyne. He's the son of Jeremy and Scarlett Ballantyne. Jeremy was the son of Dorothy Ballantyne – maiden name Fortescue – who was the fourth daughter of the first Lord and Lady Poynings."

"Why aren't Jeremy or Scarlett in line before Rod?" Figgis asked.

"Jeremy died a year ago. Scarlett was previously married to a Donovan Maguire, a petty officer in the Australian navy. He died on active service. Scarlett is simply not in the Fortescue bloodline, unlike Jeremy and Rod." Henrietta said. "There's something else."

She paused and looked at Figgis, then me.

"Before she married Maguire, Scarlett's family name was

Tuff."

There was a moment of silence. We looked at one another while we tried to work out what it all meant.

"Any a relation of the late Roderick Tuff?" Figgis asked the obvious question.

"His grand-daughter," I said.

"And, presumably, her son Rod is named after his great grandfather," Henrietta said.

"And next in line after Shirley to the Poynings title," I said.

Figgis clapped his hands together. "Prime suspects."

"We can't be sure," I said. "We don't have a shred of evidence that Scarlett or Rod has ever harmed a single hair on the head of any of the murder victims. In fact, they're both touring with the Australian women's cricket team. Rod works as the team's baggage master."

"If they're Australian and play cricket, they have to be guilty of something," Figgis growled.

"That's prejudice," Henrietta said.

"We could go to the cops with what we know," Figgis said.

"But what we know doesn't point a finger of guilt at either of them. They could easily claim we'd be wasting police time. Even though, when Alec Tomkins is running an investigation, they waste enough of their own. My main priority is Shirley's safety."

"Quite right," Henrietta said.

Figgis picked up a paperclip and bent it out of shape. A sign that he didn't know what to do.

He said: "An Australian baroness. A cricket team with killers. A gold nugget. A man who found God. I need to think some more about this. In the meantime, write a piece about Hector Pilbeam and the cabin trunk."

"But that's giving away our advantage on this story to the competition," I protested.

"Write it so that it's all a bit vague."

211

"You mean, a document was found in a suitcase somewhere in Sussex."

"Don't get clever with me. I've got newspaper columns to fill."

I felt angry. "So, let's fill those columns with what we know. Not airy speculation. Besides, we have to remember a killer is out there. Whoever they are, we don't want to tip them off about what we know. That could be really dangerous."

"Not to us."

"That's a disgraceful thing to say. We have a responsibility to the people we write about."

"We're a campaigning newspaper not the social services. That's my final word."

Figgis reached for a pile of galley proofs. A signal that we were dismissed.

Henrietta's face was drawn in shock.

We stood up and headed for the door.

As we stepped outside, I said to Henrietta: "Have you ever done anything you were doubtful about? And later regretted it?"

"Story of my life."

"That's what I feel about this Pilbeam copy Figgis wants me to write."

Less than an hour later, I arrived back at my lodgings.

Yes, I'd written the story Figgis wanted. Yes, I'd kept it vague enough to keep rival papers off the scent. And, yes, I'd included enough detail to keep our punters awake while they read it.

I should have felt down in the dumps. But I felt like a dangerous kind of exhilaration had pumped around my bloodstream. I felt I was close to solving the mystery of the murders. I had a plan of action.

And, best of all, I was about to see Shirley.

I inserted my key in the lock and gave the door a good shove.

It bounced back at me like it was on a spring. The Widow had put the chain on the door. Clearly, she was taking Shirley's safety seriously.

The door closed and I heard the chain rattle as the Widow released it from its slot. The door swung inwards and the Widow peered around the edge of it. She brandished the poker she usually kept by the coal fire in the kitchen.

The Widow opened the door wider when she saw it was me. I stepped inside as Shirley ran up the corridor and threw herself into my arms. She kissed me like I'd just returned from a three-year trek through the darkest jungle. All it needed was Mantovani and his violins to make the moment perfect.

Shirley broke our clinch.

She said: "I haven't been out all day, but Beatrice has been wonderful."

The notion that the Widow could be wonderful had never occurred to me before. Indeed, the very fact she could be thought of as Beatrice was slightly unsettling.

But the Widow would have been walking on more air than you'd find in a barrage balloon. She'd never had a real-life baroness under her creaking roof before.

Most important, Shirley was happy. And safe. And that was all that mattered.

I said: "Let's go upstairs to my rooms and talk."

The Widow moved in front of the stairs and said: "You can always talk down here."

Shirley said: "Beatrice has baked some rock cakes."

The Widow said: "I can serve them with a pot of tea."

I said: "I can't risk a broken tooth this evening."

"I've eaten two with no trouble," the Widow said.

"Yes, but your dentures look like they're made from reinforced concrete."

The Widow huffed a bit but moved away from the stairs.

I said: "I really am very grateful to you for taking such good care of Shirley. If you weren't brandishing a poker, I'd shake your hand."

Shirley said: "Come on, then," and ran up the stairs.

I needed no further invitation.

The Widow shouted after me: "Don't forget the springs in your bed squeak loudly when you subject them to excessive action."

"I better put in my earplugs," I said over my shoulder as I disappeared on to the landing.

In my room, I poured Shirley a gin and tonic from my secret supply.

I kept it behind the wardrobe in a cardboard box labelled "old socks".

I poured myself a straight tonic. I planned to do some serious driving later.

Shirley sipped her drink.

I said: "There have been some important developments today."

Shirley leaned forward and the little worry wrinkle appeared on her forehead.

I told her how we had linked Poynings to a man called Hambrook. And I told how we had tracked Tuff's descendants to Scarlett Ballantyne and her son Rod.

I ended: "We don't have a shred of evidence that Scarlett or Rod is behind the murders. But the killer seems to want revenge on the descendants of Poynings. That means we can't rule them out. The women's cricket team are playing at Arundel tomorrow. Tonight, they're staying at the Norfolk hotel in the town. I'm going to make a surprise call on Scarlett and Rod – and put some straight questions to them. We need to know whether they're guilty or not."

Shirley put down her gin and tonic and said: "I'm coming with you."

"No, you're not. It's too dangerous. If either or both of them are killers, you'll put yourself in danger. You'd be like a hunter who throws away her rifle and walks out to face a hungry lion."

"It's my life – and I need to know the truth."

"I can tell you what I discover when I return."

"I want to discover it myself. Besides, if you go alone, I won't be here when you get back."

"Now you're just being petulant."

Shirley's hands flew to her face. She held them over her mouth. She shook her head.

She took her hands away and said: "I did that in case I said something I later regret."

Her eyes opened wider and a wistful smile played on her lips. "All my life, I've lived in a kind of darkness. I've not known who my family is. Or where they come from. Or what they do. Can you understand what that's like when you're just a little girl?"

"Not without ribbons in my hair. But I might understand it as a little boy."

"When I was at school, my friends were always talking about their cousins. Telling us about the treats their grandmothers had arranged. Showing us the presents their grandfathers had given them. And there was me. Always on the outside. Always the one who had to pretend I'd left the new doll my grandmother had given me at home. Because I didn't have the doll. And I didn't have a grandmother who loved me enough to give me one. That's why I have to come tonight. Because if I don't understand what's happening to me, I don't think I will be able to live anyway."

I moved closer to Shirley and put my arms around her. I kissed her lips. I kissed her cheeks – and they were wet with tears.

"It's time for you to find the truth," I said. "Let's find it together."

***

Chapter 21

Shirley climbed out of the MGB and looked warily around her.

She said: "Jeez! This place sure feels spooky. Good job I don't believe in ghosts."

"What about ghoulies?"

"I always think of something else when ghoulies are mentioned."

I'd parked the car outside the Norfolk hotel in the centre of Arundel. A mist from the river Arun had swirled into the town. It chased itself like impish wraiths in the narrow lanes and twittens. Street lights cast a hazy yellow glow over the ancient cottages huddled on the steep slopes of the main drag. They sheltered under the shadow of the battlements of Arundel Castle. The place felt like you'd stepped back into the Middle Ages. Perhaps a knight on his charger would clip-clop into town. Perhaps a court jester would appear and wave his marotte stick at us.

Or perhaps we were the real fools here. Fools for undertaking an errand that was fraught with difficulty. And danger. For me, but mostly for Shirley.

For the hundredth time since we'd left Brighton, I regretted the decision to allow Shirley to come.

But she'd insisted. And long ago I'd learnt that when Shirl wants something, it would be easier to stop a hurricane in its tracks.

Somewhere away in the mist, a church clock sounded a muffled eleven o'clock.

I said: "This looks like the kind of place where good townsfolk will be long abed. Let's hope the cricketers have stayed up."

"Only one way to find out," Shirley said.

We looked at each other like we were about to throw ourselves off a cliff. Then I took Shirl's hand and we walked to the hotel entrance.

The hotel's lobby had a trio of red leather armchairs grouped around a handsome coffee table. The table held copies of *Country Life*, *Tatler* and *Punch* magazines. That told you all you needed to know about the people who usually stayed here. The lobby was lit by a small chandelier. The place smelt of old leather and even older money.

There was a reception desk on the far side of the lobby. Behind it, an old bloke, with a few wisps of hair, had made a desperate attempt at a comb-over. His head rested on his hand and his elbow on the desk. His eyes were closed, but one opened and viewed us malevolently as we crossed the lobby. He sat up straighter as we approached but kept one eye closed to show he didn't really care.

I said: "He looks like he could be trouble."

Shirley whispered: "Leave him to me."

She stepped up to the desk and in her heartiest Australian accent said: "G'day, Bruce."

The other eye opened. "The name is Wendell, madam."

"Never mind, you'll get over it, Bruce. Now tell me where the girls are."

"The girls, madam?"

"Yeah! The girls from down under – I guess some of them are already down under the table, Bruce. Too many tinnies. But don't worry. We'll be up with the cockroaches in the morning and put those dastardly English to the sword."

"The sword, madam?"

"The match, Bruce. The game of cricket. At the famous Arundel cricket club. We'll be there bowling our seamers and taking out those English middle stumps. Ever had an Australian girl take out your middle stump, Bruce? Wink, wink, know what I mean?"

"I'm sure I have no idea, madam. And if you are referring to the ladies of the Australian women's cricket eleven - of which

I have some doubts that you are one – you'll find what's left of them in the club bar."

"Thanks, Bruce. Now that wasn't too painful, was it? Ever thought about getting a job as a hotel receptionist? G'day!"

And with that Shirl wiggled away from the reception and headed deeper into the hotel.

I gave Wendell a pitying shrug and followed.

We found Scarlett Ballantyne at a corner table in the bar.

She was on her own. She had a pint glass of lager in front of her. It was half empty. Or, perhaps, she thought it was half full. She was staring hard enough at it. As though it were the last drink in the world.

We walked up to the table and sat down without an invitation.

I said: "Cricket is thirsty work. Can I get you another? Or would that count as nobbling the opposition?"

Scarlett looked at me through glassy eyes like she didn't know who I was. Then she looked at Shirley and a little light of recognition flickered.

"You're the batter who made forty-nine for the Eleven Ladies of Eastbourne," she said. "No half-century for you."

"Yeah! So near, yet so far. Bit like you."

Scarlett slurped a swig of her lager.

"What do you mean by that? And, no, you can't get me another. This limey lager tastes like wombat's piss."

She had another gulp and looked harder at me. "You're that gutter reporter who was at the Eastbourne match. You accused me of killing some old guy."

"Hobart Birtwhistle."

"Yeah! You can whistle off."

"We want to ask you some more questions."

"Well, I ain't got any more answers."

"You should be able to answer the first question."

"What's that?"

"Why you've hidden the fact your maiden name was Tuff."

That had Scarlett's attention.

She drained her glass and slammed it down on the table. "I will have another one, after all."

I signalled to the barman. He came to the table. I ordered Scarlett another lager and drinks for Shirley and me.

Scarlett leaned across the table. "Listen, cobber. I've never hidden nothing in my life. I'm proud of what I've done. And I'm gonna show that on the cricket pitch tomorrow."

I said: "This isn't about cricket. It's about another game. A game with rules that make cricket's look like a coin flip."

"What game?"

"The game of life. How some lives seem blessed with good fortune. And others seem cursed with bad luck."

"My family has never had bad luck."

"Hasn't it? What about the day Ned Hambrook and Roderick Tuff found a gold nugget worth a fortune? Ned ended up with the fortune and Roderick ended up dead. Am I right so far?"

Scarlett gave a tiny nod. "I knew Roderick had been screwed by Ned. Murdered by him. Roderick's son Archie, my father, told me. He seethed with hatred for Hambrook."

"But Roderick's death could've been an accident."

"We Tuffs never believed that. We always hated Hambrook for killing Roderick. And it was worse because Hambrook had disappeared. We didn't know whether he was still in Australia. I didn't think so, because I always believed he would be recognised by someone. It's a big country but it didn't have many people in those days. The fact we didn't know where he was just made us hate him more. We imagined him living in a big house with servants and plenty to eat and drink. Things we never had."

"But one day something happened that changed all that. You married Jeremy Ballantyne."

Scarlett's eyes widened in surprise. She opened her mouth

to speak. But the barman glided alongside our table with the drinks.

Scarlett watched the barman head back to the bar. "I didn't know Jerry was a Hambrook when we married. And he didn't know I was a Tuff. I'd been wed before and kept my married name, Maguire."

"How did you find out that Hambrook was Jerry's grandfather?" Shirley chipped in.

Scarlett glugged at her lager. "Between the sheets," she slurred.

"Who with?" Shirl snapped.

"With whom?" I asked.

"Who do you think? Ballantyne. Old golden nuggets. Although I never got much action from them. But, then, I was never interested in his body. His wallet had my attention."

"Was he wealthy when you married him?" I asked.

"Not so you'd lose sight of the noughts on his bank balance. But I'd never had much out of life from my Ma and Pa – bless the holes in their little cotton socks. So even a bit of cash to splash seemed like riches to me. But when golden nuggets told me that Hambrook or Fortescue, or whatever he called himself, had turned into Lord Poynings, my life changed. I hated him for being one of them."

"How did he know?" Shirl asked.

"It was his awful mother, Dorothy, an up-tight old cow with a mouth like a rat's arsehole. It was just before she died – not soon enough for me. She took a trip back to England to clear up the affairs of her mother."

"The former Shamrock O'Reilly?"

"Yeah! She'd died way back in the nineteen-thirties but the lawyers said they'd had difficulty clearing up her estate, her having changed her name and the war coming and everything. Personally, I think they just wanted to string it out so they could charge more fees. 'Let's kill all the lawyers', eh? Who said that?

Al Capone?"

"William Shakespeare," I said.

Scarlett shrugged and had a glug of lager. "Whoever. Anyway, there were papers which revealed the whole sordid story. How Hambrook grabbed the gold nugget, fled Australia, and married Shamrock. And how they changed their names. When Dorothy got back to Oz, she couldn't wait to tell golden nuggets – her beloved Jeremy. Jeez, what I had to do to worm the full story out of him. The bedsprings were never the same again."

After that information, I needed a long pull at my gin and tonic. Shirl just laughed.

I said: "How did that news affect your relationship with Jeremy?"

"Well, I couldn't hate him much more than I already did. But I certainly didn't let on that I was a Tuff. And I don't think he ever knew. I just carried on with my cricket. Made that the centre of my life. And Rod, my son, of course."

I said: "Did you tell anyone else?"

"No."

"Really?"

"You calling me a liar?"

I raised an eyebrow. "Forgetful, maybe?"

Scarlett turned to Shirley. "Is he always like this?"

"Worse, usually. You've got him on one of his good days."

I said: "When did you tell your son, Rod?"

Scarlett slurped at her drink. "I suppose you'll find out anyway. You ever had a kid?"

I shook my head.

"You don't know what it's like then when your kid comes home from school in tears because he's been bullied. Bullied because he's different from the other kids."

"Different? In what way?" Shirley asked.

"He's difficult. You know. Stubborn. Flies into a rage if he doesn't get his own way. Rages beyond reason. There are troubles in his head. Always have been. He shouldn't be like that. I tried to protect him. He needed confidence. I was determined to do something to give him a step up so he could look the world in the eye."

"And so, you told him that, unlike the other kids at school, he had an ancestor who was a lord," I said. "That he was in line of succession, even if distantly."

Scarlett said: "He locked on to that news straight away. Frightened me how he became so obsessed about it. What laws he'd make when he was a lord. How he'd treat his peasants. I had to explain to him that being an English lord wasn't like being a French aristo. Then on TV one night, he watched the film *Kind Hearts and Coronets*."

Shirl looked puzzled.

I explained: "It's a story about a distant relative who works out that he can inherit a title if he bumps off the eight heirs before him. In the film, Alec Guinness plays all eight of them."

Scarlett said: "Rod was fascinated by it. When Dorothy had visited England, she'd been given a family tree chart which showed the order of succession at that time. She'd passed it on to Jeremy. But old golden nuggets died last year. Anyway, Rod used to pore over his family tree for hours. Once asked me why I wasn't in the line of succession. I said my bloodline hadn't descended from the first Lord Poynings."

"But Jeremy was in the line of succession," I said. "As Rod was his son, he'd also be in the bloodline."

Scarlett burped, a great harrumph that rumbled round the room. She slumped back in her seat. Glanced from Shirl to me with fear-glazed eyes.

"That's what he thought," Scarlett said in barely a whisper.

Shirl and I exchanged a worried glance.

"Thought," I said. "What do you mean by 'thought'?"

Scarlett reached for her lager. Changed her mind. Rubbed her hands on her face. Looked at the door as though wondering whether to make a run for it. Decided she was in no fit state even to stagger.

"We had a row," she said. "I asked Rod whether he'd anything to do with the deaths."

"Of the Poynings' descendants?" I asked.

"Yes."

"Fletcher and Jake Woodburn?"

"Yes."

"Mungo Brown?"

"Yes."

"Tom Ryan?"

"Yes."

"And Hobart Birtwhistle?"

A silent nod.

"What did Rod say?"

"He denied everything. Completely lost his temper. I'd never seen him like that before. Screamed that the worst thing a mother can do to her son is accuse him of murder. Said he'd never liked me. Hoped I'd die a horrible death so he could be rid of me. It was too much. I screamed back at him. Told him he was an obsessive little runt who needed to get a real life. Told him no matter how many people he killed he still wouldn't become a lord."

Scarlett's hand flew to her mouth. Her eyes flared with shock. She'd said something she'd meant to hold back.

We looked at one another in uneasy silence for a moment.

Then I said: "Because Jeremy Ballantyne wasn't his father."

Scarlett looked like I'd just plunged a dagger into her heart. Her eyelids drooped like she was in pain.

"Because Rod is illegitimate," I said.

"How did you know?" Scarlett asked in a whisper.

Shirley said: "You've made no secret of the fact you thought your husband was a drongo. I guess you didn't restrict playing away to cricket."

Scarlett looked like she'd just had her face slapped.

I said: "Where is Rod?"

"When I told him he'd never be a lord, he screamed that I was a liar. Said he'd prove it. And that the only time he wanted to see me again was as a dead body. Then he stormed out. Took the hire car. I heard him rev the engine and the tyres squeal on the blacktop as he raced away."

"Do you know where he's gone?" I asked.

Scarlett shook her head.

"Did he have any money with him?"

"Not much. Couple of pounds, maybe."

"Does he have any friends in Britain he could ask for help?"

"He doesn't have any friends in Oz."

I gave Scarlett my hard look. The one I use before a tough question.

"You've not been straight with us. You know Rod has committed these murders. And you know how."

"Moonshine," Scarlett snapped.

"Not so," I said. "I know that Hobart Birtwhistle was researching the family background. I suspect he'd been in touch with you and Rod weeks ago about that. He'd discovered that Fletcher and Jake Woodburn had been murdered. He wanted to know whether you could throw any light on the matter. And that worried you. Because you knew Rod had killed them as part of his obsession to become a lord."

"Do I have to listen to this?"

"You worried that Hobart would turn up some evidence that would point the finger at Rod, as a distant heir. We know Hobart was worried because he'd asked to see Shirley. He wanted to enlist her help."

"But he was killed before we could speak," Shirl said.

"By Rod," I added.

"Where's the evidence for that fantasy?" Scarlett spat the words at me.

I said: "The police have a brief note that Hobart made. It mentioned S Ballantyne along with a date and time for a meeting. But you didn't attend that meeting. Rod did, with your blessing. And he went to kill him."

"The blue meanies will never buy that."

"I think they will. Because whoever killed Hobart tore the page with the B entries from his address book."

Scarlett flashed a supersonic hate glare at me. Her eyes were virtually on fire.

She said: "Newspaper reporters. Think you know it all. Well, Mr Smart Guy, you tell me. How did Rod kill these guys?"

"With weapons that readily came to hand."

Scarlett laughed derisively. "Like a sub-machine gun?"

I said: "None of the victims was shot. They were knocked out with a blunt instrument and then strangled – from the marks on their necks by a giant with huge hands. A cricket bat to deal the blow. And wicket-keepers' gloves to finish the job. Strangled by a powerful pair of gloves with reinforced padding. It must've been a terrible end. And Rod had the perfect cover. Baggage master for your cricket tour. What could be more innocent for him than to have a cricket bag with bat and gloves in it?"

"Total garbage," Scarlett jeered.

"Is it? When I took a look in your cricket bag…"

"You did what?"

Scarlett rose with her fists balled. But Shirley eased her back into her seat.

"Yes, at the Eastbourne match, I inadvertently got to see inside your cricket bag. There were two bats, one wrapped in a towel. And two pairs of gloves, one in a plastic bag. I'm guessing the covered ones were used for the killings. And you were minding the weapons that killed."

"Prove it," Scarlett spat.

"That's a job for the police. Their forensic guys will take a close look at those bats and gloves."

"And find they've only been used to play cricket."

"We shall see."

I didn't think there was much chance of the cops finding evidence that would survive cross-examination by a smart lawyer.

But we had Scarlett worried. She let out a long sigh. Her shoulders sagged. Her head lolled to one side.

"I've heard enough. So, you can both piss off. I've got a match to win. Poms! Life's losers! And we'll beat you again tomorrow."

We watched as Scarlett stumbled to her feet and staggered from the bar.

We climbed back into the MGB and sat there watching the mist swirl in the empty street.

After our encounter with Scarlett, we felt our emotions had been dragged through a bramble patch.

I said: "We don't have a shred of hard evidence to prove those charges we threw at Scarlett. No confession. No forensics. Only suspicion. We don't even have the page Rod must have torn from Hobart's address book. I doubt whether the cops have anything better."

I started the car, put it in gear, and pulled out into the road.

Shirl shivered as she stared through the windscreen. "I wonder where Rod is and what he'll do next," she said.

Chapter 22

I spent a restless night, but not the kind of restlessness I usually enjoy in bed with Shirley.

Our late-night confrontation with Scarlett had left both of us drained.

And with Rod on the loose, Shirley was in even greater danger. Mrs Gribble had allowed her to stay another night.

Any more of this kindness and I'd have to consider upgrading the Widow to the status of human being.

The following morning, I left Shirley munching burnt toast in the Widow's kitchen and headed for the *Chronicle*.

The action started as soon as I stepped into the newsroom. My telephone was already ringing. I sprinted around the other desks and answered it breathlessly.

Ted Wilson said: "You sound like a man who's spent a restless night."

I said: "Let's not go into that. You don't usually call before you've had your breakfast. Does that mean they're on strike at the Greasy Spoon?"

"They're not on strike at the village hall in Poynings. That's because we've got a body to examine."

That had my attention. And not in a good way. I felt the heart start pumping harder, but played it cool.

"Let me guess. Hector Pilbeam, the caretaker. Hit with a blunt instrument and then strangled."

"How did you know that?"

"Clairvoyance. I have a gift. I'll be with you in fifteen minutes."

So, the question: "where did Rod go after he'd stormed out on Scarlett?" had been answered. And the worst of it was, he'd been tipped off by an article I'd written on Figgis' orders. He'd asked me to mention the village hall. The helpful caretaker, a regular at the village pub. And the box with the mystery parchment.

The article would have led Rod straight to Pilbeam. I might as well have lined him up against a wall and painted a bullseye on his chest. I felt sick, like my stomach wanted to sink down and take up residence in my shoes.

At least I hadn't described the verse on the parchment. But that was scant consolation. The absence of key information would only have made Rod even more anxious to see the verse himself.

But there was no gain in moping. I pulled myself together. Then I pulled my Remington towards me. I wound copy paper into the carriage and typed 100 words about the Pilbeam murder, based on what Ted had confirmed. Then I added a 200-word rewrite of the earlier article to remind readers of the context.

I yanked the copy paper out of the Remington. Still angry! Handed the paper to Cedric to take to the subs. It would make the midday edition.

Then I headed for the door, cursing Figgis' name, his wizened little face, his so-called missing memoirs, his Woodbines - and everything he stood for.

There were three cop cars and two vans clogging up the lanes around Poynings' village hall.

There wouldn't have been so many law enforcement officers in the place since the witchfinders came to call.

I tucked the MGB in behind one of the vans and climbed out. I ducked under the blue "crime scene" tape and walked up to the village hall door.

The plod on the door was too busy lighting his fag to notice me. He had the ciggie dangling from his lips and his hand over the lighted match to prevent it blowing out in the breeze.

I slipped past without wishing him the time of day.

Inside, Ted Wilson was sitting at a makeshift desk. It had been rigged up from a trestle table and one of those folding canvas chairs. He had a buff folder stuffed with forms. He had his head down signing them.

He stood up as I approached. "Paperwork. I blame this new Sussex Police Force that's taking over next year. They want a requisition chit for everything."

"Too bad. They'll have you arresting real villains next."

Ted gave me an old-fashioned look. "Perhaps I should be arresting you. After all, you did know a surprising amount about this killing."

I held out my arms. "Better put the bracelets on now."

Ted sat down behind his trestle table. "Instead, I'll settle for a detailed account of what you know about Pilbeam's murder. By detailed, I mean with nothing left out."

"Well, not much."

"No, nothing."

So, I told Ted everything about my meeting with Pilbeam. How I'd found him fussing around the ruins of Poynings Old Place. How the house had been a thriving centre for weekend parties until preacher Norbert Carr appeared on the scene. How the first Lord Poynings had got religion – and then died. And how the second Lord Poynings had allowed the estate to fall into disrepair.

And I told him about the cabin trunk full of documents. And about the box with the parchment and the *Waltzing Matilda* verse.

"That's everything?" Ted asked.

"That's everything," I said with fingers crossed behind my back. "Now what do you know so far?"

"Well, the killer's target seems to have been that box with the verse. We found the cabin trunk opened and the box empty. Last night, we think Pilbeam may have noticed there was an intruder. Perhaps a light showed. Or, perhaps, he was just doing a regular round to make sure everything was locked up. Anyway, he evidently went to investigate and ran into the arms of a killer. What we can't work out is who would want to kill for a verse – and why? I mean, what's the point of poetry? Most of the poems I know start with the line, 'There was a young lady from Ealing'."

I ignored that and thought hard about what I knew – and what I wanted to reveal. Decided Ted had to know who the likely culprit was.

I said: "I believe the killer is Rod Ballantyne, son of Scarlett Ballantyne. She's leading the Australian women's cricket team's tour of England. He's the so-called baggage master. But I don't have a shred of hard evidence to put him in the dock."

I told Ted about the meeting Shirley and I had had the previous evening. About how Rod could be after revenge for a murder that took place eighty years before. Or, perhaps, Rod had it all wrong. And it wasn't a murder but an accident. I told Ted how I believed previous murders had been linked.

Ted scratched his beard while he thought about that.

He said: "And here was me thinking someone had bashed the village hall caretaker and run off with the petty cash. And you're telling me Rod could be behind four other murders."

"Five. Don't forget Hobart Birtwhistle."

Ted rubbed his forehead. Shook his head.

"This is way too complex for us. Killings in this country and Australia. I'll have to escalate this to Scotland Yard. Interpol probably. You know what that means?"

"More paperwork," I said.

I left Ted gloomily contemplating more paperwork and headed back to the *Chronicle*.

After speaking to him, I felt even angrier that Figgis had ordered me to write an article which had led to Pilbeam's death. I couldn't decide whether I should have a row with him about it. Or leave it be so that I could follow my own instincts on the story. Besides, Figgis would have heard the news and worked out the part the article had played. He wasn't a man who did remorse. But there has to be a first time for everything. Besides, he'd know I'd chop his legs off rather than listen to some weak excuse laced with self-pity.

I sat at my desk and considered what to do next. As I saw it, there were two main problems to solve.

The first was that Rod was still on the loose – and therefore posed a clear and present danger to Shirley.

The second was that he'd seized the parchment with the *Waltzing Matilda* verse. That had been written by the first Lord Poynings who'd started life as Ned Hambrook. I wondered whether the verse contained a clue about the truth of Roderick Tuff's death.

Ted Wilson hadn't asked me about the text of the verse. But then, he couldn't see the point of poetry so he probably thought it wasn't important.

I opened my notebook at the page with the verse. I stared at the words. Sang them silently in my mind to the well-known tune. Ned Hambrook had gone to great lengths in his life to disguise his identity. He'd changed his name, created a fog about his past. Passed himself off as a perfect English gentleman. A peer of the realm. Yet when he'd wanted to say something, he'd reached back into his Australian heritage. To this verse. Surely, that must be important.

I read the first line again: *Once a lucky hunter searched for a cross of gold.* Was the "lucky hunter" intended to be himself, I wondered? The penniless prospector in the Australian goldrush. Lucky because he'd discovered a priceless nugget. Or was the "lucky hunter" someone who would come along after his death and find whatever they were searching for?

Whatever it was, the second line – *Hid where it's safe – as safe as a tree* – made it clear there was something to find. Did that mean the hidden item was secreted in a tree – or near a tree. That didn't sound like a safe place to hide something of value. Trees live in the open air. They're victims of storms and squirrels. And woodcutters.

But whoever finds the cross, the verse tells them, will "understand" about their life. Understand what? How they'd lived their life in the past? How they should do it in the future? I remembered that Poynings had taken to religion in his final months. Perhaps this was some kind of moral message.

It was all a puzzle I couldn't penetrate without finding out where the "cross of gold" was.

And I had a big worry. Now that Rod had the parchment, he'd also be at work to decipher the meaning. So, this had turned into a race. But a race with no rules and no finishing post. Instead, a race to reveal the hidden meaning in a strange verse.

I leaned back in my captain's chair and looked idly around the newsroom. Over the other side Susan Wheatcroft was thumbing through the morning's *Financial Times* looking for stories with a Sussex angle. Phil Bailey had the telephone receiver glued to his ear. He'd picked up a whisper that the council wanted to build a marina in Brighton. He wanted a quote on record so he could stand up the story. Sally Martin, the women's page editor, had some kaftans draped over her desk. Bright paisley designs, too. Apparently, we'd all be wearing them if we wanted to reap the miracles of the Age of Aquarius.

I looked back to my notebook. It had fallen open at the page with my notes about Hobart Birtwhistle.

Talk about a miracle! And if mine came with compliments from the Age of Aquarius, I'd get one of those kaftans after all.

I knew there'd been an itch at the back of my mind. When Shirley and I had driven to our fateful meeting with Birtwhistle, we'd passed through a tiny village called Golden Cross. It was a road sign on the A22, a handful of houses, an empty field – and it was gone. Could this be the "cross of gold" in the verse? It was a long shot. But the fact Birtwhistle's house in Muddles Green was barely a mile away shortened the odds in my book.

And there was only one way to find out whether I was right.

***

Shirley looked pensive as I drove the MGB – roof down – past Lewes.

She said: "Jeez! The last time we came this way, I had a half-uncle who wanted to give me some useful information. Now I have a second cousin who wants to kill me. I guess that's life."

I said: "And don't forget last time you were Miss Shirley Goldsmith. Now you're Baroness Poynings."

"Yeah! I can't quite get my head around that. I wonder whether the Pirelli calendar guys will still want me. It's only my name that's changed, not my tits. Hope they don't think I've turned all snooty."

"Clearly not."

That earned me a playful punch on the arm.

We passed through a village called Laughton.

I said: "Just two miles to Golden Cross."

Shirley said: "Yeah! And perhaps when we get there we'll be no nearer the truth."

A few minutes later, I parked the MGB under a sycamore tree.

We climbed out of the car and looked around. We saw a fine brick house with a conical roof, like Kent's oast houses. We saw a windmill whose sails shuddered in a breeze. We saw a dilapidated barn, with rusting corrugated iron, and a lonely cow.

We didn't see a golden cross.

A hundred yards down the road, an elderly man was cycling towards us. He wore a tweed jacket with corduroy trousers. He had cycle clips around his ankles.

I flagged him down as he approached.

He had smiley blue eyes and a pencil moustache.

I said: "We're tourists. We've stopped off because we'd heard here's a golden cross here. Can you tell us where it is?"

The bloke swung his leg over the saddle and propped the bike on a fence.

"Golden cross? You don't want to believe everything you read on road signs. Now if you're a tourist looking for a bit of decadence, like rock and roll, I'd recommend Brighton. If you're just interested in a quiet life and an early death, then Eastbourne's straight on."

I grinned. "So, no golden cross?"

"Nope."

"Anything like it?"

"If this place wasn't called Golden Cross, I'd name it World's End."

"Bad as that?" Shirley chipped in.

"Especially on Sundays when there's no bus service. Even the chapel closed down years ago. Mind you, no one ever went there. Just an old ruin now."

"Where is the chapel?" I asked.

"The chapel? You must be desperate. See that lane off to the right a hundred yards down the road?"

We nodded.

"Head on down there, and you'll find the place behind an overgrown hedge. But be warned. I've seen people go down there, but I've never seen anyone come out."

"So no visitors?" I asked.

"Not now. They're digging the drainage ditches down there. Those big diggers growl away most of the time. You can hear the sound over the hedges. Bucolic peace? Forget it. Who'd live in the country? Good day!"

He slung his leg back over the bike and pedalled off.

I looked at Shirley. "I guess the ruined chapel is our best bet," I said.

"Our only bet, big boy."

We climbed back in the car. I turned it around and we drove down the lane.

The old bloke on the bike had been right. There was a big overgrown hawthorn hedge in front of the chapel.

By a gap in the hedge, there was a huge digger, like an over-grown tractor. It was painted yellow and had a large bucket with sharp prongs on the end of a long mechanical arm. There was a driver's cab on top with a steering wheel and levers.

I piloted the car through the hedge's gap into a grassed area, thick with dandelions.

I parked on an overgrown brick path and looked at the chapel in front of us.

"Is this it?" Shirl asked.

The red brick building had lancet windows on either side of an arched door. Both the windows and the door had been boarded up long ago. The plywood was stained by rain and had started to rot.

About ten feet from the far side of the chapel, there was a small low building. A kind of outhouse with no windows. It had a single door. The place was overgrown with ivy.

We climbed out of the car. I took Shirl's hand and we walked down the left side of the chapel. There were three arched windows and a side door, all boarded up. Clearly, visitors weren't wanted.

The door's boards had been nailed to the frame behind. In one place a Virginia creeper had grown behind the board. As it thickened, it had forced the board's nails away from the frame.

I put my fingers in the gap between the board and the frame and heaved. Part of the board broke off and a couple of nails fell on the ground.

"Oops! Careless me."

"Yeah! Could have happened to anyone," Shirl said.

In five minutes, I had stripped away the rest of the board.

I opened the door behind it and we stepped inside the chapel.

We stopped in our tracks and gawped at the sight.

"Jeez!" Shirl said. "What is it?"

I let my gaze travel around the chapel.

"It's the solution to the mystery," I said.

Chapter 23

The floor of the chapel was painted with a huge tree.

Its thick branches reached out like arrows towards the walls. And those walls were covered with a series of painted murals. Shirl turned to me with amazed eyes. "What does it all mean?"

"It's the tree of life," I said. "Remember the *Waltzing Matilda* verse said the cross of gold was *'hid where it's safe, as safe as a tree'*. The next line said, *'When you find the cross, you'll understand about your life'*."

"I don't get it," Shirl said.

"The tree of life is a symbol for what a person is like. It defines their individuality. The different branches show how that person became what he was. See how each branch points to one of the murals on the wall. I think this is the first Lord Poynings, Ned Hambrook in his early life, trying to tell us why he was like he was. Perhaps he saw this as his route to salvation."

We walked around the tree and gazed at the murals. There were eight of them, two on each of the four walls. The outside of the building may have been falling into disrepair, but the inside was neat and tidy. Free of dirt and dust. Well cared for. And the colours of the murals' paints were as bright as the day they'd flowed from the artist's brush.

"What is this all about?" Shirley asked, wide-eyed.

"It's a cross between the Bayeux tapestry and the Sistine Chapel," I said. "It's about telling the story. It's about Poynings leaving the truth behind him as his legacy – even if there was no one who believed him while he lived."

"It makes no sense," Shirl said. "No one comes here. The place is boarded up."

"I think that's the point. When Poynings commissioned this, it wasn't to show off to any Tom, Dick or Harriet. Remember, he'd got religion bad. He'd been converted by Norbert Carr. And like many of the rascals who invent their own cults, Carr would have won the unquestioned devotion of his followers. I can see Carr wagging his finger at Poynings and explaining what he had to do to gain salvation at the Pearly Gates. So Poynings buys a ruined old chapel that nobody uses any more. He hires an artist to set out his story. Not for us earthly mortals. This is for the powers in another sphere. It's the same thinking that made the pharaohs hole themselves up in a pyramid with all their possessions. Ready for another world."

"Jeez! It blows my mind."

"Let's look more closely at the murals and see whether we can work out the story Poynings wanted to tell."

At one end there was a raised area for the chapel's altar. It was a classy affair built out of oak and standing around five feet high. No cross, which I found strange, but there were two chunky candle holders. Each held a thick white church candle. In front of the altar, there were half a dozen wooden pews arranged in three rows. But none of the pews had hassocks or hymn books.

This was a chapel for spirits beyond this world. And good luck to them!

I pointed at the altar and said: "I think the sequence of murals starts on the wall to the right of the altar. Let's follow and see what we make of it."

The first mural showed two Australian swagmen, their Matildas on their backs, meeting by a billabong. They shake hands and smile at one another – like a pair embarking on an adventure together.

Shirley said: "Guess this shows Hambrook meeting Roderick Tuff for the first time."

We moved on to the second mural. We look down a deep hole a crudely hollowed-out mine. It is black but, in the distance, we see two characters. They are digging by the feeble glow of an oil lamp. Beyond the light is a bright gold object. It is like a star radiating golden rays. Both characters' hands are reaching towards the light.

"This is where the guys find the nugget," Shirl said.

We turned on to the wall at the front end of the chapel. The first mural here showed one of the characters sneaking into the darkness with a spade and an oil lamp. Meanwhile his partner sleeps next to the gold nugget. The sneaky character is looking over his shoulder to make sure he's not followed.

"Is the sneaky guy Hambrook or Tuff?" Shirley asked.

"I think it must be Tuff. It should become clear when we look at the later murals."

We shuffled on to the next. The sneaky character is back at the mine where the pair had found the nugget. He'd obviously started to descend a rickety ladder but the mural shows him falling into the darkness. His Matilda trails after him. Obviously, his intention had been to find another nugget without his partner, Hambrook.

I said: "This suggests Tuff wanted to cheat Hambrook."

"Sure, that would provide Hambrook with a motive to kill Tuff."

"Let's see where the story takes us."

We moved a few feet to our right. The next mural showed the other character – Hambrook – at the mineshaft. Way down below the terror-stricken face of Tuff, illuminated by a single shaft of light, looks up. Hambrook is rigging up a rescue cradle attached by a rope to a bracket screwed into the wall of the mineshaft. But the artist has vividly shown the splintered wood and creaking screws that won't hold the weight of the cradle and rope – let alone a man.

I said: "This clearly shows Hambrook tried to rescue Tuff."

"But is it the truth? Remember, this guy is trying to cover up a killing."

"I don't think so. Hambrook wants to rescue Tuff, but can't manage it. This whole weird business is about redemption. It's about Hambrook who's convinced he's heading for Hell's fire unless he can show he's innocent."

And when we moved to the next mural, Shirl agreed. The artist had painted a busy street in a town.

"Hey, that's Victoria Square in Adelaide. The central market's just beyond where the picture ends."

In the mural, there's a prominent newspaper contents bill outside a building. The bill reads: POLICE CHASE GOLD NUGGET KILLER. Hambrook is in the picture's foreground. He has a look of abject fear on his face.

I said: "It looks as though the story started going the rounds that Hambrook had murdered Tuff. Not surprising. There must have been a lot of violence in those gold rushes. A lot of cheated partners, too."

"But if the murals are true, Hambrook was innocent," Shirley said.

"He was a man looking at a miscarriage of justice – and the hangman's rope – unless he fled."

Sure enough, the next mural showed Hambrook boarding a boat bound for Britain. He'd changed out of the swagman's clothes. Now he was dressed like a bank clerk. Black jacket, pin-striped trousers, and bowler hat. And he was carrying a heavy case with Carruthers & Stoat embossed on the side in gold letters. The case was weighed down with something very heavy.

I said: "This solves the mystery of what happened to the gold nugget. He brought it to Britain with him and used its value to buy himself into the merchant bank that Boofy Arran told us about."

"But what happened to the nugget?" Shirley asked.

"Perhaps it's still in Carruthers & Stoat's bank vault. But I don't think so. Boofy said it was an ailing bank, so it's more likely it was melted down and sold to raise new bank capital. Whatever the truth, we know Hambrook – Fortescue after his name change – led a prosperous life, married and had children."

"But he left behind a mystery which has led to killing."

"Let's see how Hambrook hoped his story would end," I said.

We moved on to the final mural. It showed a preacher – certainly Norbert Carr – standing by the altar of a chapel. In front of him is Hambrook, now Lord Poynings, in his ermine-trimmed robes. Carr has a severe look on his face. His right hand is pointing towards the sky. Behind some fluffy white clouds, there's a hint of a celestial city. His left hand points down to an underworld inhabited by hunched creatures tortured by fires.

I said: "Not exactly subtle."

"But effective. Ever heard that expression about putting the fear of God into people. Looks like Carr was the champ in that department."

We moved away from the final mural and sat on one of the pews.

We shared a silent minute. We had a lot to absorb. Even more to think about.

Somewhere outside, an engine roared as the ditch digger sparked into life.

Shirley said: "I feel drained after looking at all this. Those pictures tell the story better than any words could."

"Including mine?"

Shirl grinned. "We'll have to wait and see. You gonna call your copy in?"

"I don't know. It turns out Hambrook didn't steal Tuff's share of the nugget after all."

"He could have given a share to Tuff's wife."

"But he was fleeing a false murder charge. Besides, Hambrook must have suspected that Tuff had gone alone to the mine at night because he planned to cheat him."

"So, Rod has embarked on a murder spree for the wrong reasons."

"Don't forget Scarlett's role in this. All that guff about his family tree and being a lord. It was as though she'd loaded the gun and invited Rod to fire it."

The roar from the ditch digger grew louder.

I said: "I didn't see the drainage ditch come close to the chapel."

"It ran in the other direction," Shirl said.

"Perhaps that digger is turning round."

Kerrrunch!

The digger's bucket smashed through the side-door. The wood splintered. The glass crashed. And the door jamb exploded out of its slot dragging plaster and bricks with it.

We leapt from the pew and ran towards the digger waving our arms.

In the cab, up behind the hydraulic arm with the bucket, we could see an outline of the driver.

He pulled levers and the arm moved from side to side.

Smash!

Up and down

Crash!

The arm quivered, like it wasn't sure of its own strength. Locked behind a part of the wall. Dragged backwards.

Crack! The wall broke away from the foundations. Held suspended in the air. Crashed to the ground.

A timber supporting the roof splintered and fell.

Tiles slid off the roof and shattered with a sound like rifle fire.

As the digger moved backwards, the driver came into full view.

It was the face of a young man who'd aged ahead of his time. His hairline had receded to reveal deep wrinkles in his forehead. There were dark bags under his bulging eyes. His nostrils flared and his lips twisted into a snarl that revealed grey teeth. Claw-like hands grasped the digger's steering-wheel.

Shirley gasped and grabbed my arm. "Jeez. That's the guy who followed me from the beauty parlour. The guy with the belted raincoat and the slouch hat – like a fifties private eye.

He's the guy with those weirdly rounded shoulders. I'd spot them a mile off."

"It's Rod," I shouted above the digger's din. "And I wish we were a mile off. Because he wants to kill us."

The digger reversed out. It left the side-door blocked with rubble and timbers.

Shirley grabbed my arm. "We've gotta get out of here."

"How? All the doors and windows are boarded up."

"Can't we climb over that heap of rubble?"

Before I had time to reply, Rod made another attack. The digger surged through the wall.

A huge section of bricks and plaster crashed feet from us.

Grey dust foamed into the air. The place looked like a London fog had drifted in.

Shirley shrieked: "Jeez! This is getting dangerous."

I tried shouting at Rod, but the digger made so much noise, he couldn't hear.

I grabbed Shirl's hand and we sprinted towards the front door. But the thing was boarded up with thick wood.

"You'd need a sledgehammer to get through there," Shirl shouted.

"Typical. You never have a sledgehammer when you need one."

"Yeah! Well, we're gonna need something or we'll be buried alive as the building collapses."

Rod reversed out. The digger disappeared behind the wall. The engine note rose.

A huge crunch shook the corner of the building. More wall crumbled away. Roof timbers collapsed. The floor shook like an earthquake had started.

Each attack by the digger left a heap of rubble that trapped us.

There was no way out.

But wait a minute!

The chapel had been boarded up for years, the bloke on the bike had told us.

Yet when we got inside, we found the place neat and tidy.

No dirt. No dust.

Well cared for.

Like the housekeeper had just visited with the vacuum cleaner and the feather duster.

How did the housekeeper get in?

And then get out?

As the digger manoeuvred for another attack, I scanned the building. No obvious doors. None hidden either. The murals – what was left of them - took up all the wall space. The artist would not be pleased.

Frantically, I scanned the chapel.

The altar.

A sturdy oak construction, five feet high.

"This way," I shouted.

Shirley and I sprinted across the room just as the digger shoved in another section of wall.

The glass in a window frame shattered and jagged splinters shot around us like arrows.

Roof supports tumbled in behind us. A section of ceiling exploded in a stream of powdered plaster.

We reached the altar. The side facing the congregation was built of solid oak panels.

We slid behind the altar. To the side which faced the chapel's back wall.

I pointed. "There," I shouted above the din.

The altar had a pair of doors. Neat hinges. Brass handles.

I yanked on the handles. Offered up a quick prayer that the doors weren't locked.

They weren't

Thank you!

Shirley and I peered in. Inside, it was like a large empty

cupboard. It smelt of dust and damp. A cobweb hung from the roof. A set of steps lead downwards.

"Should we?" Shirl said. "We don't know what's down there."

"We know what's up here."

At that moment, the digger crushed more wall. An electricity supply box tore free from its fixings. Wires wrapped themselves around the wheels of the digger. Sparks from fused power points lit up the chapel.

The digger's engine roared. The wires had slowed its progress. And then the central section of the roof crashed down.

We'd seen enough. We disappeared down the steps and into a dark tunnel.

Under a pile of timbers, the digger growled like an angry bear.

Above us, we could hear a long rumbling crunch as a huge piece of masonry fell.

Shirl grabbed my hand and said: "You take a girl to all the best places."

"I try. Let's see if we can find somewhere down here for a cocktail."

With one hand in front of me and one hand in Shirl's we edged along the tunnel.

"I can feel a draught coming from somewhere in front," I said.

"Me, too. Smells like a dead dingo. It sure ain't air conditioning."

We moved one step at a time.

"My foot's just hit something," I said.

"Hard or soft?"

"Hard."

"So it's not a body. Promising."

I felt further forward.

"It's a step," I said.

"What goes down, must come up." Shirl said.

"Let's hope it's us."

I put one foot on the first step. The other foot on the next step.

Up we went. Above me I could see an outline of light around a dark square object.

A loose-fitting trapdoor.

I pushed through it and we scrambled into a small windowless room. It was the outhouse we'd seen when we'd parked.

Along one wall was a shelf with Lux soap flakes, Fiddes Supreme Wax Polish, Windex window cleaner. There were dusters and scouring pads.

There was a rack with brooms and dustpans hanging from it.

In front of us, was a door.

I grabbed the handle, turned and pushed. The door flew open and we stumbled through.

The air was full of dust and noise.

A long rumbling roar came from the chapel.

The last walls collapsed and the rest of the roof fell in. The digger's engine died. Thick black smoke poured from its exhaust. Its long hydraulic arm collapsed on the ground.

"Looks like the cleaner will need more than a dustpan and brush to clear that lot up," Shirley said.

Frank Figgis read the last folio of my copy and added it to the pile on his desk.

He took off his spectacles and said: "I must admit you've excelled yourself this time. We're so far ahead of the other papers on this story, they might as well be in a distant galaxy."

It was late afternoon – and what an afternoon it had been.

Back at the chapel, the cops had arrived – followed by the fire brigade. They'd dug Rod out of the rubble – alive enough for Ted Wilson to arrest him on six murder charges.

I'd headed to the nearest phone box to dictate a splash piece for the front page. Then Shirley and I had high-tailed it back to Brighton. She headed for her flat. I stormed into the office and pounded out a 2,000-word detailed account for tomorrow's paper.

Figgis had just finished reading it.

I said: "After Rod had killed Pilbeam and snatched the *Waltzing Matilda* verse, he clearly worked out what it meant, too. When he arrived at the chapel, he would have been surprised to find my MGB parked outside. He decided he had to kill us – Shirley especially as she blocked his way to the peerage. He turned that ditch digger into a deadly weapon. Did more damage with it than a tank."

Figgis said: "Rod may have demolished the chapel, but that's not evidence that he murdered the heirs to the Poynings peerage. Or Hobart Birtwhistle."

"Rod had driven to the chapel in Scarlett's hire car. They found a cricket bag in the back. With a bat and wicket-keeper's gloves. The bat delivered the knock-out blows. The gloves made it seem the strangling had been done by a giant with huge hands. The cops are confident the forensic guys will find enough traces on them to nail him as the killer of Mungo Brown and Tom Ryan. But it doesn't nail him for the Aussie killings of Fletcher and Jake. That's a job for the Melbourne cops."

"Doesn't nail him for Birtwhistle's killing either."

"The slip of paper on Hobart's office spike suggested that Scarlett made the appointment. I think they'd already been in touch through Hobart's family tree research. But it was Rod who turned up on the doorstep and killed Birtwhistle."

"And no doubt thought he'd got away with it," Figgis said.

"But Rod made a big mistake there. He tore the page out of Birtwhistle's address book. The page with all the B entries. He wanted to hide the fact there were Ballantynes listed. They found the page scrunched up at the bottom of the cricket bag. He must've forgotten it was there."

Figgis leaned back in his chair and stared out of the window. Some starlings were twittering on his window ledge. He gave them one of his stares and they flew off.

He said: "Do you suppose Rod really hoped to find a gold nugget at the end of his killing spree?"

"I've thought about that a lot. I think it was old-fashioned greed that started his motor running. But, in the end, it was revenge. For what he believed was Hambrook's murder of Roderick Tuff. But the murals in the chapel suggested Tuff was the victim of his own greed. Hambrook was innocent all along. I guess Rod also thought he could become the eighth Baron Poynings."

Figgis nodded. "I get that, but how did Hobart Birtwhistle get caught up in the killing?"

"Curiosity about his family tree. After all, we all want to know where we come from."

Figgis raised an eyebrow. "Do we?"

"Hobart's father died before he was born and his mother, Bella, last year. From what we know, she'd always been secretive about her background. I'd place a large bet that her death gave Hobart the chance to rummage through family papers and start to learn some of the truth. If, as I suspect, he learnt that Sydney and Adelaide Fortescue had originally been Ned Hambrook and Shamrock O'Reilly, he'd know that his family tree wasn't what it seemed."

"This all sounds a bit speculative," Figgis said. "Is there any evidence that Hobart was on the hunt for missing relatives?"

"Ted Wilson tells me that pages from Hobart's diary show he'd tracked down Jeremy Ballantyne and spoken to him. Perhaps also to Scarlett. I think he would have learned something of the truth about the family history – including the legend of the gold nugget - from Jeremy. He died last year. I think that put Hobart on high alert that there were more secrets to uncover. When he discovered the fact Shirley was his half-niece, he hoped he'd found an ally for his search. Somehow, he must have let this slip to Scarlett or Rod. That would have made them suspicious of him. He could have uncovered their link to the Tuffs. And so, he had to die."

Figgis said: "Rod must be relieved the government has suspended the death sentence for murder."

"Murder still carries a capital sentence in Australia. Two of his killings – Fletcher and Jake - were there. Whether he dies or not, he won't see the outside of a prison cell until he's an old man. His mother, Scarlett Ballantyne, looks like she'll be joining him. I've heard the cops interrupted the cricket match at Arundel and arrested her an hour ago. She was batting. On 49 runs, too. Had to retire hurt. Missed out on her half-century. Retribution for Shirley."

I stood up with effort. My arms and legs felt tired. My brain needed sleep.

I turned to leave.

Figgis said: "One other matter. My memoirs. You were supposed to track them down."

It was the last thing I needed. I'd put up a show by interviewing Susan Wheatcroft. But I didn't want to embarrass any more of my colleagues in the newsroom. It was time to end this charade. I'd known from the start where the memoirs were. In the locked cupboard in my lodgings. I'd taken them when I'd heard that Figgis had mentioned some of my scams. How dare he. Those scams were my copyright. There was no way I wanted them broadcast to the world.

Besides, in my book, Figgis had Pilbeam's blood on his hands. He should never have ordered me to write that story. He deserved his punishment. And he'd have to take it like a man.

I said: "Last I heard, the manuscript got muddled up with returned unsold copies of the paper. It's been sent for re-pulping. I'm afraid you'll have to consider that book closed."

I opened the door and stepped into the newsroom. Behind me, I could hear Figgis explode with some choice words that never found their way into the *Chronicle*.

I didn't care. I'd had enough of pretending.

I went back to my desk and slumped in my captain's chair. At least, the story of the Poynings peerage was over, I thought.

But I was wrong.

It wasn't over for me.

And it certainly wasn't over for Shirley.

Chapter 24

Fresh trouble started when the newspapers were delivered at Shirley's flat the following morning.

I'd decided to stay at Shirl's place rather than doss down at my own lodgings. I couldn't face the endless questions from the Widow about the events at the chapel. Besides, now the Widow had twigged Shirley was a baroness, she'd invite her friends around so she could show off.

Anyway, I was sitting up in bed when Shirl stormed in with the papers.

"Look at this," she said. She pushed one of the red-top tabloids at me.

I read the splash headline on the front page: BIMBO BARONESS BEATS THE BOYS.

There was a picture of Shirl taken from one of her earlier photoshoots. She was wearing a bikini that reminded me of that song about "the itsy bitsy teenie weenie yellow polka dot bikini". Except that Shirl clearly wasn't afraid to come out of the locker. She was sitting under a sun umbrella holding a glass of champagne.

The picture had evidently made the tabloid's writer pop with purple prose. His copy started:

"Sultry sexpot Shirley Goldsmith, 27, raises a glass on becoming Britain's sauciest baroness.

"Shirley, 38-24-36, will clearly keep abreast of debates when she joins the House of Lords.

"She'll have the dukes and earls drooling at her points of order.

"Curvy Shirley is expected to wear one of her slinkiest outfits when she turns up for debates.

"So, my lords, watch out. Blonde bombshell Shirley is heading your way."

Shirl's eyes flashed with anger. "Where do they find the creeps that write this crap?" she said.

"Journalism school, I believe."

"Wrong answer, big boy. You need to take this seriously. The guy who wrote this set out to use me. To make me somebody I'm not. And that's not right."

I sprang out of bed. Crossed the room and gave Shirl a big hug. I could feel the tension in her body. The article had made her quiver with anger.

"No, it's not right," I said. "It's sloppy exploitative journalism."

Shirley said: "Women suffer this garbage in these tabloids every day. They can do nothing about it. But I can."

"What do you mean – you can?"

"Sure, about the only thing that fish-and-chip paper got right about me was that I'm a baroness. I can speak in the House of Lords. And I'm gonna do just that. Today. Better call your old friend Boofy Arran and find out how we can arrange it."

I released Shirl from our embrace.

"Well," I said. "At least I know the first thing to do."

"What's that?"

"Put on my trousers."

After a couple of calls that got me nowhere, I tracked Boofy down to his office in London.

He was preparing for another busy day pushing his new law through parliament. But he agreed to talk when I explained what I wanted.

Fifteen minutes later, I re-joined Shirley in the bedroom. She'd just finished dressing.

I said: "Better get out that slinkiest dress. You can join the Lords today."

Shirl was so pleased she didn't even pick me up on my slinkiest dress crack.

I explained: "It turns out that new peers – with a title that's not existed before – have to be introduced formally into the House of Lords' chamber. That's quite an elaborate ceremony with a lot of bowing. And you have to get into the fancy dress kit of red robes, ermine and hat. But Boofy told me that, since 1663, peers who inherit their title don't need a formal introduction. They can turn up, sign a few papers, and they're into what has been called the best club in London."

"Sounds great," Shirl said.

"The trickiest part, Boofy said, might be getting you an opportunity to speak. It all works in an informal way in the Lords. But he'll have a word with a few friendly peers to make sure it happens."

"Even greater."

"There's only one thing that worries me."

"What's that?"

"What are you going to say?"

Shirl crossed the room, gave me a big hug, and super smacker on the lips.

"You just leave that to me, big boy."

Boofy Arran met us in the Central Lobby at the Houses of Parliament at half-past two.

He shook Shirley's hand and said: "What you're planning to do is very brave. I salute you. Now, the Lords sits at three which just gives us time for you to see the chamber. There are four places where you can sit – the Conservative, Labour, Liberal or Crossbencher benches. The Crossbenchers don't align with any political party. These days, I normally sit on the Liberal benches because I can hear better from them. But you can sit anywhere."

"I'll sit near you. I'll need the moral support," Shirley said.

Boofy turned to me. "You'll need to sit in the public gallery but I've reserved you a ticket. So, let's get to our places."

Shirley turned to me. For an instant, I thought I saw panic in her blue eyes. Her lips quivered with an unspoken fear. Then she blinked, took a deep breath – and smiled.

"Go break a leg, kid," I said.

I guess I was more nervous than Shirley when I took my place in the public gallery.

She'd already taken her seat. She had Arran on one side and a woman I later learned was Baroness Asquith, the daughter of a former prime minister, on the other side.

Lord Gardiner, the Lord Chancellor, who ran the show, took his seat on the Woolsack. (Yes, a quaint English tradition. Back in the fourteenth century, Edward the Third had said the Lord Chancellor had to sit on a seat stuffed with wool to boost the trade. Only problem was, when they came to replace the stuffing in 1938, they found it was horsehair.)

The house started its business promptly. And I was surprised at how many different subjects came up. What uniforms police wear in hot weather. They keep their helmets on. The effect of sonic booms on hospital instruments. You don't want to know.

Just before five o'clock, a rumble of voices ran around the chamber: "Baroness Poynings! Baroness Poynings!"

Shirley looked uncertainly at Boofy. He flicked a hand in a stand-up gesture. Shirl glanced around her, then stood up suddenly.

A silence fell over the chamber. You could have heard a coronet drop. It was like there was electricity in the air.

Two hundred faces turned towards Shirley.

She smiled. Shifted from right to left foot and back again. Built some more tension. And then she began to speak.

The best I can do is reproduce how *Hansard*, the official parliamentary record, reported what happened.

Baroness Poynings: Hi, guys.

Lord Chancellor: Noble lords.

Baroness Poynings: Them too, boss man.

Their lordships: Oh!

Baroness Poynings: Some of you who read your newspaper this morning may have hoped to see me in my slinkiest dress. I am sorry to disappoint you.

Lord Temple Hirst: You haven't.

Baroness Poynings: I'm pleased to hear it. I am actually wearing a green Louis Féraud business suit. As you can see, it is a classic high-neck mini-dress with an A-line silhouette. And it comes with a boxy cropped jacket. It may not be my slinkiest but because it was made in this country, it has created well-paid jobs for people and put cash in their purses. I think that should be of more interest to newspaper readers than the size of my tits.

Their lordships: Oh! What? Eh!

Baroness Poynings: Sorry, guys. I meant to say boobs.

Their lordships: Oh! Oh! Oh!

Lord Chancellor: Order, order.

Baroness Poynings: You want to order the Louis Féraud mini-dress, boss man? You haven't got the legs for it.

Their lordships: Laughter.

Baroness Poynings: But I dig your wig. Does it get wet in the bath?

Their lordships: Laughter.

Lord Chancellor: Order, order.

Baroness Poynings: I came here today because I was angry about the way a newspaper described me. The paper said I would get dukes and earls drooling at my points of order. Well, drool away, guys. By the look of some of you, it's the best offer you're going to get today.

Their lordships: Oh! Oh! Oh!

Baroness Poynings: Yeah! I know that hurt some of you. But that's the point. When you say something gratuitously offensive, people are hurt whether they're men or women. But in some newspapers, it's usually women. And that's got to stop.

Lord Temple Hirst: Hear! Hear!

Baroness Poynings: Because it's not only demeaning for the women. It's demeaning for the men who write it. Guys who had dreams of being the great war reporter under fire on the front line end up writing about a woman's body. Not bombs, but bums.

Lord Whimple: What? Did someone just say "bums"?

Baroness Poynings: Yes, but don't let it worry you. They're not interested in your bum. Now go back to sleep.

Their lordships: Oh!

Lord Chancellor: It is out of order to point out a peer is asleep in the chamber.

Baroness Poynings: Well, the old guy who's snoring is certainly out of something. But there is an important thing I want to say.

Lord Temple Hirst: Hear! Hear!

Baroness Poynings: Don't get too excited. We're not dating.

I work in the fashion industry. The pictures of me help to sell the clothes I model. A lot of people work in the clothes industry – and most of them are women. In that way, the clothes industry is like the world. A world where women do most of the important work. Across the globe, women cook the meals, fetch the water, chop the wood, cherish the children, slave in the factories, tend the farm animals, tread the grapes, type the letters men dictate, bind their war wounds, and provide the love. And too often they are beaten or abused or shouted down for it. Or, worst of all, they are simply ignored. Well, I say that has to stop and it has to change. The world simply doesn't work without women. So, yes, you guys need to take that on board. And if just one of you guys changes your mind about this, it will have been worth the train fare coming here today. Thank you for listening to me. It's great to be in a place which wants to hear what women think.

Their lordships: Hear! Hear!

Earl of Arran: Good show.

Baroness Asquith: Well said.

Lord Whimple: I must have dozed off. Have I missed anything?

Jeff Purkiss poured our drinks and put them on the bar.

It was the evening after Shirley's triumph in the House of Lords. We'd chosen Prinny's Pleasure rather than one of Brighton's classier bars to avoid people pestering Shirley. Her speech had been all over the evening papers and television news.

Jeff said to Shirley: "They mentioned you in the news on the Home Service this evening."

Shirley gave me a resigned look.

I said: "You'll have to start calling it Radio Four from September."

"Calling what?"

"The Home Service."

"I don't know why they have to change these things."

Shirley said: "It's called progress."

Jeff scratched his bum. "The kind of progress I like is where things don't change."

I said: "On that basis, this is the most progressive pub in Brighton."

To avoid Jeff's interrogation, we took our drinks to the corner table at the back of the bar.

"You certainly wooed their lordships this afternoon. They couldn't get enough of you."

Shirl sipped her Campari soda. "Yeah! Well, they'll have to make do or mend."

"What do you mean by that?"

"I'm not going to make any more speeches in the House of Lords."

"Good to have a rest. Keep them waiting. Makes them appreciate it when you next deliver."

"You don't understand. I'm giving up my seat in the House of Lords. Boofy told me how. I have to send a document called an instrument of disclaimer to the Lord Chancellor within a year of inheriting the title. Then I'm out of the Lords."

I sat there with my glass half poised between the table and my lips. I'd read about the Peerages Act which had been passed four years earlier. It was the result of a campaign by an elected member of parliament called Anthony Wedgwood Benn. He'd inherited his father's title of Viscount Stansgate, which meant he could no longer sit in the House of Commons. The Peerages Act let him get rid of the title and be elected as an MP.

I said: "Are you sure you want to do this?"

"Certain. Making speeches is not my scene."

"You scored a great success this afternoon."

"That was a one-off. Besides, I couldn't have a title that's stained with the blood of six murder victims."

I drained my gin and tonic. "That's a good reason, I have to admit."

Shirley leaned across and kissed me. Not one of her power plonkers this time. A soft tender smooch which had a life-long tale to tell.

We broke apart and I looked deep into her eyes. There was something she wanted to say.

She finished her Campari soda.

"I have a final reason," she said. "I don't want to be known as Baroness Poynings. I'd rather be Mrs Shirley Crampton."

I swear my heart missed a beat. Yes, I know that's corny. But, this time, it was true. It went bonkety-nothing-bonk. I couldn't get out of my mind that when Shirl had said the words "Mrs Shirley Crampton" she'd looked so happy.

Before I could say anything, Jeff stepped alongside the table.

"Saw your glasses were empty. Like another?"

I felt that my life was moving in slow motion. Everything around me seemed suffused with a golden light. If I didn't get a grip, any moment I'd be hearing the music of the spheres. I realised I was gawping like a love-sick teenager. I took a deep breath.

I turned slowly to Jeff.

"Better make the next round your best champagne," I said.

Jeff's eyes popped. "Getting married or something?"

Shirley reached across the table and I took her hand. She curled her fingers around mine in a gentle squeeze.

We laughed and answered together.

"Yes, we're getting married – or something."

Read more Crampton of the Chronicle stories at:

www.colincrampton.com

Author's note and acknowledgements

I've mentioned before that any Crampton of the Chronicle adventure couldn't appear without help from many people. Barney Skinner has designed the cover and typeset and formatted the book for both the e-book and paperback editions. Barney is also the designer behind the Crampton of the Chronicle website. Members of the Crampton Advanced Readers' Team read the manuscript and made many helpful suggestions and corrections. The members of the team who helped are (in alphabetical order) Jaquie Fallon, Andrew Grand, Doc Kelly, Andy Mayes, Mark Rewhorn, Christopher Roden and Gregg Wynia. Thanks to you all! Needless to say, any errors that remain are mine and mine alone.

Finally, a big thankyou to you, the reader, for reading this book. If you've enjoyed it, please recommend it to your friends! In these days of internet sales, online book reviews are very important for authors. So, if you have a few minutes to leave one on Amazon and/or Goodreads, I would be very grateful. Thank you.

Peter Bartram, November 2022

About the author

Peter Bartram brings years of experience as a journalist to his Crampton of the Chronicle crime mystery series. His novels are fast-paced and humorous - the action is matched by the laughs. The books feature a host of colourful characters as befits stories set in Brighton, one of Britain's most trend-setting towns.

Peter began his career as a reporter on a local weekly newspaper before working as an editor in London and finally becoming freelance. He has done most things in journalism from door-stepping for quotes to writing serious editorials. He's pursued stories in locations as diverse as 700-feet down a coal mine and Buckingham Palace. Peter wrote 21 non-fiction books, including five ghost-written, before turning to crime – and penning the Crampton of the Chronicle series. There are now 15 books in the series.

Follow Peter Bartram on Facebook at:
www.facebook.com/peterbartramauthor

Follow Peter Bartram on Twitter at:
@PeterFBartram

More great books from Peter Bartram...

HEADLINE MURDER

When the owner of a miniature golf course goes missing, ace crime reporter Colin Crampton uncovers the dark secrets of a 22-year-old murder.

STOP PRESS MURDER

The murder of a night watchman and the theft of a saucy film of a nude woman bathing set Colin off on a madcap investigation with a stunning surprise ending.

FRONT PAGE MURDER

Archie Flowerdew is sentenced to hang for killing rival artist Percy Despart. Archie's niece Tammy believes he's innocent and convinces Colin to take up the case. Trouble is, the more Colin investigates, the more it looks like Archie is guilty.

THE TANGO SCHOOL MYSTERY

Colin Crampton and girlfriend Shirley Goldsmith are tucking into their meal when Shirley discovers more blood on her rare steak than she'd expected. The pair are drawn into investigating a sinister conspiracy which seems to centre on a tango school.

THE MOTHER'S DAY MYSTERY

There are just four days to Mother's Day and crime reporter Colin Crampton is under pressure to find a front-page story to fit the theme. Then Colin and his feisty girlfriend Shirley Goldsmith stumble across a body late at night on a lonely country road...

THE COMEDY CLUB MYSTERY

When theatrical agent Daniel Bernstein turns up murdered, any of five comedians competing for a place on a top TV show could be behind the killing. Colin and Shirley take on identical twin gangsters and tangle with an unlikely cast of misfits as they set out to solve the mystery.

THE POKER GAME MYSTERY

Colin discovers nightclub bouncer Steve Telford murdered – but can't understand why five cards of a poker hand are laid out next to the body. The tension ratchets higher when the life of a young girl is on the line. Colin must win a poker game with a sinister opponent to save her.

THE BEACH PARTY MYSTERY

Brighton is about to host its most exciting beach party ever – with the world's biggest name in rock music headlining the show. It seems a world away from the work of Evening Chronicle crime reporter Colin Crampton. But that's before fraudster Claude Winterbottom is beaten to death. The climax explodes on a pirate radio ship moored off the British coast.

THE WORLD CUP MYSTERY

It's July 1966 – and millions would kill for a ticket to the World Cup final at London's Wembley Stadium. Then café owner Sergio Parisi is murdered in his own kitchen – and his ticket has gone missing. Colin and Shirley discover the ticket's disappearance could be part of an even more deadly crime.

THE MORNING, NOON & NIGHT TRILOGY

The adventure starts in *Murder in the Morning Edition*… when crime reporter Colin Crampton and feisty girlfriend Shirley

Goldsmith witness an audacious train robbery. (Free on my website when you subscribe to the readers' group).

The mystery deepens in *Murder in the Afternoon Extra...* as the body count climbs and Colin finds himself hunted by a ruthless killer.

The climax explodes in *Murder in the Night Final...* when Colin and Shirley uncover the stunning secret behind the robbery and the murders.

Read all three books in *The Morning, Noon & Night Omnibus Edition* or listen to them on the audiobooks available from Audible, Amazon and iTunes.

Printed in Great Britain
by Amazon

10387501R00161